PRAISE FOR BRENDA

"A super-hot h
Brenda Jacks ... and characters
you fall in lov

—Lori Foster, *New York Times* bestselling author

"*The Midnight Hour* is a roller-coaster read of passion, intrigue, and deceit."

—Sharon Sala, *New York Times* bestselling author

"With a taut, over-the-top romantic thriller, Jackson revisits her popular Madaris Family and Friends series...Jackson smoothly alternates between several points of view and throws in a number of plot twists...Jackson [has a] knack for creating characters with emotional depth and distinct voices...[a] tension-packed read."

—*Publishers Weekly*

"Jackson has written another compelling drama about the Madaris family and their friends."

—*Booklist*

"Action, mystery and sensuality propel *The Midnight Hour* forward. Jackson forces readers to step outside the romantic suspense box and enter an elusive world of undercover agents and crime lords. Victoria and Drake are memorable characters who will provide hours of enjoyment for even the most cynical of readers."

—*Romantic Times*

"Drake and Tori are tough, passionate, loyal, and attractive protagonists. Their courage and fire and their strong feelings for each other can't help but appeal to readers. So, too, will the non-stop action; there are no dull moments in *The Midnight Hour*."

—*Romance Reviews Today*

MORE...

SURRENDER

"The Madaris family is one that fans will never tire of! First-time readers will also feel right at home—this is a self-contained story as well as a sequel!"

—*Romantic Times*

TRUE LOVE

"In *True Love*, Brenda Jackson writes with a smooth pen and a very distinctive voice. Prepare yourself for twists, turns, and family secrets that only add wonder to an already enjoyable story."

—*Romantic Times*

FIRE AND DESIRE

"With her inimitable style, Ms. Jackson has created another rip-roaring, seductively sensual love story that is sure to take the romance-reading community by storm. As always, her standard of excellence is evident in every scintillating page of *Fire and Desire*."

—*Romantic Times*

SECRET LOVE

"Jackson has done it again. Fantastic."

—*Romantic Times*

ALSO BY BRENDA JACKSON

The Midnight Hour

A Family Reunion

Ties That Bind

The Savvy Sistahs

The Playa's Handbook

Unfinished Business

BRENDA JACKSON

St. Martin's Paperbacks

UNFINISHED BUSINESS

Cover photography by Sharon Greene, composition by George Cornell.

ISBN: 0-312-98998-9
EAN: 80312-98998-9

Printed in the United States of America

St. Martin's Paperbacks edition / April 2005

St. Martin's Paperbacks are published by St. Martin's Press, 175 Fifth Avenue, New York, NY 10010.

10 9 8 7 6 5 4 3 2 1

ACKNOWLEDGMENTS

This book is dedicated to all the faithful readers of my Madaris Family and Friends Series who waited patiently and untiringly for Christy's and Alex's story. I appreciate all of you and I thank you from the bottom of my heart.

To my hero, husband and best friend, Gerald Jackson, Sr., and to my two sons, Gerald Jr. and Brandon.

Special thanks to my readers who are accompanying me on the Madaris Family and Friends 10-Year Anniversary Celebration Cruise to the Bahamas. Let the celebration begin.

To Cruises and Tours Unlimited, Jacksonville, Florida, the title sponsor of the Madaris Family and Friends Anniversary Cruise.

To the members of the Brenda Jackson Book Club—you are a very special group.

To Jeff Westcott, Special Agent, FBI, Jacksonville, Florida. Thanks for taking the time to answer all my questions.

To Shemell Perry. This one is for you.

And to my Heavenly Father who makes all things possible.

THE MADARIS FAMILY

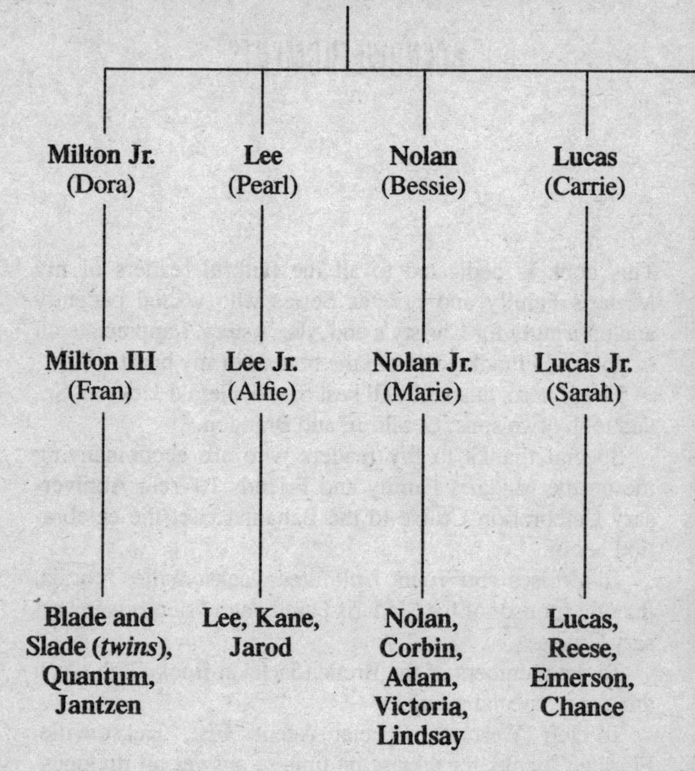

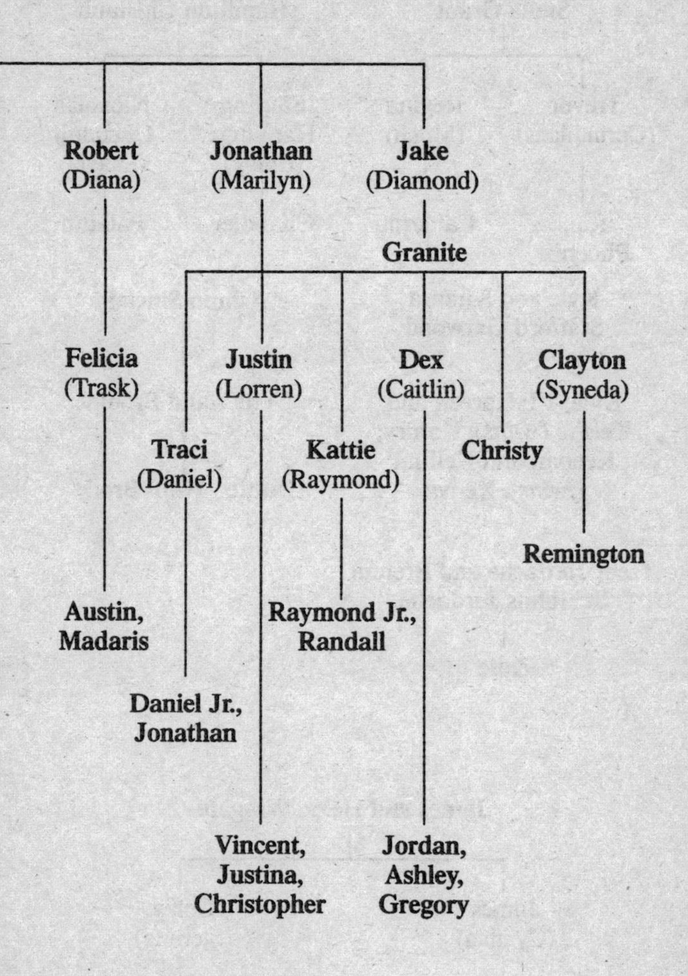
Robert
(Diana)
Jonathan
(Marilyn)
Jake
(Diamond)
Granite
Felicia
(Trask)
Justin
(Lorren)
Dex
(Caitlin)
Clayton
(Syneda)
Traci
(Daniel)
Kattie
(Raymond)
Christy
Remington
Austin,
Madaris
Raymond Jr.,
Randall
Daniel Jr.,
Jonathan
Vincent,
Justina,
Christopher
Jordan,
Ashley,
Gregory

FRIENDS OF THE MADARIS FAMILY

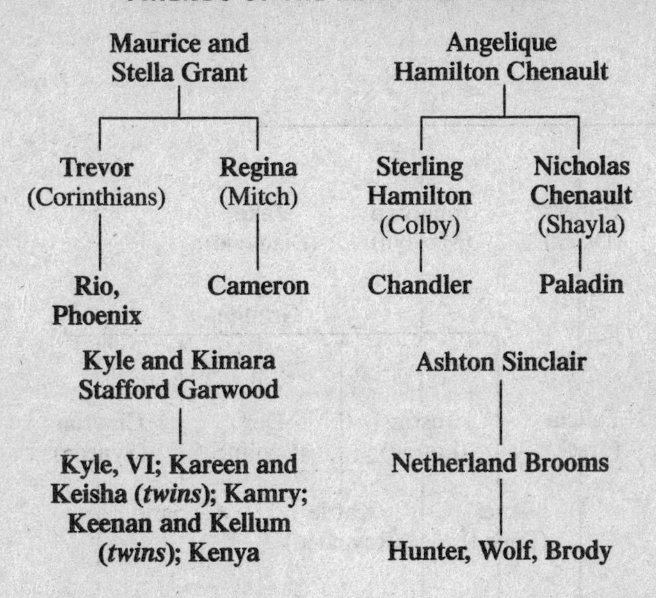

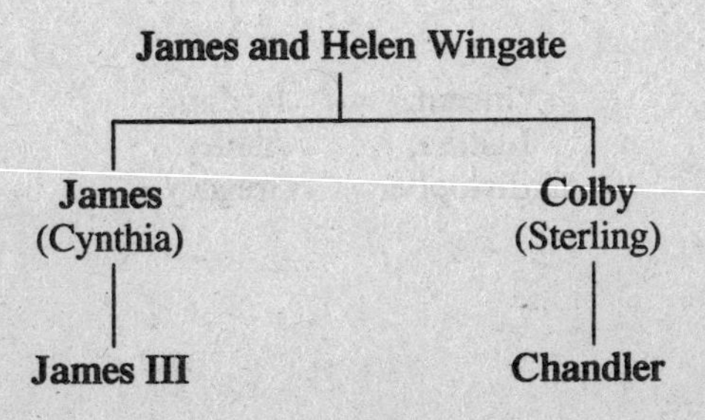

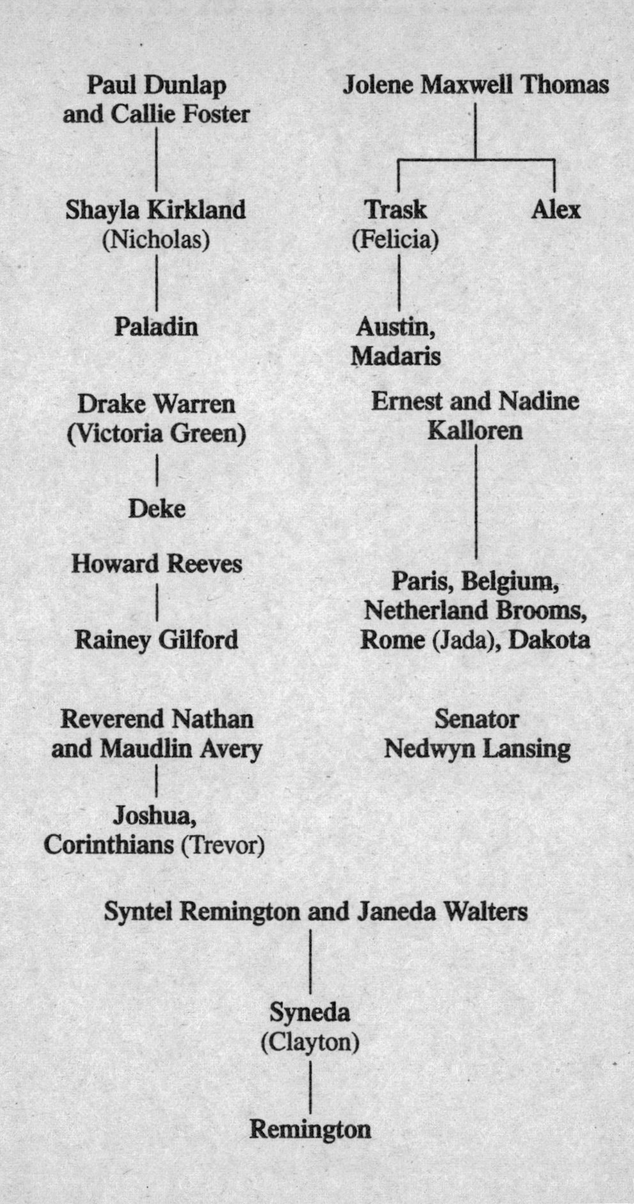
Paul Dunlap
and Callie Foster
Shayla Kirkland
(Nicholas)
Paladin
Jolene Maxwell Thomas
Trask
(Felicia)
Alex
Austin,
Madaris
Drake Warren
(Victoria Green)
Deke
Howard Reeves
Rainey Gilford
Ernest and Nadine
Kalloren
Paris, Belgium,
Netherland Brooms,
Rome (Jada), Dakota
Reverend Nathan
and Maudlin Avery
Joshua,
Corinthians (Trevor)
Senator
Nedwyn Lansing
Syntel Remington and Janeda Walters
Syneda
(Clayton)
Remington

Unfinished Business

Stop being mean, bad-tempered and angry. Quarreling, harsh words. . . . Instead, be kind to each other, tenderhearted, forgiving one another, just as God has forgiven you.

—EPHESIANS 4:31–32

PROLOGUE

Christina Marie Madaris stood at the window that faced her mother's flower garden as she remembered a quote from Albert Einstein: "In the middle of difficulty lives opportunity."

She sighed deeply, acknowledging that this had been a very difficult two years since graduating from college and returning to Houston. But now she was faced with an opportunity, one she had decided to take advantage of.

She turned slightly when she heard the sound of car doors opening and closing. Drawing in a deep breath, she glanced down the walkway that could be seen from where she stood. As she'd known they would, three men came into view, and although she could see them clearly, they couldn't see her, so she took a moment to study them. They had similar features, indicating that they were brothers. They were tall and handsome and had the gait of self-assured men.

But she knew how vastly different they were.

Justin, the physician, was the oldest of the three. He had been twenty and away at college when she was born twenty-four years ago. Of her three brothers she considered him the warm, sensitive, diplomatic one. That didn't mean she had never seen him angry. It just took a lot to get him there.

Dex, the geologist, was eighteen months younger than Justin and didn't know the meaning of *diplomacy*. Where Justin could be warm and sensitive, Dex could be hard and unyielding. Most of the time he was way too serious, but he was always a man of his word.

And then there was Clayton, the attorney. He was three years younger than Justin. Because Clayton was in high school and still living at home when she was born, she'd always had a special bond with him. He had been the fun brother, the one who would let her get away with just about anything.

She couldn't help but smile when she recalled how her birth had been a shock to her two older sisters, Traci and Kattie. They had been in their early teens, and for the longest time they could not get over the fact that their forty-something parents were still sexually active.

Christy thought of all the fun she had being the baby in the family, with three overprotective brothers and two overindulgent sisters. She had never minded how her brothers' guard-dog attitudes always scared guys away because she had truly believed that she was going to grow up and marry Alexander Maxwell. He had been their neighbor and a close friend of her brothers. Boy, what a fool she had been at thirteen to believe Alex's promise, and an even bigger fool to continue to believe it for eight solid years. But he had set her straight on the matter three years ago, and as far as she was concerned her life had been in total shambles since.

Because the Madarises and Maxwells were such close friends, it was not uncommon for her and Alex to be invited to the same functions. Each and every time she had been around him had been difficult, and returning home from college had been the worst. Seeing him was a constant reminder of what a fool she had been to believe the eight-year difference in their ages meant nothing and that he was doing just as he had promised—waiting for her to grow up.

The phone call she had gotten two days ago had been a blessing. It would give her the opportunity to pick up her life and move on, something she could not do if she remained in Houston.

She had already told her parents her decision, and the

only thing left to do was tell her brothers and sisters. She decided to tell her brothers first, since everybody knew her sisters couldn't hold water and she wanted her brothers to hear it from her. She was glad that Justin, who lived near Dallas, was in town visiting, so she could tell all three of them at the same time.

She knew they wouldn't like her news. More than likely they would try to talk her out of leaving, saying that she already had a great job as a reporter for the *Houston Chronicle* and that she didn't need to take the job in Cincinnati, Ohio.

What she couldn't tell them and what they didn't know was that the job opportunity was only part of the reason she was leaving. She needed space and a chance to do something she hadn't been able to do for three years.

Repair her heart.

And more than anything, although it would be hard for them to do, she intended to get their blessings and their promise not to interfere in her life. She would not be satisfied until they finally acknowledged that she was no longer a little girl but a grown woman. If their parents could accept that, then it was time her brothers did as well.

"Christy? Mom and Dad said you wanted to see us."

She slowly turned around and met three pair of curious and intense eyes. She shifted her gaze from one to the other, smiled, then said softly, "Yes. I have some news that I want to share with the three of you."

Seven hours later

Alexander Julian Maxwell bolted upright in bed when he heard the telephone ring. Suddenly he remembered he was back in Houston and not in Miami, where he had been for the past week. Since leaving the FBI as a federal agent a few years ago, the company he owned, Maxwell Investigative Services, was expanding, which meant more cases to solve, which oftentimes took him out of town.

When the telephone rang again, he wiped the sleep from his face before reaching over to pick it up. "Yeah?"

"Alex, sorry if I woke you, man. This is Clayton."

Alex wiped another hand down his face and glanced across the room at the illuminated clock. It was past midnight. The last time Clayton had called him in the middle of the night had been when he'd wanted him to find someone: his wife's biological father. "Clayton, what's going on?"

He heard Clayton's frustrated sigh before he said, "I need you to do me a favor, and I want you to keep it between us. That includes not telling Dex and Justin."

Alex lifted a brow. "What is it?"

"Do you still fly into Cincinnati occasionally to check on that business interest you have there?"

Alex knew Clayton was referring to the rental properties he had recently acquired as part of his investment portfolio. "Yes, why?"

"Whenever you go there, I'd like you to check on Christy, but do it discreetly because—"

"Christy? Why would Christy be in Cincinnati?"

"She's moving there."

"What!"

"Yeah, we were surprised as hell, too. She broke the news to me, Justin, and Dex this evening. She's taking a job there, claims it's an opportunity of a lifetime."

Alex took a deep breath, not believing what he was hearing. Christy was moving to Cincinnati? He couldn't believe the Madarises were letting her move way across the country, considering how overprotective they were of her. Her leaving home to attend college was one thing, but permanently relocating to another state was altogether different.

"And you, Dex, and Justin are OK with it?"

"No, we aren't OK with it, but we didn't have much choice, with the folks giving her their blessings. Of course they expected us to give ours."

Alex shook his head. "And the three of you did?"

"Yes, grudgingly. And we even promised not to interfere."

"But *you* are," Alex pointed out.

"Yeah. I need to know she's OK. So will you do that for me?"

Alex wiped another hand down his face. "Yeah, I'll check on her whenever I'm in Cincinnati."

"Thanks, man. I owe you one."

"Don't mention it."

After hanging up the phone, Alex closed his eyes and inhaled deeply. Reopening them, he had thrown back the covers to sit on the side of the bed when the phone rang again. Thinking it was Clayton calling back, he quickly picked it up. "Yeah?"

"Alex, sorry to disturb you, but this is Dex."

Alex raised a dark brow. "Dex?"

"Yes, and I have a favor to ask of you and I want it kept between us. I don't even want my brothers to know about this."

Alex nodded. "Sure. What do you need?" he asked, though he already knew the answer.

"Jake mentioned you have a business interest in Cincinnati."

"Yes, that's right."

"Good. This is what I want you to do. . . ."

A half hour later, Alex pushed his sliding glass door aside and stepped out onto his deck. The night was hot and humid, not uncommon for July. He inhaled deeply thinking about the calls he had gotten from Clayton, Dex, and Justin. They had made the same request and each wanted things kept confidential.

Alex stared into the darkness as his thoughts shifted to Christy's thirteenth birthday. He had come upon her crying and saying that no guy would ever want to marry her when she grew up because of her overprotective brothers. As a way to cheer her up, he had told her to stop crying because he would wait for her to grow up and marry her himself, and had gone so far as to take a ring he wore on his pinkie and place it on hers.

With an exasperated sigh he then recalled that night three years ago when Christy had been home on spring break from college and had reminded him of that promise. He was surprised she had remembered that time and tried to explain to her that he had only been teasing her that day. He emphasized the eight-year difference in their ages, told her that she needed to start dating guys her own age and stop waiting for him, because he had no intention of ever marrying her or any other woman. He knew his words had hurt her that night and since then she had made him her sworn enemy.

But what he hadn't been able to forget, more than anything else about that night, was the kiss they'd shared before he had given her the brush-off. Desire for her had consumed his body to a degree he hadn't thought possible. And when he had kissed her—"devoured her mouth" was a better way to describe it—he had felt things he had never felt before . . . or felt since.

He rubbed his hand down his face, admitting that was the crux of his problem. Christy Madaris was still off-limits to him. She would forever be the baby sister of three of his closest friends. But that hadn't stopped him from finally realizing that Christy was no longer a girl but a woman—a very beautiful and desirable woman.

A woman he desperately wanted.

He sucked in a deep breath. The day of reckoning had arrived. Although he had begun seeing her as a desirable woman, he had been able to control his lust because in Houston she was in a safe place, surrounded by family, and therefore untouchable. In a strange sort of way, he had been satisfied in knowing not only was she untouchable to him, but was hands-off to other men as well, mainly because of her brothers' overprotectiveness. But now it seemed the tables had turned . . . and definitely on him.

Moving to Cincinnati meant she was no longer in a safe

place. No longer protected by her brothers. No longer untouchable. The thought of that made his skin crawl, literally shook him to the core. Christy was a beautiful woman. She would draw attention. Men would take notice. They would react.

Damn.

Without her brothers' protection, she would be like a minnow in a pool of sharks, and there was no way on this earth he would allow that to happen. He wanted her and he'd damn if he would let any other man get close to her.

He glanced down at his hand and studied the ring he had placed on his finger when an angry Christy had given it back to him. As far as he was concerned, the ring represented unfinished business between them.

Unfinished business.

He sighed heavily, and at that very moment, he knew he would risk everything to finish it.

Jonathan Madaris hung up the phone and slowly shook his head.

"Was that Justin?"

He looked up and met his wife's gaze as she came out of the bathroom. A profound sense of both love and pride swept through him. She had been his wife, best friend, lover . . . his everything . . . for almost forty-five years, and he thought she was just as beautiful today as she had been the first time he laid eyes on her.

He scanned her body from head to toe. Tonight she was wearing one of those sexy nightgowns their daughter-in-law Syneda had given her for Christmas, and she looked gorgeous in it.

"Jonathan?"

He blinked. She stood leaning against the huge wooden bedpost, waiting for his response. "Yes, that was Justin and his message was the same as the ones Dex and Clayton left earlier. He's asked Alex to check on Christy whenever he goes to Cincinnati on business. Of course, like his brothers, Justin is claiming he's doing it for our benefit, so we won't be worried about her."

Marilyn Madaris chuckled as she crossed the room to her husband. "We're *not* worried. In time they'll discover that Christy is no longer a baby; she's a mature young woman who is smart, has a good head on her shoulders, and is old enough to make her own decisions. She'll do fine. I'll miss her, but it's time for her to seek her own destiny."

Jonathan nodded as his thoughts shifted back to his three sons. "They promised her they wouldn't interfere."

Marilyn shook her head, smiling. "Yes, but we knew they would anyway. Too bad they don't realize they've made a grave mistake in soliciting Alex's help. That's like asking the rooster to watch over the henhouse."

Jonathan grinned as he pulled his wife into his arms. Her skin was so soft. Over the years, with five of their six kids married and on their own, he and Marilyn had been able to do the things they'd always wanted to do. Both had retired years ago from being educators in the Houston school system and spent their time traveling to places they had always wanted to see and visiting old friends who lived all over the country.

And now that Christy had finished college and was living her own life, his main concern was this woman he held in his arms. He wanted to devote the rest of his life to her and her alone. "So, do you think we should warn them of that fact?" he asked, burying his nose in the sweet smell of her hair and bringing her still-trim body closer to his.

"No, I think we should stay out of it. Christy will be able to handle her brothers when the time comes."

"And Alex?"

She slowly shook her head. "Now, Alex is another matter altogether."

She knew the pain Alex had unintentionally caused their daughter. Marilyn also knew he had begun seeing Christy in a whole new light, and would even go so far as to say that she believed he was in love with Christy, although it seemed he hadn't figured that fact out yet. And she knew Christy was still in love with him. But unfortunately, Alex would find out the hard way that when it came to that formidable Madaris pride, love had nothing to do with it . . . at least until he could melt the hard ice encasing Christy's heart.

"No pain, no gain. I think Christy and Alex will have hard lessons to learn," she added. "And when the time comes we'll be there for them."

Jonathan said nothing for a long moment. "And in the meantime?" he finally asked, his gaze feasting on hers before he leaned down and brushed his lips over hers.

She smiled that smile she only had for him, the one that had opened up his heart the first time he'd seen it. "And in the meantime we will enjoy our children and grandchildren and, most important, each other."

He held her charcoal gray gaze captive. "I love you," he murmured softly.

"I love you as well. And I want our baby girl to share this same type of love, one that's strong, impenetrable, and endless. It wasn't easy for us in the beginning and it won't be easy for her and Alex," she said, thinking of their own rocky start so many years ago.

"What's meant to be will be," Jonathan said, pulling her closer into his arms.

Marilyn's smile widened as she gave a soft sigh. "Yes, what's meant to be will be."

Book One

The Hunt

CHAPTER 1

Christy glanced at her reflection in the full-length mirror and smiled. This particular outfit, a slip dress of that particular shade of lime green that was so popular, and her new hairdo, a work of art by Lamar, had transformed her into a woman she didn't even recognize.

Lamar had given her a haircut to complement her face. The mass of reddish curls that flowed around her shoulders looked fuller, thicker, and even more vibrant. She had turned quite a number of male heads after leaving the salon. Her brothers used to tease her about the color of her hair, which she had inherited from her paternal great-grandmother.

Christy's smile deepened at the thought that she looked somewhat older, a little sophisticated, maybe even a little daring. Her high-heeled sandals and her leather double-handled purse added the finishing touch. She was looking forward to her date tonight with Kevin, a guy she had met last weekend at a party given by a co-worker. After a rather long and pleasant conversation, she and Kevin had practically danced the night away. She couldn't remember the last time she had shaken her booty so much. And he hadn't been a bad dancer, either. When she decided to call it a night, he had walked her to her car and surprised her when he pulled her into his arms and kissed her.

OK, so she hadn't felt the passion, the zing, the torrid explosion that had ambushed her that time Alex had kissed her, but Kevin did have potential and with a little more practice his kiss would eventually graduate from being nothing more than a pleasant mouth exercise.

Although she hated admitting it, Alex's kiss had stirred a carnal desire within her that she hadn't known existed. It had introduced her to sexual impulses, hot dreams, and basic urges. Just thinking about it was a lot for a twenty-four-year-old virgin to handle. But she would handle it, since she wasn't into casual sex. The man she gave her virginity to was going to be the one who was destined to be a part of her life forever.

She glanced around when she heard the sound of the doorbell, wondering who it could be. She didn't know a lot of people in Cincinnati, since she'd been in town for only a month, and she had opted to meet Kevin at the club instead of telling him where she lived. She was still cautious, since she didn't know him that well, and although he had been the perfect gentleman at the party on Saturday night, she couldn't help but remember the number-one rule her brother Dex had given her when she had moved out of her parents' home into an apartment upon returning home from college: *Never give a man your address until you get to know him better. And if he gives you trouble, call me and I'll come kick his ass.*

She smiled knowing Dex had been dead serious. Crossing the room, she headed for the door. She glanced through the peephole, but because dusk had settled in and the person's back was to her, she knew it was a man but couldn't make out his identity. "Yes, who is it?"

"Alex Maxwell."

Sharp needles pricked Christy's heart at the sound of that name. Surely she had heard wrong and the man standing on the other side of the door was not the person she had always thought of as "her Alex" until that fateful night three years ago when he had let her know he was not "her" anything.

She quickly looked out the peephole and drew in a deep shuddering breath when he turned and she stared straight into the face of the one person she had moved over one thousand miles from her home to escape. The main question that began forming in what was left of her confused mind was, what in the world was Alex doing in Cincinnati?

Knowing he was the only person who could answer that question, she snatched open the door and gave him a hostile glare and spoke with all the loathing she felt: "What are you doing here, Alex?"

Alex stood in the doorway, transfixed, mesmerized. He doubted he would ever get used to this grown-up version of Christy. When he had seen her that night three years ago at a charity auction, it had been the first time he'd noticed how she had gone from being a string-bean wisp of a girl to a young woman with luscious curves that had been so apparent in the flirty little gown she'd been wearing.

But now, seeing her standing before him, regardless of the fact that she had a huge frown on her face and her eyes were shooting daggers at him, he was suddenly tongue-tied, and he'd never been a man at a loss for words. It didn't help matters that she was wearing a dress that resembled nothing more than a slip and it clung to her body a lot more than that other one had.

"Alex, I asked what you're doing here?"

The sharp tone of Christy's voice snapped him out of his trance as he met her murderous gaze. "I was in town on business and thought I'd drop by to see you."

The anger in her eyes darkened. "Tell that to someone else. First of all, what business could you possibly have here in Cincinnati? Second, since we're no longer friends, why would you want to see me?" Her glare deepened. "My brothers sent you, didn't they? They sent you here to spy on me."

Alex glanced around. A couple of Christy's neighbors were arriving home and seemed interested in what was going on. He met Christy's gaze again. "No, I'm not here for your brothers," he said truthfully.

Although they had asked him to check on her, he would have done so anyway. His reason for being here had nothing to do with her brothers but everything to do with the unfinished business between them. "Let me inside, Christy. We're causing a scene."

Christy noticed what he said was true and reluctantly stepped aside to let him in. This was a nice apartment complex that catered to families. She'd only recently moved in, and the last thing she wanted was for any of her neighbors to think she was having any sort of domestic issues.

Once the door closed behind Alex, she turned to him, her expression fighting mad. "You have no right to be here."

Alex sighed deeply. Over the years, her reddish-brown hair had become more vibrant and was the color of flame, which basically matched her fiery temper. But even in all her heated splendor, she looked beautiful, desirable, and the sight of her made his gut clench. "I do have business here in Cincinnati, since I have investment property that I check on occasionally. But besides that, I had to come and see you, Christy," he said, thinking she was much too tempting for her own good. "There's unfinished business between us."

"Unfinished business?" she snapped, placing her hands on her hips and taking a step closer as rage engulfed her. "Oh, trust me, any business that I thought may have existed between us in *my* little girl's mind is definitely finished. You made things perfectly clear that night. You were right, I needed to grow up and I have. I'm three years older and wiser. I know not to blindly trust the words of a man. I know how to tell the difference between pity and sincerity. And I know how it feels to give your heart—your undying love and affection—to someone just for him to trample it."

She inhaled deeply, trying to place her full concentration on her anger and not the sight of him standing in her living room. Six feet and four inches of the most gorgeous man she had ever seen. Even in Ohio, it was easy to see the word *Texas* written all over him while he was impeccably dressed in a chambray shirt, designer jeans, boots, and an expensive-looking blazer. His black hair was cut low on his head, and all his handsome features, including his dark, penetrating eyes, added depth to his semi-sweet chocolate–colored skin.

She needed him to leave before the tears started coming. She had cried her last tear over him. "I loved you and you threw that love back in my face because you thought I was too young to know my feelings," she said heatedly. "Well, I'm doing just what you suggested. I've grown up and let go of childhood dreams and fantasies. I have a wonderful job and I've even taken your advice about dating men closer to my age. Things are going just great for me," she lied, deciding he didn't have to know that. "And I intend to have a fantastic love life."

Something within Alex snapped with that proclamation. He gritted his teeth, thinking she had definitely said the wrong thing. "What the hell do you know about a fantastic love life?" he asked sharply, grabbing her arm.

She snatched her arm back, lifted her chin, and met his glare. "Nothing yet, but I intend to learn."

A rush of anger tore into him. She would learn, all right, but only with him. It would be a cold day in hell before he let any other man touch her that way. Dammit, she was his! She had loved him once, and he would see to it that she loved him again.

Suddenly his head began swimming and the first thought that came to his mind was that he was acting stone crazy. No woman had ever driven him to this point. He was dealing with emotions that were unfamiliar, hazardous, threatening to push his limit of control. He had to get a grip.

He exhaled slowly, trying to calm the rage consuming him. "Have dinner with me," he said in a strained voice.

"Dinner?" She slung back that single word as if the thought of going out to eat with him was as foreign as a six-dollar bill.

He watched as she threw her head back and all that fiery

red hair cascaded around her shoulders, making her look like a woman on the warpath, a woman who could take on anybody, including him. "I would not go out with you, Alexander Maxwell, if you were the last man on earth."

He inclined his head and glared back at her. Little did she know that he might as well be the last man on earth, since he was definitely the only man she would ever become involved with. "We need to talk, Christy."

"We don't need to do anything. I've already told you in plain English that we don't have anything to say. It's been said and, if I recall, you did most of the talking."

He shook his head. This was one stubborn woman, but he could be just as stubborn as she was. "I refuse to leave until we get a few things straight."

She crossed her arms over her chest and glared at him. "There is nothing to get straight. Now if you'll excuse me, I have a date, so please leave."

Alex's features darkened. Just the thought that she was going out with another man had him seeing red again. He knew he had to pull himself together, get himself in check. Besides, he had pushed her enough for one night, especially when she had a tendency to push back.

He would be in town for a few more days, and although Christy might wish otherwise, she hadn't seen the last of him. Before he returned to Houston, she would definitely know who she belonged to.

Without saying anything else, he turned and walked out the door.

Christy closed her eyes and inhaled deeply. How dare he? How dare Alex show up on her doorstep like this! After ignoring her for three years he thought they had a reason to talk?

She inhaled again, calmly this time, as she tried to understand why on earth he assumed there was unfinished business between them. They had not only finished things between them, but he had let her know in no uncertain terms that things should never have escalated to that point anyway.

She had felt as stupid as any one woman had a right to feel when he had looked into her face, after she'd reminded him that he had given her that pinkie ring as a promise of marriage on her thirteenth birthday and said, *Christy, you know I was just kidding with you that day, don't you?*

No, she hadn't known he'd only been kidding. Wearing his ring had meant everything to her, but he had looked her dead in the eye and said, *It meant nothing!* She had found out the hard way that humiliation could make a person feel so awful, so low, that for as long as she lived she would never forgive him for making her feel that way. And tonight she couldn't help but notice that the ring was back on his finger. She was surprised he hadn't tossed it away when she gave it back to him.

A sharp pain she had tried so hard to ignore for the past three years touched her heart, reminding her of the reason she had fallen in love with him at thirteen. In her mind he had been her soul mate. To her he had been *Alexander the Great,* just like the nickname she'd given him in her preteen years. Even when she had gotten old enough to know what she wanted, it had always been Alex Maxwell. Alex who'd always had an older, sophisticated, and mature air about him. Alex with his smooth, sure walk, articulate talk, tall, lean, well-built body, an impeccable dresser, sharp, intelligent, all the things she wanted in a man.

There had always been this calm and collected spirit about him. He had always been a person in complete control, never showing any deep ingrained emotions. To her he had been Mr. Cool and she had admired that quality about him, but now she hated it with a vengeance. That night three years ago, she had seen just how ironclad that cool control was. She had seen him lose his anger but never his control. She would love pushing him to the limit, seeing him snap, but doubted such a thing was possible.

Deciding she didn't want to think about Alex any longer, she grabbed her purse off the table. More than anything, she intended to have fun tonight and was determined to erase the forever cool and in control Alex Maxwell from her mind once and for all.

Alex had had a ton of messages waiting for him when he returned to his hotel room. Most of them, he figured, were from the Madaris brothers. He was too upset to talk to anyone tonight and decided to wait until morning to return their calls.

He pinched the bridge of his nose, not believing how angry he was. He was like a man possessed. If he didn't know better, he would think he was in love. He let out a frustrated sigh. Dammit, he knew better than that since he was incapable of loving anyone; unable to show that emotion . . . thanks to his poor excuse of a father.

He walked over to the hotel's window and looked out, and recalled just when he'd realized how Carl Maxwell's disappearing act had left a scar on him. He hadn't quite reached his first birthday when his father had walked out on his wife and two sons. But the child in Alex had loved the missing parent anyway, and had actually believed that because of that love, his father would one day miraculously return. No one, he had thought in his young, naïve mind, would not accept that much love. He was proven wrong when his father never returned to the family he had deserted.

The day he had realized the truth, that all the love in the world wouldn't make his father return, he had lost control and totally trashed his bedroom. On that day he had promised himself that no matter what, he would never fall in love and no one would ever make him lose control of his emotions again. By the time Alex left for college at sixteen, he had learned a hard lesson in life and had vowed never to put stock in the power of love.

His thoughts shifted back to Christy and he felt a deep pounding of his heart in his chest. If it wasn't love he was feeling, than what was it? What had him in such turmoil at the thought of her with someone else?

He rubbed his hand down his face, feeling both mentally and physically exhausted. Moments later, he released a slow breath. He might not want any part of love, but he did want Christy.

And no matter what, he was determined to have her.

CHAPTER 2

"So, how was your date last night with Kevin?"

Christy glanced up as Shemell Parker dropped down into the chair next to her desk. It was at the party Shemell had given where Christy and Kevin had met. He had recently moved into Shemell's apartment complex and she had invited him.

Shemell was twenty-six and was the first one to welcome Christy to the *Cincinnati Enquirer* when she began working there a month ago. She was a reporter for the entertainment section and was determined to find the perfect man to marry before her thirtieth birthday.

Christy smiled thinking of her date with Kevin last night. "It was fun. In fact, we're going dancing at the club again tonight."

Shemell beamed. "Umm, two nights in a row. Things are sounding serious."

Christy shook her head as she tossed the file she'd been working on aside. "Trust me, it's not. He's just a lot of fun and I have a lot of nervous energy to work off."

There was no need to explain that it was probably more anger she was working off than nervous energy. Alex showing up at her place unexpectedly last night hadn't been a good thing. And to make matters worse, it had been Alex and not Kevin who had intruded into her dreams, igniting some of those basic urges that would come to the forefront whenever Alex was around.

"Well, I'm glad you and Kevin seem to be hitting it off. I don't know a lot about him, but he seems to be a—"

Shemell stopped talking in midsentence when her gaze latched on to someone who had entered the newsroom. Christy glanced over her shoulder to see who had gotten Shemell's attention, and all she saw was a middle-aged white woman who was walking toward her boss, Malcolm Wilcox's office. It seemed everyone had stopped what they were doing and was staring.

"What's going on?" Christy whispered, curious as to what was happening.

Shemell shook her head sadly. "That's Morganna Patterson. Her family used to be one of the pillars of the communities until around five years ago, when their manufacturing company went bankrupt and the family hit rock bottom. But the Patterson name still carries some weight in this town, especially since her great-grandfather was one of the founders of the *Enquirer*."

Christy nodded. "Why do you think she's here?"

Shemell sighed. "Probably because her daughter has contacted her again with more information."

Christy raised a brow. "I don't understand. What kind of information?"

Shemell leaned closer to Christy and whispered, "Two years ago Mrs. Patterson's fourteen-year-old daughter, Bonita, ran away from home. She used to get into all sorts of trouble around town, not being able to handle the family going from riches to rags. So it wasn't surprising when we heard she had run away without a trace, leaving a note letting her parents know she thought they sucked, because of her financial ruin, like it had been deliberate. She was nothing but a spoiled, ungrateful kid."

Christy nodded, thinking it was sad that teenage runaways in this country were becoming an epidemic. She had written a report on the problem while working as a reporter in Houston. "Did she ever come back?"

"No. Mrs. Patterson claims her daughter is dead somewhere and she knows it for certain because periodically she gets messages from Bonita from the grave."

Christy blinked. "Really?"

Shemell rolled her eyes upward. "Well, of course we all know she's off her rocker, but the woman is convinced there is some diabolical international organization that's kidnapping teenage runaway girls and shipping them to some foreign country and using them in a slave trade."

"Wow," Christy said. "Has anyone reported this to the FBI?" She asked since she knew kidnappings fell within their jurisdiction.

Shemell nodded. "Yes, but their investigation ended when they couldn't find anything to support Morganna's claim. Everyone around these parts figures Morganna Patterson has a few screws loose, but because of her family's name they pretend to believe her. Her family's former ties with this paper are the reason she brings any news here instead of taking it to the police. Cincinnati's finest won't give her the time of day, because they are short staffed, and the FBI refuses to take anything she has to say seriously anymore."

Shemell leaned back in her chair. "Malcolm is a longtime family friend and just to make her happy he usually will assign one of his reporters to take down the latest development, assure the woman we'll investigate things, and then a few days later we discreetly file the information away."

Christy sighed deeply. "If people assume she's not operating with a full deck, then why doesn't her family get the necessary help for her?"

Shemell smiled. "Again, because of the family name. She's harmless and not hurting anyone, except maybe someone who's nutty enough to believe her story. Morganna's mother's side of the family were from Louisana. I understand her grandmother was supposedly psychic, which is probably why Morganna actually thinks she's communicating with the dead."

Christy nodded, thinking Mrs. Patterson's story was probably more interesting than the one she had covered that morning about the cat that had gotten trapped in a sewer and had to be rescued by the fire department.

She knew that it was time she had a talk with Malcolm. She was an investigative reporter and wanted assignments she could sink her teeth into. Who knew? If she became so absorbed in her work, then she wouldn't have time to think about Alex Maxwell.

Alex sighed deeply as he hung up the phone and leaned back in the wingback chair in his hotel room. Justin and Clayton had been satisfied to hear he had seen Christy and that she was doing fine. Dex, however, had wanted in-depth information such as whether or not she was eating properly, if her apartment was in a safe location, and whether she was dating and, if so, who the guy was and how serious it was.

Alex had decided to tell the brothers as little as possible; after all, he'd meant what he had told Christy. Her brothers were not the reason he was in Cincinnati. They deserved to know she was doing OK, but that was it. Besides, the shit would hit the fan when they discovered his true reason for being here. He fully understood that when the depth of his relationship with Christy was revealed, he'd have the Madaris brothers to deal with. But at the moment that concern was the least of his problems. Right now he had to first go about establishing that relationship. And Christy was being deliberately difficult.

It was evident that she was not in a forgiving mood. But he was a patient man and she deserved at least that from him. So while he waited for her to come around, there was one thing he could do.

Eliminate the competition.

Be careful what you ask for because you just might get it.

Christy sighed as she gazed around Morganna Patterson's

modest home. She had gone into Malcolm's office to have a heart-to-heart talk with him about the type of assignments she'd been getting. He had listened to her complaints and then had turned the cards on her by giving her the one assignment none of the other reporters wanted: to investigate Mrs. Patterson's story—or at least pretend to be doing so.

Christy had to admit the woman seemed kind and sincere, and when she had arrived at the Pattersons' home she felt awful to see it in such disrepair. Before leaving the office she had pulled the Patterson file out of dead storage to take it home and read. Although everyone had pretty much written it off as fiction, Christy figured it would be interesting reading for the weekend, if nothing else.

She glanced up when Mrs. Patterson reentered the room with a pitcher of cold lemonade. The woman was such a gracious hostess, and Christy's heart went out to her. Malcolm had said the woman's daughter had run away and her husband had died within the same year, so she was living all alone.

"You look too young to be a reporter," Mrs. Patterson said, smiling, pouring lemonade in two glasses.

Christy smiled. She was getting used to that comment. "Yes, I'm probably the youngest reporter Malcolm has on his staff right now. I graduated from college two years ago and worked as a reporter for the *Houston Chronicle* before deciding to take the job here."

Deciding to jump right into the interview, Christy clicked on her tape recorder and said, "Tell me about your daughter, Mrs. Patterson."

She watched as sadness crept into the woman's eyes. "Had she lived, Bonita would have celebrated her sixteenth birthday two days ago."

Christy lifted a brow. "That was the most recent day she came to you in your dreams?"

"Yes."

"And you said when she came to you it was to warn you that another girl was about to be abducted?"

"Yes."

"And did she give you any information about the girl? A name? The town where she lived? Anything?"

Morganna shook her head. "The only thing she could tell me was that her name was associated with Christmas."

Christy frowned. *Christmas? Would the girl's name be Mary? Angel? Star?* "Is there anything else you can remember?"

"No, I've told you everything. My heart goes out to that young woman's family, whoever she is. Bonita explained once in an earlier dream how after being taken, she was put in the cargo section of this boat with other young women—all of them had been snatched and were frightened for their lives. They were told that no harm would come to them if they did what they were told and accepted how things would be from then on."

A gentle smile touched the woman's features. "Of course that was probably Greek to Bonita, who always had a mind of her own. Being rebellious came naturally to her. After a few months of being some man's love slave she couldn't take it anymore and tried to escape. It was then that she met her death."

A lump formed in Christy's throat. She didn't want to ask, but she had to. "And how did she die?"

The woman hesitated, then took a deep breath as tears filled her eyes. "Bonita was beheaded in front of every other woman to show what would happen to them if they tried to escape like she did."

Christy didn't say anything, and for a moment she had forgotten that whatever Morganna Patterson was telling her was nothing but a figment of the woman's confused imagination, although it had sounded real.

"And this place that your daughter was taken, where is it?"

The woman shook her head. "I don't know, because Bonita was never sure. All she knew was that it was in a foreign country, where the men spoke a language she didn't understand.

She was put in this harem with other teenage girls between the ages of fourteen and nineteen, from all over the world. Each girl was to serve whatever man chose her as his plaything. Some of the men she claimed were Americans."

Christy's eyes widened. "Americans?"

"Yes."

"Military men?"

"No, dignitaries. Men in power. She even said one was an American senator, although she never knew his name." More tears formed in the woman's eyes. "Bonita said he was one of the most abusive."

Christy took a huge sip of her lemonade thinking this woman really did have a wild imagination. "Do you know what you're saying, Mrs. Patterson?"

The woman nodded slowly, sadly. "Yes, I know what I'm saying, which is the reason I know all of this is a cover-up by our government. I was told by one FBI agent that Bonita is probably someplace alive and doesn't want to be found, but I know that's not true. I also know that everyone thinks my ability to communicate to my daughter from the grave might sound crazy, but it's the truth. I think I may have inherited psychic powers from my grandmother. Bonita comes to me in my dreams, and although she knows it's too late for her, she's trying to reach out and save the others."

Morganna Patterson reached out and took Christy's hand in hers. For several moments an air of sadness, desperation, and hopelessness hovered in the room. Christy couldn't help but see the heartfelt plea in the desolate eyes locked with hers. "Will you help me save them, Miss Madaris? Will you help me save all the others?"

CHAPTER 3

Christy inhaled sharply when she glanced through the peephole in her door. She couldn't believe that after all she'd said to Alex last night he would come back. She assumed he had left town to return to Houston that day. Evidently she'd been wrong on both counts.

She frowned. Apparently she hadn't made herself clear to him. She didn't need him snooping around on her brothers' behalf, and she most certainly didn't need him rehashing that night he had crushed her pride. It was over, done with. That time had passed and she wanted to get on with her life without any thoughts of him in it.

Her session with Morganna Patterson had lasted longer than planned. She had decided that unlike the other reporters she would not file the woman's story away and forget about it. Tomorrow she intended to go back over the file to see if there was anything in it worth checking out.

The doorbell rang again, grabbing Christy's attention. She wondered if she didn't answer the door Alex would assume she wasn't home. She shook her head. That was a coward's way out and the one thing she wasn't was a coward. She snatched open the door.

"Why are you here, Alex?"

Without waiting for an invitation, he walked past her. "We don't want to give your neighbors anything to talk about, do we?"

Alex turned and took note of the outfit she was wearing,

a rather short skirt and a pullover blouse. He always thought she had a gorgeous pair of legs and remembered that she had been a majorette while at Howard University. Her vibrant reddish brown hair, her most noticeable feature, caught his attention again tonight. The way she had it styled around her face and shoulders totally accented her toasted almond–colored skin. "You look nice, by the way. Another date tonight?"

Christy slammed the door shut, her facial features taut and her glare as icy as the North Pole. "Yes, and what's it to you? Do I need to call my brothers to let them know you've done your snooping and it's time to call you home?"

Alex stared at Christy. "I thought I made myself clear last night when I said I'm not here because of your brothers."

Christy placed her hands on her hips and stared back. "That's right. You claim there's this unfinished business between us. OK, then let's finish it so you can catch a plane back to Texas and get out of my life."

Alex met her glare. "There's no way we can finish this tonight, and as far as me getting out of your life, you can forget it."

The deep intensity of Alex's voice startled Christy. "Who the hell do you think you are, Alex? Three years ago you all but told me—although in a nice way—to go to hell, and now you have the nerve, the gall, the damn audacity, to stand here and tell me that you don't intend to get out of my life the way you asked me to get out of yours? I'm not someone you can kick to the curb, then come back and call out to play when the mood suits you."

"I was wrong, Christy."

Christy raised a surprised brow. Not in a million years had she expected him to admit that. She sighed. Too bad. He was a day late and a dollar short. "You're right, Alex, you were wrong. Now please get out of my life."

"Can we at least talk about it?"

"For what? It won't change a thing. It happened. It's over.

There's no way we can go back, wipe the slate clean, or start over, and it's all your fault."

Alex eyed her thoughtfully, then said, "That night you claimed you loved me. If you could fall out of love with me so easily, then I was right all along. It truly wasn't love you felt after all, was it, Christy?"

The darkening of Christy's eyes showed her seething rage. "How dare you tell me that I didn't love you! I've loved you since I was thirteen. I never took any of my dates seriously and my brothers' extreme case of overprotectiveness never bothered me because I always assumed that no matter what, I had you. I wore that ring proudly because as childish as it seemed, I truly believed in my heart that ring stood for something special. And in one night you showed me it hadn't stood for anything. None of it did—the ring, my love, my dreams—nothing. In one single night you destroyed it all."

"Christy, I—"

"No, I really don't want to hear it, Alex. No matter how I might have felt before, I'm no longer in love with you, and if you really care about my feelings, the decent thing to do is walk out that door and leave me alone."

Alex swallowed deeply. He refused to believe he had messed up so badly that it was beyond repair. He knew the Madarises well, and the one thing he did know about them was that when they fell in love it was forever. But then he also knew from his close association with Dex and Clayton that when it came to the issue of the Madaris pride, they could be unforgiving.

Christy was no different from her brothers. He had hurt her pride that night and there would be hell to pay before she found it in her heart to forgive him. But he refused to give up and let go.

He met her gaze. "I can't leave you alone, Christy."

A lump formed in Christy's throat. Why was he putting her through this? Telling him that she didn't love him was the hardest thing she'd ever had to do, and knowing it was a lie had made it even harder. But for now, the hurt and humiliation she had endured that night overshadowed any love she felt, and she would make sure it continued to do so. She could not think of forgiveness when she still felt pain. She had learned a valuable lesson and would not let Alex—or any man, for that matter—have control of her heart again.

Before Christy realized it, Alex took a step forward and drew her into his arms. Her breath caught in response to his closeness, the masculine scent he was emitting, and the sensuality of every single thing about him. She knew she had to resist him. She needed to ask him to step back, insist that he leave, but she couldn't get the words to form in her mouth. And at the moment pulling away from him wasn't an option, either. It seemed his deep, penetrating gaze had her transfixed in place.

Then the memories of that night three years ago flooded her mind, but not in the way she wanted them to. Instead of remembering the harsh words he had spoken, she was seized with memories of the kiss they had shared; just thinking of it had her light-headed, barely able to draw in her next breath.

Desire between them had flared that night, raged out of control, and then exploded in such a way that it had their tongues mating, licking, sucking, devouring all and resisting none. She believed that if it hadn't been for his ironclad control, combined with his ingrained sense of honor, he would have made love to her right there, in her parents' house. And she would have gladly given herself to him as she succumbed to the love she had for him as well as to the urgent hunger he had elicited within her.

"Christy?"

She blinked, returning her thoughts back to the present when she heard him say her name. She met his gaze and felt heat turning in her stomach when he reached out and softly stroked her cheek with his fingers. His gaze remained locked with hers. "I am sorry, Christy, for every damn thing I said that night, and I promise that I will make it up to you."

His whispered words had Christy taking a deep breath. She wished she could believe him, wished she had the will to turn her heart over to him for safekeeping. She had done so once and it had gotten ripped in shreds, and she couldn't let that happen again.

She watched as his mouth slowly lowered to hers. "I don't want this, Alex," she heard herself say, knowing it was a lie even as she said it. Her heart was resisting and she wished she could get her mind in sync. He was going to kiss her and she wanted it as much as she had wanted anything in her life. This would be their last kiss, she reasoned, and she knew if it was anything like the one they had shared that earlier night, it would remain inflamed in her mind forever.

Before Christy drew her next breath, Alex captured her mouth with his. Her initial reaction on contact was a slow moan that emitted from deep within her throat as a silky heat started forming in the pit of her stomach. Those sexual urges that she had discovered upon their first kiss were revving, taking over her mind, her body, and making her focus on what he was doing to her mouth as it moved slowly, steadily, and intensely over hers, inviting her tongue to join in the stimulating foray and mate with his.

He so easily made the kisses she had shared with Kevin obsolete, a waste of good time, expulsionable. Her heart pumped wildly, and when he tightened his hold on her and deepened the kiss, desire thickened her tongue. That same tongue he was a master at capturing with his, mating with and inflaming it so potently and powerfully. Christy felt fire move through all parts of her body. She felt her knees weaken, felt her brain turn to mush, and felt her vital sexual organs become alive and aroused with a need for something they never had before.

Alex had felt her initial resistance but continued to break down that resistance with passion. He was an experienced man and although he knew he had to be patient and not push her too far, their desire was burning too hot and too bright.

He drew her hard against him, needing the feel of her body close to his.

This was the second time he had kissed her. The last time she had been not more than a girl. But no mere wisp of a girl could have driven him close to losing control as she had that night, challenging his resolve and making such mind-whirling sensations grip him as they had. He could now admit that one of the reasons he had unleashed his fury on her that night was because he had not expected her to have such power over him, a man known for his control. She had done something no other woman had ever done. Rock his world. She had made a hunger well up in him so profound he'd been tempted to yield to anything and everything she demanded of him.

Even now, a part of him wanted to kiss her forever, wished he had all the time in the world to do so. He had longed for this again so many times. Every time he had seen her at some function or other, he had wanted to cross the room and take her into his arms. But his stubbornness, his refusal to believe that anything could happen between them had forced him to keep his distance. There was an eight-year difference in their ages. And the biggest reason: she was the baby sister of three of his closest friends. But then, over a period of time, he had slowly come to realize that none of those things mattered. He wanted her. He had fought it, cursed it, and tried to deny it. But now he could only accept it. He deepened the kiss and pulled her closer; so close the hardened tips of her breasts were scorching his chest and her delicious scent was filling his nostrils.

Suddenly, Christy pulled away. She backed up, breathing heavily.

"That was a mistake," she said softly, fully aware of the quiver in her voice.

"Nothing we do together will ever be a mistake," Alex said in a deep, husky voice. "That kiss was the best thing we could have done," he added. His smile was slow and easy. "I enjoyed it and so did you."

Christy frowned. She *had* enjoyed it, but would never admit it to him. "I have a date tonight, Alex. You need to leave."

He continued to stand there and stare at her. He was filled with so much raw desire that he couldn't think straight. Knowing she would be spending the evening with another man wasn't helping matters. "Who is he? Is he the same guy you went out with last night?"

Christy stiffened and glared at him. "And what if he is?"

"Then I think you should forget about him."

Before she could gather her thoughts and give him a blazing retort, he said, "Spend time with me this weekend, Christy. Show me around Cincinnati. I want to see the places you enjoy going."

Christy stared at Alex, trying not to let her jaw drop. He was serious. The damn nerve of him! He honestly thought that one kiss, one that still had her veins sizzling, could erase everything? "I will not forget about Kevin, nor will I spend the weekend with you, Alex. And when you leave here this time, don't come back."

"You enjoyed our kiss."

"It didn't mean anything."

He leaned forward, his lips mere inches away from touching hers. She could feel the heat of his breath, could almost taste it. "Oh, I think it meant a lot." A challenging smile touched the corners of Alex's lips. "And I *will* be back, Christy." He then slowly pulled away.

She watched as he turned and walked out her door.

CHAPTER 4

There were times when a man had to do what a man had to do.

Alex had been given that bit of advice a few years ago by his good friend Ashton Sinclair. It was why he was discreetly entering the door of the Shades of Blue nightclub.

The advice had been given during the time Ashton was in heavy pursuit of Nettie, the woman he had eventually married. But their beginnings hadn't been easy, since Nettie had been determined not to get involved with a military man and Ashton was military through and through—a colonel in the Marines, in fact.

Ashton had taken it upon himself to do what he'd said a man had to do to get the woman he loved, which hadn't just stopped at rigging a charity auction but had also included kidnapping. Alex didn't intend to go that far. Besides, Ashton was blessed with the gift of vision, so he'd had an advantage in knowing how his future with Nettie would turn out.

Unfortunately, Alex wasn't quite that certain about Christy, since she was still pretty pissed off with him. If he were to kidnap her she would probably press charges just to see him rot in jail . . . that is, if the Madaris brothers didn't kill him first.

Not wanting to think about the possibility of either, Alex glanced around wondering what was worse, the crowd of people that filled every nook and cranny or the band who was performing at a near deafening level. His jaw tightened when he spotted Christy sitting at a table with a man who he assumed was this Kevin she had mentioned. He guessed the guy looked decent enough, if you were a woman who went for the cover model type.

Alex was lucky to find a table in the back where he could observe but not be seen. So what if what he was doing could be labeled as spying? He was merely protecting his interests, he reasoned, even if Christy wouldn't see it that way.

After leaving her apartment he had circled around the neighborhood to wait until her date arrived, only to see Christy leave minutes later by herself, which meant she was meeting the guy instead of letting him come to her place to pick her up. A smart move, especially if she hadn't known the man for a while.

"What would you like to drink?"

Alex glanced up at the waitress who was smiling at him. Like everyone else in the place, she looked young, in her early twenties. He wasn't old, but he would bet at thirty-two he was the oldest person here. He took a quick glance back at Kevin and figured him to be probably the same age as Christy. More than ever he regretted the day he had told her to date guys her own age.

He looked back at the waitress. "I'll take a Bloody Mary."

The young woman's smile widened when she teasingly said, "You got her." She then walked off.

Alex sighed. The waitress was totally wrong. If he had her, he wouldn't be sitting in a crowded nightclub watching *her,* the woman he wanted, with another man.

"Are you sure you don't want anything else to drink, Christy?"

Christy glanced up at Kevin and smiled. She'd only had one drink in the hour or so that she'd been here, but for some reason she was beginning to feel light-headed, loose, brazen. She sighed as she shook her head, wondering what was wrong with her. "No, I'm fine."

Kevin smiled at her, showing a dimple that added charisma to his face. "Yeah, baby, you definitely are, and I'm dying to find out just how far that fine goes."

At any other time a remark like that from any man would be a total turnoff, but for some reason she liked it. In fact, it made her feel good to know another man wanted her. So *there*, Alex, she wanted to say. Leaning forward she whispered. "Do you think you're up to it?"

He chuckled. "Oh yeah, I'm up to it all right. Slide on over here and feel how up to it I am."

Christy laughed. "O Kevin, you're simply outrageous."

"I'm also hot for you. Let's leave this—"

At that moment Kevin's mobile phone rang. He snapped it open, and after a few short words he looked over at Christy. "Excuse me. I need to take this call. It's my job."

Christy nodded. He had told her that he worked as a computer engineer at some huge Fortune 500 company, but for the life of her at the moment she couldn't recall what company it was. What was wrong with her? She usually was sharp at remembering things.

"Don't go away. I'll be right back, and when I return, we're leaving here and going somewhere where we can be alone. All right?" he said, smiling.

Kevin's words intruded on her blurred thoughts. She felt herself returning his smile. "All right." She then watched as he walked off.

Alex's eyes narrowed as he watched Christy's date get up from the table and head in the direction of the men's room. This was the opportunity he had been waiting for. He hadn't liked the way the man had been hanging over Christy when the two had danced together earlier. He had held her too damn close.

On two occasions it had taken all of his control not to cross the room and snatch Christy out of the man's arms. But causing a scene was the last thing he wanted to do. If he thought Christy was pissed at him now, if he went so far as to embarrass her in any way she would write him off forever.

But dealing directly with Pretty Face Kevin was an entirely different story. It was time the two of them met. Getting up from his table, Alex headed towards the men's room too.

"Hey, man, your date is really wasted. What did you give her?"

Kevin smiled over at his friend as he zipped up his pants after using one of the urinals. "I dropped Trina a huge tip to slip something into her drink, something guaranteed to loosen her up. She's been playing hard to get and I intend to get into her stuff tonight. The beauty of it is that she won't remember a damn thing about it in the morning."

The other guy chuckled. "You're finally going to find out if she's really a redhead, huh?"

Kevin laughed. "You know it."

Alex stopped dead in his tracks, just inside the bathroom doorway. Fury coursed through him. The bastard had given Christy a date rape drug! He burst into the men's room ready to kill somebody.

The two men turned around and Kevin said, "What the hell!"

Alex went straight for Kevin, grabbing him by the throat. "You bastard!"

The other man grabbed Alex from behind. Alex elbowed him in the stomach before giving him a quick jab to his midsection, followed by a hard kick that sent him sprawling against the wall, where he collapsed, unconscious on the floor.

Alex then turned his attention back to Kevin, who'd remained pinned up against the sink. "What'd you give her?" he asked, his voice deadly.

Kevin was clearly terrified. "Hey, man, I don't know what you're talking about. I didn't give anybody anything."

Alex snatched him up and brought his face within inches of his own. "Then maybe a little flushing might help you remember."

With a firm grip on the collar of Kevin's shirt, Alex pulled him into one of the stalls and dunked his head in the toilet and held it there, then pulled him back up. "Can you remember anything now?"

Sputtering, Kevin nodded. "I . . . I had the waitress, who's a friend of mine, put some ketamine into her drink."

Ketamine! Alex's stomach muscles tightened. That was one of the most potent sexual assault drugs on the streets. He was well aware of the effects it had on a person. "How much did you give her?"

When Kevin didn't answer fast enough to suit Alex, his head got another dunking. "N-not much, just enough to do what I planned to do to her," Kevin said, sputtering water again. His hazel eyes were bulging and he was fighting for breath. "L-look, I-I didn't mean any harm."

In Alex's book that was the worst thing the bastard could have said. "You didn't mean any harm? Then in that case, neither do I." He grabbed Kevin up out of the stall and threw him against the wall.

Kevin matched Alex in weight and height, and although he tried putting up a good fight, he couldn't compete with the skillful Alex. Moments later, when Alex had beaten Kevin to a pulp and he lay sprawled on the bathroom floor barely able to move, Alex stared down at him in disgust. Alex knew there was no way he could turn Kevin and his waitress friend over to the authorities without getting Christy involved.

"If you ever come within a mile of Christy Madaris again I'll kill you." Without looking back he left the men's room.

He glanced around. Evidently Christy had gotten bored waiting for Kevin to return, as she was sitting at the bar chatting away with a woman. Alex could tell from the way she was talking to the woman that she was someone Christy knew. Damn, he needed to get her out of this place.

He quickly crossed the room to her, coming up from behind. "Christy, we need to leave."

Both women turned and looked at him. A surprised Christy then smiled. That smile alone was a definite indication that she wasn't herself. He couldn't remember the last time she had smiled at him. "A-Alex, what are you d-doing here?"

He sighed deeply. Her speech was slurring already. "I came to take you home."

She smiled at him again. "That's sweet, but I'm supposed to leave with Kevin."

Alex's eyes darkened. "Not tonight you aren't. Come on; let's go."

The other woman stood, blocking Christy from him. "Hey, who are you and where do you think you're taking her?"

Alex narrowed his eyes. "And who are you?"

"I'm Shemell Parker, a friend of Christy's. We work together at the *Enquirer*."

He nodded, feeling the woman could be trusted, but still he wouldn't tell her but so much. "And I'm Alexander Maxwell, a friend of Christy's who's in town for a few days visiting from Houston. Now if you'll excuse us, I'm sure you can see she's had a little too much to drink, and I want to take her home."

The woman stared at him for a moment, and then as if she had reached the conclusion that he could be trusted she moved aside.

"Come on, Christy," he said, reaching out and gently pulling her into his arms.

"Umm, I want to dance with you before I go, Alex," Christy murmured softly, wrapping her arms around his neck and blatantly rubbing her body against his.

"No, I'm taking you home."

"No! I want to dance."

Alex stared at her, saw the stubbornness lining her features, and quickly decided if one dance was what it would take to get her out of this place without causing a scene, then so be it. The band had taken another break and taped music was playing. The song by OutKast, "The Way You Move" was just beginning to play. "OK, let's dance," he said, taking her hand and leading her to the dance floor.

Although Alex knew he didn't have to worry about embarrassing himself on the dance floor, since he felt that he was a pretty good dancer, he was not prepared for the dance moves Christy was throwing his way. Damn, but he loved the way she moved, just like the song said.

He couldn't help but watch her body shimmy to the beat of the music as she threw everything she had into it—breasts, hips, hands, legs. And he couldn't ever recall seeing a pair of buttocks wiggle like hers.

Perspiration began forming on his forehead as he kept dancing and watching her. Regardless of the fact that she was, technically, dancing under the influence, never before had he seen any woman work her body like this. If she shook any more, she would be shaking herself right out of her short skirt.

When she suddenly eased up to him and shimmied, rubbing provocatively against him, he had to forcibly remind himself that she was not herself. And although he was aware of that fact, the combination of her outfit, shoes, hairstyle, and deliciously moving body parts was enough to push that not so minor detail to the back of his mind.

Almost but not quite.

When it came to Christy he would always be driven to do the right thing, although he had a strong feeling that before the night was over, doing the right thing would nearly kill him.

When the music ended, Christy sagged against him. He gently picked her up and carried her off the dance floor. He took the time to swing by the bar to grab her purse from Shemell before walking out of the club with Christy nestled in his arms.

A few blocks from the nightclub, Alex pulled his car off to the side of the road and turned to Christy. For someone who'd been completely drained when he'd taken her off the dance floor, she now appeared to have gotten zapped with an overabundance of energy. "For Pete's sake, Christy, do you want me to have an accident?"

He knew she was still under the influence, but he wished she would keep her hands to herself. They had barely gotten out of the club's parking lot when she unsnapped her seat belt and leaned over and began licking around his ear. Then she had reached down and begun rubbing her hand over his crotch while her fingers slowly inched their way to his zipper.

"I want you, Alex," she said, leaning over and licking his lips with her tongue.

What she was doing to him felt good, and he was trying like hell to ignore the effects it was having on some of his body parts. He sighed deeply and gently pushed her back in her seat and reached over and snapped her seat belt in place. Alex knew it was the drug talking and before tonight was over things would get worse. Ketamine wasn't a drug to mess with. Besides causing an increase in sexual desire, impaired motor functions, and slurred speech, it could result in aggressive or violent behavior if the person didn't get the sexual fix she needed. When Alex thought about what the night held in store for Christy, he had a good mind to go back to the club and kick Kevin's ass all over again.

"You don't know what you're saying, Christy."

"I *do* know what I'm saying."

He shook his head, already detecting aggressive behavior. He knew for now the best thing to do was go along with her . . . at least let her think he was doing so. "And I want you, too, baby, but wanting each other won't do us any good if we're dead. I need you to behave and let me drive you home safely. Then after I get you home I'm going to take care of you."

She reached out and placed a hand on his thigh and started rubbing it. The eyes looking into his were filled with hope, excitement, and anticipation. "Promise?"

He removed her hand when it began inching toward his crotch, and placed it in her lap. "Yes, Christy, I promise."

She didn't have to know that his idea of taking care of her was getting her tucked into bed and hoping she slept off the effects of the drug, although he knew that was a lot to hope for.

However, apparently she believed his promise, because for the rest of the ride to her house she stayed in her seat and behaved. It was a Friday night and it was late. In a way, that was a blessing, since it seemed none of the residents in her particular apartment building was out and about. Parking the car, he quickly went around to the passenger side, and after opening the door he gathered her into his arms.

"Don't forget your promise, Alex," she reminded him softly when he reached her door.

He glanced down at her while trying to fish her keys out of her purse. "I won't."

Once inside her apartment he quickly turned on the lights in the living room before heading straight to her bedroom. The first thing he needed to do was ply her with coffee.

He placed her gently on the bed and then he looked at her. No woman, under the influence or not, had a right to look this sensual, this mouthwateringly sexy. He tried ignoring that look as he began taking off her shoes. "I want you to strip down to your slip, then get into bed, Christy. Can you manage to do that?"

"No. If you want me you're g-going to have t-to undress me you-yourself, Alex. I don't think I can do it."

He cursed. Her speech was getting even more slurred and it was apparent she was losing coordination. "OK, I'll undress you."

Like a docile child she stood, leaning against the bedpost for support, as he knelt and reached under her skirt to remove her panty hose from her body. Beads of sweat formed on Alex's forehead and his breathing was becoming irregular when her heated scent inflamed his nostrils.

Once the panty hose were removed, he gently unfastened her skirt and tugged it down her hips. Next he removed her blouse, which left her in a very thin slip, her bra, and panties. "Now please get under the covers," he said in a voice that trembled so much he could feel it.

She looked at him. "But what about the rest of my clothes?"

"I'll take them off later," he lied.

"All right. Now aren't you going to take off your clothes, too?"

"Not yet. I want you in the bed, and I'll be back."

He pushed back the bedcovers and watched as she slipped between the sheets. Then he quickly left the room to go into the kitchen to get the coffee started. He checked his watch. The major effects of ketamine were known to kick in at least two and a half hours after a person had received the initial dose. What Christy was now experiencing was the prelude, which was mild in comparison to the real thing. He just hoped he could handle an oversexed version of Christy.

Deciding he needed to check on her, he left the kitchen and quickly returned to the bedroom. He stood in the doorway and smiled. Christy was still nestled under the covers, and it appeared she had drifted off to sleep. He let out a deep sigh of relief. Kevin had said he hadn't given her much of the drug, so there was a possibility she would sleep off the rest without any problems.

But still, to be on the safe side, he decided to watch over her during the night. Kicking off his boots and removing his jacket, he moved to the recliner next to the bed. He picked up a thick file labeled *"The Patterson Report"* that was lying on her nightstand table and decided to read it, hoping that doing so would keep him awake while he watched over Christy. He settled back in the chair and as he began reading he hoped that the worst was over.

Alex woke to the sound of someone thrashing about in the bed. He became alarmed when he saw Christy quivering uncontrollably, and then he remembered another effect of ketamine was fluctuations in body temperature.

He moved to the bed and reached out and touched her. She felt ice-cold. He quickly removed his shirt and jeans and got under the covers with her and pulled her nearly frozen body into his arms, sharing his body heat.

"I-I'm cold, A-Alex," she said through chattering teeth.

"I know, baby, and it's going to be OK. I'm not going to let anything happen to you." And he meant it as he held her.

He knew if he didn't get her temperature back to normal he would have to take her to the emergency room. He was trying to avoid having to do that, since there would be questions asked and he wanted to spare Christy that. Another alternative was to call in a contact at the Bureau to see if there was a doctor in the area who was willing to make an unofficial house call. Alex knew from having worked as an agent that every city had physicians willing to discreetly do what they could to help federal agents.

He continued to hold her as her body shivered uncontrollably. A half hour later her trembling had stopped, her temperature was back to normal, and she had drifted off to sleep again.

Alex's eyes slowly opened when he felt a hot, soft body cuddle against his back, a very hot, naked soft body. And at the same time he felt the tip of a tongue move around in his ear. "Make love to me, Alex," a feminine voice whispered in that same ear. "I need you. I'm aching."

Alex sighed deeply as he slowly turned around. Christy wasn't going to sleep anything off after all. "Christy, I—"

Before he could get out another word, she had straddled him and was kissing him with that incredible mouth of hers. And if that weren't bad enough, he felt her breasts, bare breasts that were pressed up against his chest, and the heat of her below as she was grinding against his midsection.

Damn. What had happened to her slip, bra, and panties? He was still wearing his briefs, but that didn't stop his erection from pressing into the the area between her thighs. He knew that he had to garner all the control he could muster and get her off him before . . .

But then he enjoyed kissing her, devouring her mouth, mating hungrily with it. And he liked the way her soft hips were cradling his thighs and how her body was rubbing sensuously against him, making his erection just that much harder.

Closing his eyes, he felt a rush of heat flare to his groin and knew he had to stop her before things got too out of hand. He groaned deep in his throat and after opening his eyes he flipped over, pinning her beneath him. "Behave, Christy," he quietly ordered her.

She ignored him and darted her tongue out to insert it inside his mouth, moving it around and around, driving him mad with desire in the process. He quickly pulled back. "I said stop it!"

She suddenly went still and her gaze clashed with his and he knew the aggressive and violent behavior had set in. She glared at him. "I want you, Alex. Make love to me."

He knew that tomorrow she wouldn't remember a thing about tonight, but he refused to take advantage of her that way. "No."

She met his gaze. "Kiss me then," she whispered, looking straight into his eyes.

"Aw, hell." There was no way he could deny a plea like that. He leaned down and kissed her in a way he had never kissed a woman before, full of all the passion that he felt.

She kissed him back and just when he thought he was about to lose control she deliberately bit him. He pulled his mouth away, tasting blood from his bruised lip.

"What the hell did you do that for?" he asked, not believing she had done such a thing, but the pain in his lips was proof that she had.

She glared at him. "Because you lied to me, that's why. You broke your promise!"

He sighed deeply. Yes, this was the aggressive and violent

behavior he had hoped to avoid. He continued to pin her down in the bed. "You will behave or I will continue to hold you down like this."

She glared up at him. "Make love to me."

"No."

"Please."

Alex growled deeply. "No."

She growled back. "Do it!"

Shaking his head, he tried not to stare at her full and firm breasts as he held her arms over her head and manacled her wrists with one hand while using his other hand to search under the covers for her missing articles of clothing. He found her slip and proceeded to hold her down to tug it over her head. It wasn't an easy task, since she was determined to struggle against him all the way. He pulled her into his arms in front of him, wrapping his firm thighs across her legs to keep her immobile.

"Now go back to sleep," he said. He could feel his lip swelling and knew he would have a beauty of a bruise tomorrow.

"No!" Then she smiled sweetly up at him. "Kiss me again."

He glared at her. "Not on your life. Now go back to sleep."

"Make love to me, Alex. Please."

He glanced down into large dark brown eyes that were staring at him after she made such a desperate plea. "No," he said softly. "Go to sleep, Christy."

A pout formed on her lips, but she cuddled closer into his arms as he held her, and moments later he could tell that she had drifted back off to sleep.

Knowing the risk of temptation if he stayed in bed with her warm, barely covered soft body snuggled so intimately to his, Alex eased out of bed. He studied her as he put his jeans and shirt back on. She was sleeping with a peaceful and contented look on her face. He didn't want to think what would have happened tonight if he had not been there. He hated that men such as Kevin existed and hoped after tonight the man would think twice before doing something like this to another woman.

Alex sighed, settled back into the recliner and picked up *"The Patterson Report"* and continued reading.

CHAPTER 5

Christy slowly opened her eyes, wondering why her eyelids felt heavy, why her throat was dry, and why her body was aching so badly. She forced her gaze to move when it seemed that her body couldn't, and relaxed when she saw that she was in her room, her bed. But for the life of her she couldn't recall how she had gotten there. In fact, she was having problems remembering much of anything.

She closed her eyes, wondering what was wrong with her. She opened them again and forced them to move to the side and gasped when they collided with Alex's deep, dark penetrating gaze. "What are you doing here?" She forced out the words in a hushed yet shocked voice.

For a brief silent moment he continued to look at her, hold her gaze. There was a dark shadow under his chin that meant he needed to shave. She had never seen him first thing in the morning, and maybe it was a good thing she never had. She didn't think that any man could look so sexy this early. Even needing a shave, Alex was the closest thing to male perfection she'd ever seen.

"How do you feel?" he asked.

His question pulled her thoughts back to the situation at hand. She slowly eased up in bed, clutching the bedcovers securely around her. "What are you doing here?" she said again, determined to get answers. The last thing she remembered was meeting Kevin at the club last night and enjoying dancing and talking with him. After that, everything else was a total blank. What was Alex doing sitting in a chair in her bedroom like he had every right to be there? And why was she in bed wearing only her slip?

She watched as he leaned forward in the chair, still holding her gaze. Then he said, "You were drugged last night."

She blinked, not certain she had heard him correctly. "What?"

"I said you were drugged. That guy you met at that club drugged you."

She bristled at his words, refusing to believe what he said. She knew how to protect herself from such a thing happening. Her brothers had pretty much drilled her on the rules countless times. She knew not to accept drinks from people she didn't know, she opened any containers herself, she kept her drink with her at all times, she didn't share drinks, and she didn't drink anything that tasted or smelled strange. So what was Alex talking about?

She stiffened her spine and glared over at him. "That's impossible. Kevin could not have drugged me."

Alex was out of the chair in a flash and in her face in an instant. She saw the line of angry fire in the eyes locked with hers. "That bastard drugged you!" he said, and the anger in his voice matched that in his eyes. "And he bragged about it to one of his friends and even admitted it to me right before I kicked his ass."

His words hit Christy like a ton of bricks. None of what Alex was alleging made sense. "Listen, Alex, I—"

"No, *you* listen. I followed you to that damn club, and it's a good thing I did. I walked into the men's room while he was bragging to one of his friends about setting you up for the night by giving you a date rape drug. After giving him a behind whipping that he won't forget, I had a hell of a time getting you out of the club without causing a scene. The drug had already begun taking effect. You wanted to dance, so we danced, and then you almost killed the both of us when I was taking you home and you couldn't keep your hands to yourself."

Christy was hearing his words, but she had a hard time believing them. "How did I get in bed?" she asked; her mind and thoughts were getting more confused by the second.

"I put you to bed."

She leaned up and brought her face even closer to his. Her glare deepened. "You undressed me! How dare you!"

"Dammit, I dared all right. But all I did was remove your clothes and panty hose. You did the rest yourself." He blinked, trying not to focus on that incredible mouth of hers that was too dangerously close to his.

Christy dropped back down in bed. Hearing what Alex was saying was too much. Could it be true? She looked back up at him. He was mad, madder than she had ever seen him before, even madder than he'd been that night he had kissed her three years ago. She had to think. What if what he was saying *was* true? She lowered her head, not wanting to think of what could have happened to her.

She slowly raised her head and met Alex's intense gaze. She could tell he was still mad. Although she didn't remember anything, she had to admit that what he was saying made sense; otherwise they wouldn't be having this conversation. What other reason could there be for him to be here in her bedroom with her? And why would she be feeling like she had a hangover this morning? She had known Alex a long time—all of her life—and she knew he had no reason to lie about what he was telling her.

"What drug was it?" she asked quietly. An article on date rape had been one of the first pieces she had done for the *Houston Chronicle,* so she was familiar with them, especially the most popular three on the streets.

"Ketamine."

"Oh God," she said softly, covering her face with her hands. Ketamine was a favorite with some men because it was known to make a woman have intense sexual cravings to the point where she became the aggressor.

She slowly removed her hands and met Alex's intense gaze. "How much did he give me?"

"Enough."

She lifted a brow. *Enough? What the hell was enough?* She then studied Alex's bruised and swollen lip. He said he had kicked Kevin's ass. Was the condition of his lip the result of that incident? "What happened to your lip?" she asked, wondering what else he'd suffered because of her.

"You bit me."

She blinked. She must have heard him wrong. "I bit you?"

"Yes."

She stared at him for a moment, then asked, "Why would I bite you?"

Christy watched as a small smile touched the corners of his bruised mouth. "Because I wouldn't make love to you."

She swallowed the lump in her throat, hoping she had heard him wrong, but knowing the effects of ketamine, she realized that she probably hadn't. "I asked you to make love to me?"

Alex stared at her, deciding to be completely honest. She needed to know just how things had been last night. "No, you didn't ask. You *begged* me to make love to you, Christy, and turning you down was the hardest thing I've ever had to do in my life."

Christy looked away, not able to meet his gaze any longer. Damn Kevin for having done that to her. Damn her for not being smart enough to catch him doing it. And damn Alex for being there to witness it all.

Alex knew how Christy was probably feeling and reached out and gently grabbed her chin to make her look at him. "It wasn't you acting that way, Christy, it was the drug. You were under the influence. I knew it and that's why I didn't act on it."

She sighed deeply. But many other men probably would have. Like her brothers, Alex operated on an honor system that wasn't practiced a whole lot today. "I'm sorry," she said softly.

He frowned, seeing the tears that misted her eyes. A stubborn and difficult Christy he could handle. A weepy one he could not. He never could and doubted that he ever would. That's the reason he had given her his ring in the first place when she had been thirteen, because of her tears. "There's no reason for you to be sorry. Like I said, it wasn't your fault."

She moved away from him, fire replacing the tears in her eyes. "Yes, it was my fault. Somehow I didn't follow all the rules. I knew what to do to avoid date rape and I didn't take the necessary precautions."

"You did follow the rules. He had help."

Her eyes widened. "What?"

"He paid the waitress to put the drug into your drink. There was no way you could have known and you had no reason to suspect the person who served the drink to you."

A long moment passed before Christy nodded, accepting what Alex had said. Then she thought of something, knowing Alex's respect for the law. "The police?"

He shook his head. "No, I didn't call them, although I was tempted to. There was no way I could do so without getting you involved."

Christy let out a sigh of relief. The last thing she wanted or needed was some sort of scandal involving her name. She met Alex's gaze. "Thanks."

"I don't want your gratitude, Christy."

She frowned. "Would you prefer that I not be grateful?" she snapped.

"Damn it, be whatever you want," he snapped back, moving away from the bed, away from her. A part of him was still angry at what could have happened to her last night. He needed time alone to deal with his emotions and moved toward the bedroom door.

"Where are you going?" Christy asked, not understanding what had him so peeved with her. She had apologized for biting him and had thanked him for all he'd done. So what was his problem?

He turned back around. "I'm going to rummage through your refrigerator to see what I can prepare for breakfast. I suggest you get up, shower, and get dressed. After breakfast we need to go get your car."

She nodded. When he turned back around to leave she called back out to him, "Alex?"

He turned back around, pausing at the bedroom door, and met her gaze. "Yes?"

She didn't answer right away, then quickly said, "My brothers. You won't tell them about this, will you?"

Alex saw the worried look on her face and wanted to cross the room, take her into his arms, and kiss her. "No, I won't tell them anything about this."

He saw relief flood her eyes. "Thanks."

Without saying anything else, he turned and left the room.

When Christy finished her shower, she toweled off and then went to her closet to decide what to put on. After a few moments she slipped into a printed lounger her sister-in-law Lorren had given her a few months ago as a birthday gift.

There were still questions for which she needed answers. Alex had said she had begged him to make love to her and he had refused her. Yet she knew for a fact they had shared a bed. His masculine scent was all over her bedcovers and pillows. Why had he gotten into bed with her if he hadn't intended for anything to happen? The very thought of being in bed with him was enough to add heat to her already steamy shower.

Christy sighed deeply. She needed to stop thinking such things. If Alex stopped Kevin from doing anything to her and he didn't do anything to her himself, then that meant her virginity was still intact, and she was glad about that. A lot of women her age would be bothered by such lack of sexual experience, but she was not. It always bothered her how some of the girls in her dorm in college would deliberately seek out guys to rid them of what they considered "that little problem."

She'd had no problems saving herself for the man she would marry—whoever he was. She just had to completely get over Alex, which she fully intended to do. In the meantime, she would patiently wait for her soulmate to come into her life. Too bad she had already wasted all those years thinking that Alex had been the one.

She walked over to the window and looked out. An overcast sky was making it difficult for the sun to shine through and she needed to see the sun. Gramma Laverne always said there had to be a little rain in your life to appreciate the sun, and today of all days Christy needed to see the sun.

She smiled when she thought of her grandmother. In her late eighties, Laverne Madaris still got around pretty good and was one feisty lady who, along with Christy's mother, had instilled within her old-fashioned rules of decorum. Christy appreciated the role her grandmother had always played in her life. Also like her mother, Christy's grandmother was her confidante and had always been so. But Christy would make sure when they had their weekly telephone chat tomorrow that she didn't mention anything about what had happened at the club.

But she would mention to her grandmother about Alex's arriving in Cincinnati and coming to see her. Her mother and grandmother were the only two people she'd confided in about what had happened between her and Alex three years ago.

Christy turned away from the window when she heard her phone ring. She figured Alex wouldn't pick it up just in case it was one of her family members calling. He wouldn't want to explain what he was doing at her house so early in the morning.

She quickly crossed the room to answer it. "Hello?"

"Christy? Are you all right?"

Christy smiled upon hearing Shemell's voice. "Yes, I'm fine. Why wouldn't I be?"

When moments passed and it was obvious that Shemell was hesitating, Christy repeated herself. "Why wouldn't I be OK?"

"I was at the club last night. I talked to you. Don't you remember?"

Christy frowned. No, she didn't remember. "And?"

"And you weren't yourself. It was as if you'd had a lot to drink. You were sort of . . ."

Christy inhaled deeply, not sure she wanted to really know, but asked anyway. "Sort of what?"

"Sort of wild, loose and brazen. You were flirting with several men and when that guy Alexander Maxwell wanted to take you home you almost made a scene until he danced with you. And that was after you had plastered yourself all over him. I've never seen you act that way before."

And Christy intended for Shemell to never see her act that way again. "Well, I, uh, had too much to drink," she said, quickly deciding not to tell anyone the true story.

"Yeah, that's what I figured, and I'm sure Kevin was to blame. I'm just glad Mr. Maxwell was there. He knew just what to do. And he was really protective of you. I was OK with letting you leave with him. But I have a feeling that he would have taken you with him whether I approved or not."

Christy nodded, knowing that was probably true. "Yes, more than likely he would have. Alex is a good friend of my brothers. He's also a former FBI agent, so he's used to taking charge and doing things his way," she said quietly.

"A former FBI agent? Wow! That explains a few things."

Christy raised a brow. "A few things like what?"

"About what happened to Kevin. After Mr. Maxwell carried you out of the club—"

"What do you mean, he carried me out of the club?"

"Just what I said, he carried you out in his arms. It was like a scene from one of those romantic movies."

Christy rubbed a hand down her face. This was worse than she'd thought. "Now what about Kevin?" she asked, deciding the less she knew about Alex carrying her out of the club the better.

"He staggered out of the men's room after the two of you left. Someone had worked him and his friend over pretty good. But it appeared Kevin got the worst of it. If Mr. Maxwell was involved in a brawl with Kevin and his friend, I don't recall seeing a scratch on him anywhere. And you'd better believe I checked him out real good. There wasn't even a bruised lip."

Christy sighed. She didn't want to tell Shemell that Alex had a bruised lip now, thanks to her.

"I couldn't believe a man could look that darn good. Do most men in Texas look that way?"

Shemell's question recaptured her attention. "Look what way?"

"Drop-dead gorgeous, like you'd love to have one for breakfast, lunch, and dinner, someone who takes making you drool to a whole other level."

Christy shook her head. Evidently Alex had made quite an impression on Shemell. "Yes, I guess, pretty much." She didn't want to say that in her book Alex was in a class all by himself. For her he'd always been.

"Does he have any brothers?"

"Yes. Trask Maxwell. But he's married to my cousin Felicia."

"Trask Maxwell? *The* Trask Maxwell? Former NFL great?"

Christy couldn't help but smile. "Yes, that's him."

"Wow! I remember one of my older male cousins having his jersey. And he's married to your cousin?"

"Yes."

"Hey, what are you all trying to do? Keep it in the family?"

Christy rolled her eyes to the ceiling. "There's nothing going on between me and Alex. We're nothing more than friends." And even saying they were friends was really stretching it. Although he had gotten her out of a tight spot last night, she could not forget that he was the man who had crushed her heart and trampled her pride.

"Some friend," Shemell said. "I'd love to have a friend like that."

"Well, look, Shemell, I have to go. Thanks for calling and checking on me."

Christy decided not to tell her that Alex was in her kitchen preparing breakfast. She was hungry and whatever he had whipped up smelled good. There was no doubt in her mind that he could cook, since, like all of her brothers' friends, at one time or another he had been a student—whether willing or not—in Gramma Laverne's cooking classes.

"That's what friends are for. Do you need me to get you anything?"

"No, I'll be fine. I'm going to stay in all weekend and read 'The Patterson Report.'"

Shemell chuckled. "Why? It's all fiction."

"Yeah, probably, but I thought I'd read it just the same."

"OK. If you need me for anything just give me a call."

"I will."

After she hung up the phone, Christy sighed deeply. Once Alex fed her and took her to get her car, there would be no reason for him to hang around. After all she'd heard about what had happened last night, when he left she would look forward to a relatively long, quiet, and boring weekend.

CHAPTER 6

Trained to hear even the slightest sound, Alex turned when Christy walked into the kitchen. He leaned against the counter and looked at her. The lounger she was wearing made her look sexier than was probably legal. It wasn't that the outfit was blatantly seductive, but on her it just looked that way. Add the coloring of her hair framed around her face, along with her dark brown eyes and willowy curves, and he couldn't help the increased beating of his heart as well as the sizzling of his heated blood through his veins.

He had needed time alone and had gotten it while preparing breakfast. Now seeing her brought a lot of things into perspective. Over the years he had dated but had been careful not to mislead any woman into thinking he had more to offer than just going out and having a good time. He'd been too busy establishing Maxwell Investigative Services to even consider more than that. And he'd always been an ace at keeping a firm rein on his tightly controlled emotions. But he was finding that when it came to Christy she could wreak havoc on them each and every time.

Like now.

More than anything he wanted to cross the room and pull her into his arms and hold her and kiss her. Then he wanted to pick her up and carry her into the bedroom and make love to her, all day and all night.

"Something smells good."

Her words intruded into his thoughts and reminded him he was standing there staring at her. "I made Texas quiche and I hope it tastes as good as it smells. I felt lucky that you had all the ingredients I needed."

God, she loved Texas quiche. Christy smiled as she crossed the room to the refrigerator. Most people needed coffee first thing in the morning. She needed her glass of apple juice. "Gramma Laverne would have my hide if I didn't keep a stocked kitchen. Besides, cooking is more cost-effective than eating out each day."

Alex nodded, knowing money was the last thing Christy had to worry about. He knew that because of her uncle Jake Madaris, financial wizard and genius as well as wealthy Texas rancher, Christy had a nice investment portfolio. Jake was her financial adviser just as he was Alex's. He couldn't help but admire her for not being overextravagant when she could do so without any problems. Instead, she had a charming apartment in a nice area of town. What he liked most about her place was that she had decorated it modestly, sticking to the basics and making it a home instead of a museum.

Christy turned from the refrigerator and looked at him. "Need anything out of here while I have the door open?"

"No thanks. I have the coffee going. That's what it takes to kick my butt into gear every morning."

She closed the door, not wanting to think about his butt. From the time she'd hit puberty, Alex's butt had fascinated her. After he'd left for college she looked forward to his returning during the summers, when she would catch glimpses of him jogging around the neighborhood. She had found out just how good tight sweats could look on some men.

"So you gave up the peanut butter but not the apple juice."

Christy chuckled as she poured a cold, tall glass of the juice. As a kid she had loved peanut butter and apple juice with a passion. "Hey, there are some things a girl can't give up."

He returned her smile. "Evidently." Then he said, "I heard the phone but thought it would be best if you answered it."

She nodded. "It was my friend Shemell, calling to make sure I was OK. She thinks I indulged in too much to drink last night, and I'm going to let her continue to think that. I prefer she not know what really happened."

She glanced around, not at all surprised at how well Alex had made himself at home in her kitchen. It was his way. While growing up he had spent just as much time over at her house as he did in his own, so making himself comfortable at any Madaris place probably came second nature. "Is there anything you need me to do?"

"No. Everything is ready."

"You didn't have to fix breakfast, but I'm glad you did. I've wanted to taste someone else's food for a change."

Alex chuckled. "Yeah, I know what you mean. That's why I'm glad I have a standing invitation over to Trask and Felicia's place," he said, carrying a covered platter over to the table.

"And how are they?"

Alex glanced back over his shoulder. "They're doing fine. Austin is getting tall, and Madaris is simply beautiful. The last time I was over there she was trying to walk already."

Christy grinned. "How old is Madaris now?"

Dimples appeared in Alex's cheeks when he turned around and smiled. "Almost ten months, and we're calling her Aris for short."

"I can't wait to see her when I come home in a couple of weeks."

Alex glanced over at her. "You're coming home?"

"Yes, just for the weekend to attend Blade and Slade's birthday party." Her twin cousins would be celebrating their thirtieth birthday in a few weeks.

Thinking that she could at least take the tray of hot rolls to the table, Christy tried making herself useful. "These smell good," she said.

"I'll take that. The tray is warm," Alex said, reaching out

and taking the tray from her hand. Their fingers brushed in the exchange and their gazes immediately connected. They both went still.

Christy swallowed. This wasn't good. She was working hard to get over Alex and his presence, his closeness, his masculine scent. And the way he looked walking around in her kitchen barefoot wearing jeans and a shirt was enough to send all of her emotions into overdrive.

"I guess we should sit down and eat now," he said huskily, his voice low and breaking into her thoughts.

"Yes, I guess we should." He was holding her gaze way too long, she thought. But then, she was also holding his. It seemed like everything around them had gone quiet and they were cocooned into private, intimate space. A powerful sexual attraction existed between them. But this wasn't the way things were supposed to be. When it came to Alex, there had always been more to her feelings than a mere sexual attraction. When he had taught her to ride her first bike when she was six, she had felt a bond between them.

A bond that had meant more to her than to him.

She took a step back and tried to think of something to say to break the heated moment. "Is there anything you need me to bring to the table?" she asked, glancing around.

Alex stared at her for a while, knowing what she was trying to do and for the moment letting her do so. "No, that's about it, unless you want me to bring you the pitcher of apple juice."

"No, I can get it. You pour your coffee."

"All right."

But neither made an attempt to move. Then Christy watched as he took a step forward, closing the distance she had placed between them. His gaze held hers and he lowered his head slowly, hesitated, then lowered his head still more.

She studied his lips so close to hers, the bruise she had inflicted the night before. Then seemingly of its own accord, her tongue darted out and she ran it lightly, gently, over his lips, soothing the part she had bitten, and when she heard a deep groan emit from his throat seconds before his lips parted she slipped her tongue inside his mouth.

Alex took over from there. He pulled Christy closer to him, needing to feel the length of her against him, needing her in his arms, needing her taste everywhere in his. Like an alcoholic who knew he was taking his last drink, he sipped her, then lapped her like she was the sweetest brandy he'd ever tasted. He was becoming addicted to her taste. What they were sharing was delicious as well as dangerous.

He knew he had to slow down. Alex slowly pulled back and felt Christy sigh against his lips. "Did I hurt your mouth again?" she asked in a low, hushed tone.

"No, you didn't hurt it," he replied, holding her gaze, then allowing it to drift downward to her lips, wet and moist from his kiss. "We really should eat so we can go get your car."

She nodded. "OK. You get your coffee and I'll get my juice."

Christy moved away from him and Alex stood there and watched her go. He would be leaving to return to Texas in a few days, and before he left he intended for them to have that conversation, the one she didn't want them to have.

Five minutes later they were sitting together at the table eating the breakfast that Alex had prepared. As far as Christy was concerned, she'd screwed her head back on straight and was determined that another kiss between her and Alex wouldn't be happening.

She glanced across the table at him. He hadn't said much since they'd sat down. Chances were he was thinking the same thing that she was: *Why waste perfectly good kisses on each other when they don't mean anything?*

"That 'Patterson Report.' What's going on with that?"

Christy lifted her head and met Alex's gaze. She hated it whenever his dark, penetrating stare bored into her like this. It always did something to her insides. "I'm initiating an investigation to see what's fiction and what's real. Did you read it?"

"Yes, I read it. Not all of it, but enough."

"What do you think?" As a former FBI agent and now private investigator, Alex was skillful and sharp. On numerous occasions he had been instrumental in saving people's lives, even members of her own family. She shuddered, remembering when a madman had wanted her uncle Jake dead. It had been Alex who had figured out the man's identity in time to save her uncle's life.

"Do you want my honest opinion?"

She smiled. His expression told her what that opinion was. "That Mrs. Patterson's not wrapped too tight, right?"

"No, I don't think that way at all."

Christy lifted a brow, surprised. "You don't?"

"No. The FBI has used psychics on a number of occasions to help them locate missing people. Although I'm not totally convinced of this woman's claim that her daughter, who she believes is dead, is coming to her in her dreams, I wouldn't discount her theory about the kidnappings. There are known cases of young women disappearing, never to be heard of again. If you recall a few years ago, that would have been Corinthians Grant's fate had Trevor, Ashton, and Sir Drake not figured out what was happening and intervened."

She did remember. She was away at school at the time but had heard the entire story when she came home for a visit. "But how would Mrs. Patterson know about the kidnappings if not for her dreams?"

Alex leaned forward. "People can dream about a lot of stuff that does happen. Dreaming about girls being kidnapped doesn't add credit to her story. There has to be proof of a connection; something very compelling that she couldn't have known about unless she'd had inside information."

He took a sip of his coffee and then added, "I didn't see anything *that* compelling, but there were a number of things I found rather interesting and need to be checked out further."

"What?" she asked, curious what those things were.

"It seems that every time Bonita supposedly visits her mother in a dream, it is to warn her of an impending abduction. Since all the other reporters assumed what Morganna was telling them was pure fiction, they never took the time to follow up to see if a kidnapping actually took place. What if there were kidnappings like Morganna predicted?"

Christy sighed. Now there was a thought. She then remembered what Mrs. Patterson had told her about another kidnapping that was to take place, and that the young girl's name would be linked to Christmas in some way.

"This won't be an easy investigation, Christy."

Alex's words intruded into her thoughts. She met his gaze. "No, but I intend to find answers. I won't file this report away like everyone else has done and do nothing."

Alex chuckled. "No, I didn't think that you would."

Deciding they had discussed the Patterson Report enough, Christy said, "Breakfast was great, Alex."

"Thanks. When you get ready we can go pick up your car."

"All right." A part of Christy really didn't want to go near the club again, not even to the parking lot. She would always be reminded of what had happened there.

As if he'd read her thoughts, Alex said quietly, "Put it behind you, all right?"

She met his gaze; her chin was propped on her fist. "I'm going to try."

Alex nodded, knowing that she would.

It was around noon when Alex returned to his hotel. Instead of following her back to her place, he decided to go to the hotel to shower and change.

He wasn't at all happy that she had turned down his invitation to dinner again.

He threw the keys on the desk. If Christy thought she'd seen the last of him, then she had another thought coming. If space was what she needed then, he would give her that, but he would see her again before returning to Texas. And he fully intended to return to Cincinnati in a couple of weeks.

He picked up the phone to retrieve his messages when he saw the red light flashing. Both were from his office.

He hung up the phone five minutes later, annoyed. He had received a subpoena to appear in court on Monday regarding a case he'd worked on. That meant he needed to return to Houston immediately to prepare with the attorneys.

Sighing heavily, he picked up the phone and dialed Christy's number, which he had already committed to memory.

"Yes?"

"Christy, this is Alex. Something has come up and I'm flying back to Houston tonight."

"Have a safe trip."

Alex rubbed a hand down his face. Was that all she had to say? He forced a smile. The woman was taking erecting a brick wall to a whole new level. She had no intentions of forgiving or forgetting. "I'm thinking of coming back next week."

"Why?"

He forced himself to smile harder. "I'm beginning to like this town."

"That's fine, Alex, and you do know you don't have to look me up every time you come through, don't you?"

"Yes, but I think I will anyway."

"For my brothers?"

Not bloody likely, he thought, taking a deep breath. Evidently she still wasn't absolutely convinced her brothers hadn't played a part in his visit. "Your brothers were the last people I was thinking about when I was kissing you, Christy."

All he had to do was close his eyes to remember each time he had ever kissed her. The way he would cover her mouth with his; the sounds that came from her throat when she succumbed to his kiss, responded, and joined in. The way her tongue would mate with his, making every nerve cell acknowledge her as the woman he wanted. "And when I come back, it will be more of the same, Christy."

He heard her quick breath. "I don't think so."

Unfazed he said, "I don't have any other choice. Take care until I see you again."

Instead of responding, she hung up the phone. Alex shook his head. It appeared they were back at square one. He'd dealt with stubborn people before, but Christy was giving the word new meaning. But then, he fully understood the Madaris pride and knew it was something he would have to break down piece by piece.

And he would.

CHAPTER 7

"What the hell happened to your lip?" Clayton Madaris asked Alex as they sat across from each other in Sisters restaurant.

Clayton smirked. "Looks like some woman got ahold of it and gnawed you pretty damn good."

Alex gave him a dry look. "I guess you would know." Everyone had heard at least once the story of the woman Clayton used to date who got turned on from biting her dates.

"Look, you two," Dex Madaris said, crossing his arms over his chest and pinning both men with a penetrating glare. "I'm not here to discuss Alex's love life. I'm here to talk about Christy."

Alex shook his head. Little did big brother know . . . "I told you when you called me at the hotel that she was doing fine."

"You asked Alex to check up on Christy when we promised her we wouldn't interfere?" Clayton Madaris asked Dex, surprised.

"Yeah, what of it?" he responded in a defensive tone.

Clayton chuckled. "So did I."

Both men grinned. "What about Justin? Do you think he did, too?"

Clayton nodded. "Probably."

Satisfied, Dex turned his attention back to Alex. "I know you said you talked to Christy, but did you actually see her?"

Alex took a sip of his drink. If Dex knew just how much

of Christy he'd seen, the man would probably kill him. "Yes, I saw her, and she's fine." Alex could tell from Dex's expression that he still wasn't convinced. Of the three Madaris brothers he was the most intense.

"Maybe we ought to pay her a visit."

Alex cocked his brow. "I wouldn't if I were you. She thought the only reason I was in Cincinnati was because of you guys. She got pretty pissed although I tried to convince her otherwise," he said truthfully.

"But you *did* convince her?" Clayton asked. "We promised her that we wouldn't interfere, and nobody can hold a grudge like Christy when she's mad about something."

Do tell, Alex thought, taking another sip of his drink. He then released a deep, drawn-out sigh. "I tried, but whether she believed me or not, who knows?"

Neither brother said anything for the longest time, and Alex decided to add, "She'll be coming home in a few weeks for Blade and Slade's birthday party. The two of you will see her then." He then quickly seized the opportunity to change the subject. "Anything happen while I was gone?"

Clayton chuckled. "If you're asking if anybody else got pregnant, the answer is yes, the epidemic continues. Sterling and Colby are expecting again, and so are Jake and Diamond."

Alex shook his head. "Don't married people have anything else to do with their free time?"

Clayton smiled. "I can only speak for myself. I guess Syneda and I can spend our free time playing poker. But we tried that once and it turned out to be a game of strip poker with the same end result, so the answer is no. So far I haven't found anything else I'd rather do with my free time."

Clayton then leaned forward with a mischievous glint in his eyes. "Try it, Alex; you might like it," he said.

A teasing smile touched Alex's lips. "What? Playing strip poker with Syneda?"

Clayton glared at Alex. "Don't act crazy, OK? I was talking about a serious relationship with a woman."

When thoughts of Christy suddenly entered Alex's mind, he cleared his throat, deciding it was definitely time to switch to another topic. "Hey, I heard that Harding got cut from the Texans."

By Monday Christy hated to admit it, but she missed Alex. After seeing him for three solid days, now she felt like she was going through Alex Maxwell withdrawal.

She had awakened that morning thinking about the kisses they had shared. As far as she was concerned, nobody kissed like Alex. The man's tongue was simply dangerous and one touch could make a desperate sexual yearning grip her insides like nobody's business. And she was powerless to prevent it from happening. All she was capable of doing was standing there and putting her heart and soul into it.

The tips of her breasts swelled against the hard wall of his chest, her thighs rested so intimately between his, and her mound pressed tightly to the huge bulge straining his zipper. And just when she thought he was done with her, hoping that he wasn't, but needing air to breathe, he would draw back for a mere second, then start the process all over again.

She was so caught up in her memories that she jumped when the phone on her desk rang. She picked it up immediately. "Christy Madaris."

"Ms. Madaris, please come to my office."

Christy swallowed upon hearing the curt summons followed by the loud click in her ear. Evidently Malcolm had seen her expense requisition. Sighing deeply, she grabbed her notepad and headed for the man's office. Everyone knew that Mondays weren't his good day, and if he played lousy golf over the weekend, his bad mood could very well stretch into Tuesday. But she could handle moody men. She had three older brothers and five uncles who all had different temperaments.

She rounded the corner and took a deep breath before she entered Malcolm's office. She had spent the majority of the weekend going over the Patterson Report, following up what the other reporters had failed to do. After doing extensive research on the Internet, she had reached a startling conclusion. Just as Mrs. Patterson had predicted, there had been kidnappings. Although Christy would be the first to admit it would be hard in some situations to tie the kidnappings to Mrs. Patterson's dreams, she felt confident what she had found was compelling enough to further pursue the investigation.

To convince Malcolm of that might be a hard sell. She would have to play hard on his veteran reporter's hunger instincts to make or break a story. She plastered a huge smile on her face and opened the door. "Good morning, Malcolm. You wanted to see me?"

He lifted his head from some document and the look he gave her told her that he wanted her—roasted over an open fire if that's the way he could have her.

"What's the meaning of this, Ms. Madaris?" he asked, holding up the piece of paper she had slipped onto his desk before he had arrived that morning.

"Oh, I see you got my request," she said, unable to keep the smile out of her voice. Although he strongly encouraged everyone to call him by his first name, he had a problem with calling anyone by theirs.

"Yes, and I need you to explain what this is about. There is no ongoing investigation on the Patterson case. You were supposed to talk with Morganna, take down what she had to say, and file it away like the other reporters do."

Christy sat down in the chair in front of his desk although he hadn't invited her to do so. "We may have made a mistake in doing that, Malcolm."

Thick gray bushy eyebrows lifted as he peered at her. "What are you talking about?"

"I'm talking about the fact that had we followed up Mrs. Patterson's predictions, we might have found a link between what she was trying to tell us and reported cases of teenage girls being kidnapped in certain areas of the country."

Malcolm leaned over his desk. "Are you trying to tell me there's a possibility that what Morganna is saying is true?"

Christy shrugged. "All I'm saying is that it's worth checking out. Although I can't definitely link those kidnappings to Mrs. Patterson's predictions, there are enough similarities to substantiate an in-depth investigation. And I want to do that."

Malcolm leaned back in his chair and gazed at her thoughtfully. Christy inwardly smiled. She had him considering the idea. She decided to push a little further. "All I'm asking is that you give me the okay to find out the truth about Bonita Patterson's disappearance once and for all. Don't you think you owe that to the Patterson family?"

Christy sighed deeply. He was staring at her, but she knew his mind was at work. He was thinking, playing with figures in his head, trying to see how he could work what she had requested amongst all those budget cuts.

"There's no way I can approve the amount you've requested," he finally said. "Cut that figure in half, and the investigation is yours."

Christy smiled. She had deliberately padded the figures knowing the bottom line would probably get sliced. "That won't be a problem."

"Good. You only have four weeks, and I want the final report on my desk."

"Four weeks?" Christy was hoping she would get more time than that.

"Yes. That's all the time I'm giving you so you'd better get busy."

Alex stood looking out his office window in the Madaris Building. It was a beautiful summer day, and people were out and about doing whatever made them happy.

His day in court had gone rather well and now he was back at work, ready to tackle another case that might take him heaven knows where. He turned and glanced around his office. It didn't seem like it had already been a year since he had moved into the building, one of the first to sign on as a tenant when the Madaris brothers, along with their uncle Jake, had decided to build this office park.

The original plan was for a four-story office building in downtown Houston. But thanks to Mitch Farrell, millionaire land developer, an exclusive fifteen-story building surrounded by a cluster of upscale shops, restaurants, and a beautiful park had been erected on a huge tract of land located on the outskirts of town instead.

The Madaris twins, Blade and Slade, had been commissioned as the builders. It had been a huge undertaking for the two young men, but they had done a fantastic job. Since then more building contracts had poured in. The Madaris Construction Company had been recognized last month in *Black Enterprise* as one of the fastest-growing and most profitable construction companies in the nation.

Alex sighed. All morning, thoughts of Christy had consumed his mind. Leaving Cincinnati had been the hardest thing he had to do. He was anxious to stake his claim on the woman and these delays were making him more anxious.

He had wanted to return to Cincinnati this weekend, but he had just taken on a new client so he had no choice but to wait to see Christy again when she came to Houston next weekend.

His phone rang and he quickly walked over to his desk. It was his private line. "Yes?"

"Alexander, we need to talk."

A slow smile spread across Alex's lips. Only one person called him Alexander. "Ms. Laverne, how are you?" he asked the woman who was grandmother to the Madaris brothers.

"I'll be better once you get your act together."

Alex lifted a brow. "Pardon me?"

"I'll decide whether I will after we talk. Meet me downstairs in the park at two o'clock. I'll be sitting on a bench near the pond."

Wondering what on earth Laverne Madaris wanted to talk with him about, he meekly said, "Yes, ma'am." She then hung up the phone.

Alex replaced the phone, shaking his head. The last time he'd been summoned by the matriarch of the Madaris family had been a few years ago to tell him he wasn't attending church enough. He couldn't wait to hear what she needed to read him the riot act about this time. He checked his watch. In a couple of hours he would find out.

Christy picked up her phone on the second ring. "Christy Madaris."

"Just like Bonita said would happen, another girl has been kidnapped."

Christy immediately recognized the voice. "Mrs. Patterson?"

"Yes. Did you read this morning's paper?"

Christy was too embarrassed to say that although she worked for the paper, she hadn't yet read this morning's edition, as it was already a little past noon. "No, I haven't."

"Then you don't know about that girl, the one whose family is saying she was kidnapped, although the authorities are claiming she's a runaway. Her name is Holly."

Christy placed her coffee cup on her desk. *Holly?* "Give me a chance to read the article and I'll get back to you, Mrs. Patterson."

The woman didn't say anything for a moment; then she said, "All right. Just remember that I'm depending on you to save the others. Good-bye." The phone then disconnected.

After hanging up the phone, Christy immediately went to the news service on the Internet to check out the article Mrs. Patterson was talking about. A few moments later, after reading the article about the alleged kidnapping of the teenager in Birmingham, Alabama, she leaned back in her chair.

Although the paper hadn't come right out and said the runaway had been kidnapped, it said she had left home over a year ago and that her parents had received a call from her saying she was ready to come home. They had waited for their prodigal daughter's return, and when she never did, they called the authorities.

The girl's family would not accept the possibility that she'd had changed her mind about coming home, and they suspected foul play. In one conversation to her parents, the teenager had mentioned she was being stalked. Because of the family's allegations, the FBI was called to initiate an investigation. End of story.

Christy sighed. That would have been the end of the story if the girl's name hadn't been Holly. In the dream, Bonita had warned her mother that the next kidnapped girl's name would be associated with Christmas. It might all be just a coincidence and thinking of Christmas holly might be stretching it a bit, but Christy got an eerie feeling in the pit of her stomach that she was on to something.

Deciding to dig further, she pulled up the photograph the wire service had posted of Holly Johnson. Her resemblance to Bonita Patterson was astounding. Both were Caucasians with blond hair and blue eyes.

CHAPTER 8

Alex could barely hide his smile when he saw the old woman sitting patiently on the park bench near the pond and the man sitting at her side.

Apparently bored, Luke Madaris had clearly been drafted to be his grandmother's chauffeur.

Anyone who saw him would be hard pressed to believe that twenty-nine-year-old Lucas "Luke" Madaris, nationally known rodeo superstar, was anywhere but sitting on a feisty bronco or flying off some raging bull.

"Afternoon, Ms. Laverne," Alex said to the older woman. He then turned to Luke and offered him his hand in a firm handshake when Luke stood up. "Good seeing you, Luke. I didn't know you were back in town."

"Only for a little while," Luke Madaris said, grinning from ear to ear. "How are things going in the PI business?"

Alex smiled "They're going. And how's the rodeo circuit?"

Luke grinned. "Other than a few scrapes, it's going great. No broken bones so far this year."

"Luke, take a walk. Alexander and I have important matters to discuss."

Both men turned to look at Laverne Madaris. A frown was puckering her brow as she stared back at them. Her silver gray hair was pulled back in a thick bun on her head and her dark eyes were as shrewd as ever. They were eyes that both men knew missed nothing. Her wooden cane was by her side, and Alex had a feeling that if the need ever arose, she would use it for more than walking. He could see her bringing it down on someone's head if he made her mad enough.

Alex couldn't help but smile. She was one tough lady. She had to be in order to raise seven sons on her own after her husband's death, and overseeing a huge family spread like Whispering Pines. She had kept her husband's promise that all seven of her sons would be highly educated. All had eventually left home to attend college, but it had been her youngest, Jake Madaris, who had returned home to make ranching his life.

Alex glanced over at Luke, who chuckled and whispered, "My great-grandmother really knows how to give an order, doesn't she?"

"Luke, I said walk."

With a smile Luke winked at Alex before turning to walk away. When Laverne Madaris was satisfied he was out of hearing range she turned her full attention to Alex. "Sit."

Alex obediently did what he was told, sitting down beside her on the bench. He then glanced over at her. "You wanted to see me?"

"Yes," she said staring at him. "How have you been, Alexander?"

Alex blinked. Evidently she planned to get the pleasantries out of the way before cutting into him . . . for whatever reason. "I've been fine, and you?"

"I'm alive, so I'm blessed."

Alex nodded. He then watched as she leaned forward, holding his gaze mercilessly. "Now to get down to the point of why I called this meeting."

A lump formed in Alex's throat. "Yes, ma'am?"

She reached out and her bony finger poked him in the chest. "I want to know just what your intentions are toward my granddaughter."

Alex knew he had one of two choices. He could either play dumb and pretend he didn't have a clue what Ms. Laverne was talking about. Or he could decide just how much to tell her before she punctured his rib with her finger. Evidently she knew something or she wouldn't be asking.

"I want Christy."

The old woman snorted. "I already know that. Known it for years. Evidently I knew it before you did. What I'd like to know is what's your definition of *want*?"

He lifted a brow. "Excuse me?"

"No, not this time, Alexander. I will no longer excuse you. It's time you made important decisions involving Christy."

He raised a brow. "What kind of decisions?"

"Whether you love my granddaughter or merely want her?"

Alex nearly cursed under his breath. *Love?* Ms. Laverne was definitely pushing it. He didn't love anyone. That was an emotion that had become as foreign to him as living on another planet.

He breathed in deeply, and since he knew she expected an answer, he decided to give her one. The only one he had. "I care for Christy."

The older woman slowly shook her head. "That's not good enough."

He opened his mouth to tell her that as far as he was concerned, it *was* good enough, when the look she gave him made him decide to do otherwise. "And why won't it be good enough?" he asked, deciding to take a detective's way out and let her do the talking.

"It won't be good enough, Alexander, because you've hurt her and she doesn't intend to ever forgive you."

Alex was surprised by Ms. Laverne's words. "She told you that?"

"Yes, but she really didn't have to. I know her. I know how her mind works. She's a Madaris, cut from the same cloth as her father and grandfather." She chuckled softly. "You can even call her Dex Junior. Cross them and there will be plenty of hell to pay. Destroy their pride and they may never come around."

That wasn't what Alex wanted to hear.

"I know you saw her last week," Ms. Laverne said.

Alex sighed, wondering how much of what had happened last week she knew about.

"And I know from talking to Christy during our regular chats on Sunday that she thinks the only reason you came to see her was to check up on her for her brothers."

Alex took a deep breath, no longer willing to hold his peace. "And something was wrong with wanting to know that she was all right?" he asked in an agitated voice.

A smile touched the older woman's lips. "No, not if the only thing you want to be is her protector. But I expected for you to have done something more dashing, like sweep her off her feet."

Alex snorted. "Considering the way she feels about me, that would have been pretty hard to do."

"You should have done it anyway. That's the only way you'll put a dent in that damn Madaris pride. My husband was worse than all his sons put together when it came to the issue of that pride, so I know what I'm talking about. You have to prove to Christy that you're worthy of her love all over again. But just wanting her isn't going to be enough, Alexander. She is a beautiful woman who will encounter plenty of men who only *want* her. For Christy, there has to be more and especially from you. She will need your love."

The older woman stopped talking and stared at him. For a split second Alex swore he saw an odd expression on her face. He wondered if she had looked into his eyes and seen what he had tried to bury years ago—the picture of a child full of hope and love—and when love had let him down, how the man he'd become protected himself from sharing that emotion with anyone again. The Madaris brothers always claimed their grandmother had a sixth sense. Now he was beginning to believe them.

"So . . ." she said softly. "What will it be?"

Alex's protective impulses kicked in. "I don't know," he said truthfully. "Like I said, I care for Christy. I don't know if I'm capable of loving anyone."

Ms. Laverne nodded slowly. "Then I suggest you start doing a lot of soul searching because without love, you can kiss Christy good-bye. For too many years you were her knight in shining armor, the man she dreamed of marrying. When you messed up, you messed up pretty bad. It's going to take a lot to get back in her good graces, so you will have your work cut out for you. A man who merely wants her will eventually give up and walk away. But a man who loves her, truly loves her, will hang in there no matter what, because Lord knows the child can be difficult."

When Alex didn't say anything but gazed thoughtfully at her for the longest time, Laverne Madaris smiled, laid a hand on his forearm, and said, "There. I've done what I felt I must. Now the rest, Alexander, is up to you."

Horace Mansfield, head of Cincinnati's office of the FBI, stared at the woman sitting across from his desk. In his mind she was the typical reporter, who was always digging for a bone. But in this particular case, he was determined the bone she was digging for would remain well buried.

He leaned back in his chair. "I'm sorry, Miss Madaris, but I can't help you."

"You can't or you won't?"

He sighed deeply. She was getting agitated and being difficult. "There are rules I have to follow. The Bonita Patterson case is officially closed."

Christy glared at him. She hadn't liked the evasive answers she'd been getting since she had arrived. "All I want to know is whether or not at some point the Bureau checked out Morganna Patterson's story and noticed a link between her dreams and reported teens' kidnappings."

The man met her stare without blinking. "That would be

classified information I couldn't share with you even if we had. I can only assure you that we routinely followed our customary procedures and will initiate a full-scale investigation when we feel one is warranted."

Christy sighed deeply. She wasn't getting anywhere with this man. She stood. "Good day, Mr. Mansfield. I apologize for taking up so much of your time." She walked out of the man's office.

Horace Mansfield watched Christy leave. As soon as he was certain she was gone, he picked up the phone on his desk. When the person on the other end answered, Mansfield said tersely, "We might have trouble brewing."

Alex slid his fork through the flaky crust of the apple pie and immediately thought about Christy. When she was little she'd loved apples as much as she had loved peanut butter.

He pushed the dessert aside, suddenly not feeling hungry. The conversation he'd had with Laverne Madaris earlier that day was still on his mind.

He stood and walked over to his kitchen window and looked out. Everything the older woman had said led him to thoughts of one person.

Christy.

He inhaled sharply, suddenly feeling the need to hear her voice. He quickly crossed the room to pick up the phone and punched in her number.

"Hello?" a sleepy voice said.

Damn. He'd forgotten how late it was. "Christy, this is Alex."

Christy came fully awake. "Alex?"

"Yes, sorry, I didn't mean to call so late and wake you. How are you doing?"

She frowned. "Did my brothers ask you to—"

"Hey, don't get uptight and go there, OK? I'm calling

because I had you on my mind. I've been thinking about you a lot today."

Christy swallowed and slowly closed her eyes. She refused to tell him that she had been thinking about him a lot that day as well, although she hadn't wanted to do so. "How was your day in court?" she asked, remembering the reason he had returned to Houston early was a subpoena he had received.

"It was OK. And how are you doing with that Patterson Report?"

She sighed, thinking that talking to him about it would distract her from how good it felt knowing he was on the phone and had thought enough to call. She didn't want to place too much stock in it.

"I think I've made a connection with Mrs. Patterson's dreams and the kidnappings of other teens," she said excitedly. "I visited the FBI office here today but they weren't cooperative."

Alex chuckled. "People would always say that when we didn't tell them what they wanted to know or wanted to hear."

Christy smiled. "OK, I admit I might have been a little pushy."

"A little."

"Well, maybe a lot. That guy rubbed me the wrong way. He acted like he didn't want to answer a few questions."

"A few?"

"All right, there might have been more than just a few."

"OK, let's talk about it. What are the possible links?"

Christy spent the next ten minutes discussing all the things she had discovered, including the connection of the kidnapped girl's name to Christmas and the similarities between her and Bonita. Alex listened and he asked questions that made her think.

"In your research, if you find similarities between Bonita and the other kidnapped girls as well, there might be a reason for it. If these girls are being shipped out of the country to be used as some man's playthings, these men may be requesting girls with certain features."

He sighed deeply. "There was once a baby-kidnapping ring that we busted that did that very thing. When desperate couples went to them wanting to 'adopt' a child with certain features, they would go out and kidnap a child to fit that couple's specifications. The same thing may be happening here."

"That's sick."

"Anyone who would kidnap another human being to use for profit *is* sick. They are also dangerous. I'm not saying that all the girls who have been kidnapped will have blond hair and blue eyes, but it might be something you will want to check out. And don't be surprised if you find young boys have been abducted as well."

"Now I know why you're so good at what you do," she said moments later.

His soft chuckle sent shivers down her spine and made a ripple pass through every part of her body. "Why?"

"Because you're sharp."

"Umm, at the moment I'm also missing you."

Christy bit down on her bottom lip. The way he'd spoken the words gripped her with the utmost tenderness and filled her with a unique feeling of warmth. But she knew she couldn't get pulled in by the intensity of the emotions he stirred. "Don't, Alex," she said softly.

"Why not?"

"It's too late for us."

"I refuse to accept that, Christy. I screwed up, but I intend to make things right."

"You can't. Good night, Alex."

For the longest time Alex held the phone in his hand after Christy hung up. Moments later he sighed deeply. She may be one of the most stubborn people he knew, but when it came to getting something he wanted, he was one of the most persistent.

He would complete this new case he was involved with.

Then he would start work on what he considered the most important assignment in his life.

Christy spent the next few days going through loads of documentation, articles, and tons of microfilm while researching information on all the reported kidnappings she had linked to Morganna's dreams.

Satisfied more than ever that she was on to something, she decided to make a day trip to Columbus, the last place Bonita Patterson was seen alive, and talk with Clara Jenkins, the woman who owned the boarding house where Bonita had lived.

When she had told Shemell what she intended to do, her friend had looked at her like she'd gone crazy, not believing she would waste her time chasing leads to Morganna's story. But she was doing that very thing, Christy thought as she walked up the steps to the Home Sweet Home boarding house to meet with Clara Jenkins.

Christy had left Cincinnati early and the drive down Interstate 71 had been uneventful except for the heavy traffic she had encountered. During the ride, she had tried not to think of Alex, but she had thought of him anyway. Butterflies had engulfed her stomach at the thought that she would be seeing him this weekend when she returned home to attend the twins' birthday bash.

She knew he had left Houston for an assignment in South Dakota, but the last time they talked he had indicated that he would be back in time to attend the party. He had called her twice this week, and it still baffled her that he was suddenly taking an interest in her when three years ago he hadn't wanted anything to do with her.

A shiver ran down Christy's spine when she thought about the last time they had seen each other and the kiss they had shared in her kitchen. His bruised lip hadn't hindered his abilities one bit.

Thoughts of Alex suddenly left Christy's mind when the

door to the boardinghouse was snatched open before she had a chance to knock. She looked into the face of the elderly, bedraggled woman who was staring at her.

"Christy Madaris?" the woman asked her.

Christy nodded. "Yes." She and Clara Jenkins had spoken on the phone earlier in the week, and the woman was expecting her.

The woman moved aside. "I saw you pull up. I'm Clara Jenkins. Come in."

"Thank you." Once inside Christy glanced around. The room was crowded. Junky was a more appropriate word. Potted plants were crammed into every corner, and boxes filled with . . . "stuff" . . . were everywhere. There wasn't much furniture and what there was looked worse than second-hand. The only thing that looked relatively new was the television.

"I collect things," the woman said when she saw Christy glancing around.

Christy met the woman's gaze. "I don't want to take up much of your time, but I was wondering what you could tell me about Bonita Patterson."

The woman offered Christy a chair. "Not much," the woman said, sitting on the sofa across from her. "Most of the time the kids who stay here don't want you to ask them any questions so I don't. I feel good in knowing that at least I'm providing them with shelter over their heads so they won't sleep in alleys and on the streets."

Christy nodded as she took out her writing pad. "And how long did Bonita live here?"

"For about three months."

"Did she have any friends?"

Mrs. Jenkins nodded. "When she wasn't working, she hung around with another girl by the name of Lindsay."

Christy raised a brow. "Bonita worked?"

Clara Jenkins absently picked up a sewing basket that was sitting on the table between them. "Yes, she worked at the car wash on the corner. I'm not sure what Lindsay did, but she always had plenty of money to pay her rent on time."

Christy sighed. She didn't want to think about what Lindsay could possibly be doing. "Is Lindsay here? I'd like to talk with her."

Clara shook her head. "No, I haven't seen her but once since Bonita left."

"Is there anything you could tell me about Bonita's activities, any visitors she might have had, and any other people besides Lindsay that she may have hung with?"

Clara stared down at the basket in her lap, as if trying hard to remember. She then looked up. "No, other than Lindsay, Bonita stayed to herself and kept her place clean."

Christy closed her writing pad and met the woman's gaze. "Mrs. Jenkins, do you think something happened to Bonita?"

The older woman snorted a breath like it was an absurd question. "Heavens, no. I think she just moved on like everyone else eventually does. Most of these kids are on the run from something, usually their parents, who oftentimes hire someone to find them. They don't want to be found, which is sad because unless they get help, some of them will die from some kind of assault, illness, or suicide."

Christy nodded in agreement. "Do you have any idea where Bonita may have gone when she left here?"

"No, in fact I didn't know she was leaving since her rent had been paid up for two weeks. But I figured there was a reason she had to get away fast like she did."

Christy stood. She planned to drop by the car wash where Bonita had worked to see if she could find out anything there. "Here's my business card. If you see Lindsay around again, please let me know."

The woman placed the sewing basket back on the table and got to her feet. "What about Bonita? What if I see her again?"

Christy pushed a wayward curl from out of her face. She didn't want to tell the woman she was operating on the premise that Bonita Patterson was dead. "If you see her, definitely give me a call."

Christy gazed at the young man who'd told her his name was Michael. "Are you saying that Bonita thought she was being stalked?"

He glanced over his shoulder, not missing a beat in putting wax on someone's car. "Yep. In fact she asked me to take her home the last time I saw her. It was dark, and she was afraid of walking."

Christy frowned. "Did you mention this to anyone?"

The guy, who looked to be around seventeen, stopped long enough to shrug his shoulders. "Nope. There was no reason to. When she didn't come back to work, I figured she decided to split. She always said she was here temporarily and intended to leave one day soon."

"Did she say where she would be headed?"

He shook his head. "She didn't say and I didn't ask, but I could tell she was pretty scared that night."

Christy nodded. "When you took her home, did you see or notice anything unusual?"

"Nope. I didn't see a thing."

Christy reached into her purse and pulled out a business card. "If you can remember anything else about that night, please give me a call."

Michael watched as Christy drove off. When she was no longer in sight, he pulled his cellphone out of his back pocket and punched in a few numbers. When the person came on the line, he said, "Hey, I thought you'd want to know. This redhead broad, who claims she works for a newspaper in Cincinnati, just left here and was asking questions about Bonita."

CHAPTER 9

Alex walked into the ballroom where the birthday party for the Madaris twins was being held. He had arrived in town a couple of hours ago from his last assignment, and had gone straight home from the airport to shower and change. Now he stood in the huge decorated room and his gaze was searching for one person and one person only.

He saw her, at least he spotted the vibrant color of her hair, and quickly moved in that direction. At the moment, he could barely control his emotions. He had dreamed of her every single night, and in those dreams she had taunted him, teased him, offered him everything, and then haughtily given him nothing. Her goading actions had only made him want her that much more. He had felt entrapped, snarled, wanting her with a passion the likes of which he'd never felt before.

He'd barely functioned to his full capacity while in South Dakota. The only thing that had occupied his mind the entire time was the thought of seeing Christy again, taking her into his arms, and kissing her with the intense hunger he felt. And in his current frame of mind, even death at the hands of the Madaris brothers wasn't enough to deter him from that goal. He was that far gone. That much out of control.

He continued walking toward her and came to a sudden stop when Syneda Madaris abruptly blocked his path.

"Alex, welcome back."

He blinked and stared into the sea green eyes holding his.

"Thanks, Syneda," he quickly said, and then made a move to step around her but found that he was surrounded by two other Madaris women. "Caitlin, Lorren," he acknowledged, wondering what the hell was going on and why the three had singled him out.

"May we speak with you privately for a moment?" Syneda asked, taking his hand and letting him know they would do so whether he assented or not.

He raised a brow. "What's this about?"

No one answered as the three women escorted him out of the crowded ballroom toward a secluded balcony. He sighed deeply. Whatever was going on must be serious, since Corinthians Grant and his sister-in-law, Felicia, were already there waiting. He turned and faced all five women. "Will someone tell me what's going on?"

It was Syneda, the most outspoken of the five, who answered. "We've taken it upon ourselves to keep you alive."

She then placed her hands on slender hips, and tossed her head in a way that sent thick golden-bronze hair flying about her shoulders as she glared at him. "What the hell were you thinking, Alex? Jeez. Did you actually believe you could stroll in here and walk straight to Christy and kiss her in front of everyone? And don't deny that's what you planned to do, since the intentions on your face were clear as glass. What do you think Clayton would have done?"

"Or Justin?" Lorren Madaris added.

"And let's not forget Dex," Caitlin Madaris said, as if anyone could forget the most extreme of the three.

"And what position would your actions have placed Trask in?" Felicia asked softly. "He's your brother, but he's also Clayton's best friend."

"And let's not leave out Trevor," Corinthians added. "The last thing we want tonight is an outbreak of war. It's the twins' party. Tonight is not the night to expose your feelings for Christy to the world. Besides, don't the two of you still have issues to resolve? I would think you'd want as few people as possible in your business until then."

Alex sighed deeply, deciding maybe it wasn't a good time to point out that the five of them were all in his business, so what would a few more people hurt? But then again, he fully understood what they were saying. When he had first entered the ballroom he had been acting out of control. Now his head was screwed back on straight and they were right. Tonight was not a night for an outbreak of war, and as much as he and the Madaris brothers were close friends, they would not readily accept the fact that he wanted their sister.

Alex stared at the five women as curiosity ruled his thoughts. "How did you know?"

Corinthians smiled. "We've seen how you've watched her at other times, at other functions—Gina's wedding, Rio's first birthday party, Sir Drake's wedding. I can go on and on and on, Alex. There was always this longing in your features, so much desire in your eyes. I honestly don't know how the guys haven't figured it out. I guess that just goes to show they're too observant in some things but clueless in others."

"Your secret is safe with us, Alex," Syneda Madaris said softly. "When the time comes for the brothers to find out the truth, they will. And we will be there to give you and Christy our support."

He nodded, knowing when that time came he would need all the support he could get. "Thank you." He then realized with a sudden rush of affection that the five women standing before him weren't just beautiful on the outside; they were beautiful on the inside as well. Their husbands were definitely very lucky men.

His thoughts shifted back to Christy. Thinking of her sent his senses reeling, and a deep awareness of desire raced all through him. He still wanted to hold her in his arms, kiss her.

As if reading his every thought, Lorren Madaris smiled.

"Give us a few minutes to find a way to occupy our husbands' time."

He smiled with appreciation in his eyes. "Thanks."

He watched as the women walked away, leaving him on the balcony alone. He sighed deeply, thinking about the mistake he'd almost made earlier. When it came to Christy, he needed to have better control of his senses.

Deciding it was time to return to the party, he left the balcony, and the first thing he did upon returning to the ballroom was walk right into Dex Madaris's hard, solid chest.

Alex swallowed deeply as he glanced up and looked around. Now he found himself staring into five pairs of eyes belonging to the husbands of the women who'd just left him. He knew the men were probably wondering why he'd been out on the balcony with their wives.

"Evening, everyone," he said in as normal a voice as he could muster. "I guess you're wondering what I was doing outside on the balcony with your wives," he decided to cut to the chase and say. Although he didn't have a clue as to what reason he would give them.

Justin Madaris smiled. "We already know."

Alex lifted a brow. "You do?"

"Yes, we do," Clayton said, grinning. "And I hate to say, although it shouldn't surprise anyone, that my wife is the one behind it."

"I hope you told them that you didn't know a damn thing," Dex Madaris added.

Alex frowned, wondering what the hell they were talking about, but quickly decided to play along. "Yes. I think I convinced them that I didn't."

"Good," Justin Madaris said. "Under no circumstances are we going to divulge the ingredients of that tea recipe. No matter what tricks they have up their sleeves. Understood?"

All the men nodded as Alex released a deep sigh of relief. They were talking about the Whispering Pines tea. The tea's secret recipe, which contained a special blend of herbs and spices, had been in the Madaris family for almost a hundred years and could only be shared with the men in the Madaris family, but only after they had reached their thirty-fifth birthday. Alex figured that although he wasn't quite that old, that wouldn't have stopped the womenfolk from picking his brain anyway, just in case he did know something.

He glanced around the room, his gaze seeking Christy out again. He spotted her. She was standing near where the band had assembled and was talking to her uncle Jake and his wife, Diamond, as well as Sterling and Colby Hamilton and Nicholas and Shayla Chenault.

Then as if Christy felt someone staring at her, she glanced over in Alex's direction. Their gazes locked. And the desire he felt for her intensified several degrees at that very moment.

"So, Christy, how do you like living in Cincinnati?" Diamond Swain Madaris asked the beautiful young woman who was standing beside her at the punch bowl.

After Diamond had received a deliberate nod from Syneda, she'd known what she needed to do. She smiled. This was definitely a role she could handle. After all, she was a semi-retired Hollywood actress.

"I like Cincinnati, but I miss home," Christy said. "However, my present job project will keep me quite busy for a while."

"Oh, what's it about?"

Christy tried to keep her attention on her conversation with Diamond and not on Alex. He was standing across the room staring at her, and for the life of her she couldn't help but stare back. He looked gorgeous; tall, dark, and utterly handsome. And although she tried to tell herself that tonight Blade, Slade, and Luke looked just as handsome, just as earthshakingly gorgeous, she was convinced that most of the single women present were checking out Alex.

"Christy?"

"Umm?"

Diamond smiled, fully aware of who was holding Christy's attention. "This project you're working on. What's it about?"

Christy was about to switch her gaze from Alex to Diamond when her heart began beating fast. He had moved away from the conversation he'd been holding with Kyle and Kimara Garwood and was headed straight toward her.

No! She couldn't talk to him now. Not when she lacked the control she needed to deal with him. She had to leave, walk away, before he reached her. She couldn't handle it if he were to touch her, breathe on her. . . .

"Christy, are you all right?"

She blinked and, visibly shaken, looked up at Diamond. "No, I'm suddenly not feeling well. I need to leave."

Diamond reached out and touched her hand. "OK. I'll find Jacob and have him drive you home. Why don't you wait for him in the lobby? I'll send him right on out."

Christy nodded and then quickly walked away. Diamond smiled moments later when Alex reached her side. A concerned frown was on his face. "Is something wrong with Christy?"

"Oh, Alex, I'm glad you're here. She isn't feeling well and needs to go home. I was going to ask Jacob but I don't see him around now. Do you mind taking her home?"

A smile touched the corners of Alex's lips. "No, I don't mind. It will be my pleasure."

Ashton Sinclair couldn't help but chuckle as he watched how the scene unfolded. As a marine colonel and former member of the Marines Special Forces, he was a man trained to be alert, observant, and ready for action, at any place and at any time, so it wasn't unusual that he had picked up on the sideshow that had been going on.

He glanced over at the man standing beside him and, upon seeing the grin on his face, knew that he was aware of the happenings as well. Drake Warren had also been a marine and had recently retired as a CIA agent, and a damn good one. "So, what do you think, Sir Drake? How much longer before the Madaris brothers figure things out?" Ashton asked his good friend quietly, so his voice couldn't be heard by his wife, Netherland, and Drake's wife, Tori, who had a side conversation going on regarding some new shopping mall that was opening somewhere in Houston.

"I'll give it less than a month, since it appears Alex is getting bolder. It won't be long before he says to hell with the risk of dying and claims his woman."

Ashton nodded. "And when he does there's bound to be trouble. Should we give Trev a heads-up?" he asked, thinking of the good friend of theirs who was also a former marine and who happened to be a close friend of the Madaris brothers.

Sir Drake shook his head. "No. This is one of those situations where we should just keep our mouths closed."

"Keep your mouths closed about what?"

Drake lifted a brow when his wife, Tori, glanced over at them and asked the question. Damn, he hadn't wanted her to hear what they had been talking about. Sometimes he wondered if she had bionic ears.

"Yes, Ashton, what are the two of you keeping your mouths closed about?" Netherland Sinclair asked her husband when it seemed that Drake wasn't going to give Tori an answer.

The two men smiled at each other and, as if they read each other's minds, pulled the women they loved into their arms, looked directly into their eyes, and simultaneously said, "Nothing."

Christy paced the lobby wondering what was taking her uncle so long. She hated bothering anyone, but there was no way she could stay and subject herself to Alex's presence without her full guard of armor. It wouldn't have been so bad if he hadn't dominated her every waking thought the past couple of weeks. Even trying to bury herself in the Patterson investigation hadn't completely helped.

"Christy, are you OK?"

She smiled when she glanced around and saw Gina Grant Farrell and her husband, Mitch. They were just arriving. "Hi, Gina, Mitch. Yes, I'm fine but have a slight headache," she lied. "I'm waiting for Uncle Jake to take me home."

"If you'd like we can take you," Gina offered, smiling.

Christy waved off her offer. "No, that's not necessary. Besides, the two of you just got here and I wouldn't want you to miss the party. The band is simply wonderful."

A couple moments later she found herself alone again in the lobby while she waited for her uncle.

Alex watched Christy pace back and forth. His reaction to seeing her, being so close—closer than he'd been since arriving nearly an hour ago—was instantaneous. A rush of blood shot through his veins and his heart suddenly began a rapid pounding.

The outfit she was wearing, a short dress that emphasized the beauty of her long, slender legs, was multicolored and blended well with the coloring of her hair and her complexion. She was strikingly beautiful. There was no other way to describe her.

He was a man who desired her, and naturally his sexual needs were rising. It had been a long time since he'd been with a woman. He hadn't been able to bring himself to touch anyone, sleep with anyone, or think of anyone since that night with Christy. So for the past three years he had buried himself in his work trying to rid himself of the deep, intense desire he had for her.

Taking a step out of the shadows and into the light, he asked, "Are you ready to go?"

The sound of that particular male's voice reverberated through Christy, causing sensations she'd rather not deal with at the moment. And when she swirled around, her gaze collided with clear dark eyes belonging to the one man she had wanted to avoid tonight. Being so close to him was unnerving, so she took a step back, needing to put distance between them. "Go where? I'm not going anywhere with you."

Alex drilled her with a penetrating stare. "Diamond said you weren't feeling well and needed to leave."

"Yes, but Uncle Jake is going to take me home."

"I'm the one taking you home."

Christy shook her head. "But you got here less than an hour ago. I'm sure you want to stay and—"

"No," he said, the word spoken strongly, his look compelling. He took a step forward, reclaiming the distance she'd put between them earlier. "The only thing I want is to make sure you're OK."

Christy pressed her lips together, deciding for the moment not to say anything, trying not to let his words that were spoken with such compassion and care touch her, send flooding warmth through her. She looked up at him, taking in his tall height as he towered over her, his shoulders massive, chest broad, and features as arresting as any male features could get.

"Come on and let me take you home, Christy."

She drew in a slow breath, wondering how she could tell him that he was the reason she wanted to leave and that his very presence unsettled her. There was no way she could go anywhere with him. But when he reached out and took her hand in his, somehow his touch calmed whatever turmoil had been brewing within her. And when his fingers closed tightly over hers, he willed her his strength and his reassurance; of what she wasn't certain, but she no longer felt ruffled and unsettled. And she remained that way as he led her out the door to his car.

CHAPTER 10

The moment the car locks clicked in place, Christy glanced over at Alex and her breath caught when she found him staring directly at her.

"Are you OK?" he asked in a low and soft voice. "Should we stop somewhere to get you something? A soda for an upset stomach? Aspirin for a headache?"

She shook her head. "No, just take me home and I'll be fine."

He nodded and then she watched as he started the car's ignition, resulting in a soft purring sound. It was moments later when they reached the interstate that she remembered this was how things had started out three years ago, on a car ride home. It was after the charity auction and everyone in her family had left to be with Trevor at the hospital as he waited for Corinthians to give birth to their baby. Christy's brothers had asked Alex to take her home.

She shifted her body and leaned against the soft cushion of the leather seat. Now this was one thing that was different. The car. That night he had been driving a BMW. Tonight he had a Lexus sports car. It was fast, sleek, and he was handling it with unerring precision that appeared to come naturally to him. As natural as breathing. Kissing her. Or anything else he did well.

"Marriage agrees with Sir Drake, doesn't it?"

She swallowed the lump in her throat, glad he had

interrupted her thoughts, since they had been way out there. "Yes, it does," she said. "I don't think I've ever seen him so calm, relaxed, and human."

Alex's soft chuckle rippled through the air. It also rippled through her, the sensation headier than she would have liked. The inside of the vehicle was intimate, deliciously warm. "Yes," he said. "Tori is definitely his perfect soulmate. She's all the woman he needs."

Christy nodded, tempted to ask him what type of woman he needed; definitely not one eight years younger. He had made the difference in their ages a big issue three years ago. She was curious as to what he thought about it now. A few weeks ago he had apologized and said he regretted the things he'd said to her, but still a part of her couldn't thaw out a portion of her heart that his words had frozen. She couldn't let go and get beyond the humiliating pain.

And you won't let go until the two of you talk about that night, a voice inside of her taunted. *He's asked you to discuss it, but you've refused to entertain the notion there is unfinished business between the two of you like he says. You won't risk him melting that ice in your heart.*

When the car came to another traffic light Alex couldn't help but glance over at Christy and release a slow breath. The air-conditioning was filling the car with the warmth of her scent. She looked simply incredible and smelled deliciously edible. He wished he could use his mouth to taste her from head to toe.

His gaze moved to her hands, which were resting in her lap. For eight years she had worn his ring on her left hand. A ring that had meant nothing to him but everything to her. Now, more than anything, he wanted to place that ring back on her finger. He took a shaky breath, not believing he was thinking that way.

Christy had a way a making him not think straight, which

was something no other woman could do. There was never a time when he hadn't been in full control of any relationship he'd shared with a woman. Things were done his way or no way, on his terms and not theirs.

But Christy Madaris came with a whole set of rules. She could break through his primitive impulses without even trying. And she could make him desire her to the point where he would be tempted to say, "The hell with it," and fill the sexual need she had the ability to arouse in him.

Deciding that silence had ruled the interior of the car long enough, he asked, "How's the Patterson investigation going?"

Christy met his gaze briefly as he slowed down to exit the expressway. "I spent the first part of the week going through a ton of documentation, articles, and microfilm. Then on Thursday I took a day trip to Columbus where Bonita Patterson was last seen to talk with Clara Jenkins, the woman who owns a rooming house where Bonita had lived. Mrs. Jenkins is convinced Bonita just moved on."

Christy sighed before continuing, "But I did talk to a guy at the car wash where Bonita worked. He said she asked him to take her home one night because she was afraid of walking. She thought someone was stalking her."

Alex raised a dark brow. "What about those other runaways?"

Christy glanced over at him. He had brought the car to a stop at a traffic light. She tried concentrating on his question and not on the sensual lining of his lips or the mesmerizing look in his eyes. "There were three others, two girls and one guy. Only Holly Johnson's parents are still convinced there was foul play. The others now think their runaways are somewhere alive and don't want to be found."

"What do you think?"

Christy swallowed thickly, trying to concentrate on their conversation and not on Alex. "I think just the opposite. In each of Morganna's dreams, she provided some kind of clue as to each of their kidnappings. I can't believe at some point she wasn't taken seriously."

Christy's comment made a frown pucker Alex's brow. If Morganna's dreams and those kidnappings had been brought to the attention of the FBI, he wondered why they hadn't picked up on the connection as well?

"It's a beautiful night, isn't it?"

He glanced over at her as he pulled into her parents' subdivision, the same one where he'd also grown up. "Yes, it is," he answered.

Moments later they were pulling into the driveway of a spacious two-story house. Alex brought the car to a stop.

"Thanks for bringing me home, Alex. And it was nice seeing you again and I hope that—"

He didn't give Christy time to finish, since he had opened the car door and was walking around the passenger side of the car. He opened the car door for her. He met her gaze, tried not to notice the irritation in her eyes when she said, "You don't have to walk me to the door, Alex. I know my way." She made the statement firmly.

He flashed a smile. "Since you've lived here all of your life I'm sure you do, but that's not why I'm walking you to the door."

Christy gritted her teeth as he assisted her from the vehicle. "Then what is the reason?"

"You'll know when we get there."

The silence that followed as they strolled up the walkway was unnerving. At least Christy thought it was. A quick glance over at Alex indicated he was calm, relaxed. Nothing appeared to be bothering him at all, but on the other hand, she was dying of curiosity. What would she find out when they got to the door? She'd made this walk thousands of times, but never had it appeared so long.

"I told your parents you weren't feeling well and that I was taking you home."

Christy stopped. She turned to him. "Why?"

Alex raised a brow. "Why what?"

"Why would you tell them that?"

He looked at her as if the reason were obvious. "So, they wouldn't be worried when they didn't see you."

"Diamond would have told them."

"Yes, I'm sure that she would have, but *I* wanted to tell them. I wanted to assure them you were in good hands."

Speaking of hands . . . Christy glanced down at his. Currently they were in his pockets, but she had a feeling he planned to take them out and use them in some capacity before she went into the house. She had always admired his hands, big, firm, with lean fingers. And as he and Christy began walking again she tried not to think about the fact that he was still wearing the ring she had returned to him.

And she didn't want to think of all the history the two of them had shared on this patch of ground. Although he'd been one of the youngest of her brothers' friends, since he was Trask's brother, that had made him an automatic member of the group. It had never bothered him when she adoringly followed him around with hero worship gleaming in her eyes.

He had taken up so much time with her while they'd been growing up. And like her brothers, he had always been there for her. She had truly convinced herself that he was the man she would grow up and marry. He was her prince who had delivered the shoe that fit, the one who had awakened her from a deep sleep, all the things that those fairy tales' true love and happy endings were based on. But in one single night he had snatched her out of fantasyland and made reality stare her cruelly in the face when he let her know he was not a prince and she was definitely not his princess.

"What time are you leaving tomorrow?"

She answered without looking over at him. "Tomorrow evening."

"Then maybe we can have brunch at Sisters before you leave, unless you've made other plans."

"I have," she lied. "I thought I'd spend some time with Traci and Kattie before I leave." He didn't have to know that she had spent time with her sisters and their families on Friday when she arrived.

She and Alex finally emerged from the semi-darkness of the long, winding walkway to the doorstep. As usual, the porch light had been left on. "Thanks for seeing me to the door, Alex."

"Let's go inside, Christy."

She frowned. "Why?"

"So I can kiss you."

Struck by the force of his direct, cut-to-the-chase statement, Christy tried to fight back the shivery tingles that escalated down her spine, then moved to every nerve ending in her body. "No, I don't think so," she said, breathing deeply and looking levelly into his dark, mesmerizing eyes.

"I hate to contradict you, but I *do*. We can do it either out here or inside. Personally, I prefer doing it inside, but either way, I intend to kiss you."

She glared at him. "And I won't have anything to say about it?"

He smiled. "No. Your mouth and tongue will be way too occupied to say anything."

Of all the nerve! As she tried to ignore the turbulent yet sensuous quake that was shaking her body, her glare deepened. "Don't push me, Alex."

Their gazes held. Locked. Dueled. Then he said, "I'm going to kiss you, Christy. The pushing comes later. Now are you going to open the door or will I have to? Have you forgotten that like you I have a key?"

She swallowed. She *had* forgotten. Alex was the last to move out of the neighborhood, and since her parents began traveling when they retired, it had made perfect since to leave a spare key with him so he could check on things while they were away. They had never felt the need to ask that the key be returned, since they considered him and his brother, Trask, family.

She breathed in deeply and decided to use another tactic. "You will force yourself on me?"

She watched his lips quirk. "I won't have to do that. You'll want my kiss, and if I recall, you once begged for it . . . as well as for something else."

Christy pursed her lips. He was not being kind to remind her of that. "I was under the influence then."

He nodded. "True. Are you under the influence of anything now?"

She lifted a stubborn chin. "No."

"You're absolutely sure about that?"

She wondered what he was getting at. "Of course I'm sure," she snapped.

"Good."

She didn't see it coming or she would have dodged the attack when his mouth swept down on hers, stealing her next breath and weakening her knees in the process. The tongue that immediately plunged into her mouth was powerful, skillful, and hungry. It was also sensuously persuasive. In no time at all, her own tongue had succumbed, and it didn't take long for her senses to follow.

This was a master kisser at work, an experienced seducer. He was a man with the golden touch and she was getting firsthand treatment. She felt the extent of his body pressed against hers, his powerful chest to the hardened tips of her breasts, his firm, solid stomach flattened against the soft contours of hers, and his muscled thighs cradling hers in one hell of an intimate squeeze. But it was the feel of his aroused body that both panicked and excited her.

She knew the safest course of action was to break off the kiss and demand that he leave. That was the logical thing to do. But then, her mind wasn't thinking logically and was refusing to do so. How could it think rationally when his tongue was embedded deep inside her mouth, doing irrational things to it? And if the kiss wasn't messing with her mind, then the scent of him, hot and musky, was taking control of her nostrils. He was pure male. Unadulterated. And when he intensified the kiss she felt hot, on fire, all the way to her loins.

Just as swiftly as the kiss started, it ended when he lifted his mouth but not all the way. He held his lips within inches of hers. "Tell me to take you inside and kiss you again. Tell me," he murmured softly against her moist lips.

Her eyes were heavy with desire as she stared at him. *There's nothing wrong with giving in to the temptation of his kisses,* she reasoned. After all, he wasn't the only guy she'd ever kissed. But then she quickly concluded that he was the only guy who'd really ever kissed her in the full sense of the word. He made any other kisses seem obsolete. He had the adept technique of a man who knew what he was doing. Gifted, talented, cunning, and slick. And she wanted to experience it all over again with him.

"Take me inside and kiss me again, Alex," she whispered. She watched his gaze lock on to her mouth and felt the heat of his breath against her lips when he whispered huskily, "Give me your key."

She placed the key in his hand. The feel of their fingers touching made her heart thump wildly in her chest, and the heated sensation of something intense was making butterflies dance around in her stomach.

She watched as he inserted the key into the lock and slowly opened the door. He then moved aside for her to enter. She had reached the middle of the living room when she turned upon hearing the sound of the door closing behind them. She inhaled. It had been in this very same room three years ago that they had kissed for the first time. It had also been in this room that he had set her straight about a number of things.

Alex sighed deeply. He could tell from the emotions lining Christy's features that she was remembering their last time together in this room. Tonight he wanted to replace those memories with pleasant ones. He knew it would take more than torrid and heated kisses to make her forget, but at least that would be a start.

"Come here, Christy."

He watched as she stiffened her spine. "You being here is a mistake."

"It's no mistake. Come here."

She lifted her gaze up to him and he knew she was inwardly fighting him. "Three years ago I hurt you in here, and tonight I want to take some of that pain away," he said softly.

"And I told you that you can't."

"And I've asked you to let me try. What do you have to lose?"

"My heart again."

Overwhelming frustration gripped Alex. Why couldn't she believe that he wouldn't hurt her again? Why couldn't she see that he wasn't the same man she had poured her heart out to that night? He'd had three years to come to terms with a lot of things, including wanting her.

He sighed as he crossed the room to her. Maybe it was time that she knew just how deep that desire went.

He swept her off her feet into his arms, kissing the gasp off her lips and effectively destroying her resistance. He walked over to the sofa and sat down with her cradled in his lap as he continued to devour her mouth, determined to let her know just how much he wanted and needed her.

Warm pleasure shuddered through Christy when, with his mouth still locked on hers, he began unbuttoning the top part of her dress and with a quick flick of his wrist unsnapped the front fastener to her bra, spilling her breasts from their confinement.

His mouth suddenly left hers and she shivered when she

felt his lips slide slowly down her throat before easing lower and letting the tip of his tongue touch the hardened nipples of her breasts, first one and then the other. She inhaled sharply at the contact and closed her eyes as something hot and heavy seemed to pull in the pit of her stomach and spread to the middle of her center.

She blew out a long breath between her lips as he continued the torture, the pleasure, a combination of both, as she pressed her breasts against his mouth, loving the feel of what he was doing to her, as he greedily licked the mounds of flesh that no man before him had ever seen, let alone tasted.

"Alex . . . ," she murmured gently as fire raged through her bloodstream. Something, a sensation she had never felt before, tore through her stomach and was making its way between her legs, the intensity of which was overtaking her senses. And as if he knew just where she was burning, he reached his hand under her dress and expertly moved past the crotch of her panties to slide his finger inside of her. Another first for her.

Christy's hips bucked in his lap when he lightly began stroking her, making the same small circles inside of her body with his finger that his tongue was making around the nipples of her breasts. Over and over, nonstop, increasing the pressure, easing it, and then increasing it again.

And then it happened. Every part of her seemed to explode in a million pieces, sending her spiraling to a place she'd never been before. She heard herself scream just moments before he covered her mouth with his. She moaned deep within his mouth as sensations continued to rip through her, from the top of her head to the soles of her feet.

He turned her into his arms and continued to hold her gently in his lap while the sensations slowly subsided. Their gazes locked and she knew what she had just shared with him was more special than he would ever know.

Alex took several long, deep breaths. It didn't take much

to see that the glazed eyes staring back at him were in awe at what she'd just experienced. Her response to him had been a touching blend of sensuality and inexperience, which could only mean one thing. He had given Christy her very first orgasm.

That thought overwhelmed Alex and he kissed her again, long, leisurely, deeply, before standing and placing her back on her feet. Holding her soft, warm body in his arms when she'd exploded from the pleasure he'd given her was something he would never forget as long as he lived.

He pulled her closer and rubbed his face against her neck and sighed deeply, loving her scent, every damn thing about her. "Since you can't have brunch with me tomorrow, how about breakfast?" he asked, kissing the corners of her lips.

"I may not be able to make either. I'm on standby for an earlier flight back to Cincinnati if I can get one. My boss gave me only four weeks to wrap things up with 'The Patterson Report' and I need to get my butt in gear."

He leaned back and gazed down at her. "Need my help? I'm pretty good at finding people and solving puzzles."

She appreciated his offer but knew the last thing she needed was constant contact with Alex. "Thanks but no thanks. Besides, you have a business to run and the budget I got from my boss can barely cover my expenses, let alone yours."

Alex decided to let it go for now. *For tonight anyway*. But he had already made his mind up about a few things concerning her. "Come walk me to the door."

He pulled her into his arms when they reached the door, and kissed her with all the desire and wanting he felt. Releasing her, he opened the door, then leaned against the jamb. He reached out and gently caressed her cheek. "If I don't get the chance to see you tomorrow before you leave, have a safe trip back to Cincinnati, all right?"

"All right."

He smiled and then he turned and strolled down the walkway. Before closing the door, Christy watched as he got into his car. She leaned against the door, inhaling deeply. Giving her heart to Alexander Maxwell for a second time was something that she would not do. No matter what.

Book Two

The Chase

CHAPTER 11

It was Monday morning and Christy had just returned to her desk after attending a staff meeting when the phone rang. She picked it up. "Christy Madaris."

"Ms. Madaris, this is Clara Jenkins."

Christy sat down at her desk. "Yes, Mrs. Jenkins?"

"You told me to call you if I saw her again."

A knot formed in Christy's stomach. "Saw who?"

"That girl. You know, the runaway."

Christy breathed deeply. "You saw Bonita Patterson?"

"No, but I did see that other girl. The one Bonita used to hang around with. Lindsay. She's back in town."

Christy picked up a pen and notepad off her desk. "Is she staying at your rooming house?"

"No, but I heard she's taken a place at the Bottom Lot."

Christy's brow lifted. "The Bottom Lot?"

"Yes. It's a rooming house on the other side of town."

Christy scribbled the information. "I'll be coming back to Columbus, Mrs. Jenkins. To talk to her if I can."

"All right. Do you need a place to stay? I have a nice room I can let you have real cheap."

Christy smiled. "No thanks, I'll have a place to stay."

Moments later Christy hung up the phone. As soon as she let Malcolm know where she was headed and changed the voice mail on her telephone to indicate she'd be out of the office, she would go home, pack a few things, pick up a rental car, and get on the road to Columbus.

• • •

Trask Maxwell stared long and hard at his brother, not believing what he was hearing. "You mean you're actually taking a vacation, time off work that's not business related?"

Alex smiled as he continued to pack. "Yes. Do you have a problem with it?"

Trask chuckled. "Are you kidding? I think it's about time you stop playing Sherlock Holmes for a while and enjoy life. So where are you headed?"

Alex sighed. The less Trask knew, the better. "Umm, a number of places. If you need to reach me you can always get me on my mobile phone. Vaughn will be running things in my absence, and I have all the confidence in the world he can handle things." *I have more important matters to take care of,* Alex thought. He wanted Christy, and he'd be damned if he let anything or anyone stand in the way of him having her.

Not even Christy herself.

He felt that gentle tug to his heart, the same sensation he always got whenever he thought of Christy and how much he wanted her. But he refused to give in to the possibility that he loved her. That was more than he dared to think about at the moment.

Christy parked the rental car and looked around. This wasn't exactly the best neighborhood, but it was the one Clara Jenkins had sent her to, that is, if she had followed her directions right, and there was no reason to think that she hadn't.

The house was worn down and probably wouldn't be missed if it was eventually torn down, but then, the same could be said for all the houses in this particular neighborhood.

Getting out of the car, she glanced around, grateful there was still plenty of daylight left. Rule number one was: Know your surroundings.

She quickly walked up to the door and knocked. "Who is it?" a young female called out.

"Christy Madaris. I'd like to ask you a few questions about Bonita Patterson."

The door was snatched open immediately and an African-American girl who couldn't have been any more than fifteen stood before her. "Look, I told you people all I knew. Why can't you leave me alone and go out and find her?"

Christy lifted a brow, trying to make sense of what the girl was saying. "Go out and find who?"

The girl narrowed her eyes and looked at Christy. "You aren't the cops or the Feds, so who are you?"

Christy swallowed at the way the girl was glowering at her. "I'm Christy Madaris, a reporter for the *Cincinnati Enquirer*. I'm also an acquaintance of Bonita's mother."

The girl's eyes narrowed even more. "Then why should I tell you anything when her mother is the one who had her kidnapped?"

Christy blinked. "Why do you think that?"

"Because Bonita would not have gone back home on her own, so her mother hired someone to kidnap her."

"And why would she do something like that?"

"To make Bonita bend to her will. That's what rich people do when their kids don't behave the way they want and they feel the need to control them. It's my guess her mother has her locked up somewhere and plans to keep her that way until Bonita conforms to her will."

Christy frowned, wondering where the girl had gotten such an idea from. "Did you tell anyone else this theory of yours?"

"Yeah. I told the police and the Feds when they came around asking questions."

Christy nodded. "And why do you think someone kidnapped her?"

"Because Lindsay saw them take her."

"Do you know where Lindsay is, so I can talk to her?"

"She won't tell you anything. When she told the policemen what she saw they didn't want to believe her, and the

Feds weren't any better. I think Bonita's mother paid them all off."

Not bloody likely, Christy thought. "And you said Lindsay actually saw Bonita get kidnapped?"

"Yes. No one knew Lindsay was there, but she watched as two men grabbed Bonita and put her in a car."

"And she didn't try to help?"

"She was afraid to do anything. She ran all the way here and told me, but when I got there it was too late. They were gone."

"And you told all of this to the police?"

"I said I did, didn't I? Look, I'm not answering any more of your questions."

Christy heard the increased agitation in the girl's voice. "Will you at least tell me your name?" At first she wasn't sure that the girl would do so; then she said, "Tiffany."

Christy nodded again. "Look, Tiffany, I don't know why you believe what you do, but I know for a fact Morganna Patterson did not have her daughter kidnapped and is not holding her hostage somewhere until she comes to her senses. If you witnessed a kidnapping, then it wasn't one Bonita's mother orchestrated. I believe someone else might have taken her. I'm going to be in town for another day and would love to talk with you and Lindsay about Bonita's disappearance."

Suddenly the door opened wider and another teenager appeared by Tiffany's side. She was holding a baby in her arms, a little girl who appeared to be slightly over a year old.

Instead of saying anything to Christy, the young woman spoke to Tiffany. "I told you something wasn't right with that kidnapping. I don't care what those FBI guys claimed."

Christy stared at the girl. "What FBI guys are you talking about?"

The girl turned and met Christy's curious stare. "I'm Lindsay, and I'm talking about the men who investigated our claim that Bonita was kidnapped, and who came back later and said she was unharmed. We know that's a lie, but unlike

Tiffany, I don't think it was her mother who snatched her."

Christy lifted a brow. "And who do you think did it?"

Lindsay met her gaze and held it. "An organized group called the Body Snatchers."

"The Body Snatchers?"

"Yes, that's the name the runaways gave them. Last year when I was in Philadelphia, there was a rumor of a group of men who went around kidnapping teenage girls to ship overseas."

Christy frowned. She'd never heard of such an organization. "And the Philadelphia Police Department knew about this group?"

Lindsay nodded. "Yes. Word had begun spreading among the runaways to be careful. I heard the organization was expanding to other cities, including Columbus. When I returned here, I warned Bonita about them and told her to be on her guard. Then a few months later, she told me about this guy trying to talk to her. She didn't have a good feeling about him, and he asked a lot of questions, wanting to know about her family and how close she was to them and if they stayed in contact. When she described him to me, he sounded like one of the men the runaways were told to avoid."

Christy lifted an arched brow. "Who is he?"

"Don't know but he started coming around the car wash and always drove an expensive car. Bonita wouldn't listen to my warning and continued to talk to him. She was determined to find out any information she could to take to the police in case he was one of those snatchers."

"Did she go to the police with her suspicions?" Christy asked, her words coming out automatically.

"Yes, but they didn't believe her, so I convinced her to call Detective Mark Tyler in Philly. He was involved in investigating this organization."

"Detective Mark Tyler?"

"Yes, but you can't talk to him."

Christy lifted a brow. "Why?"

"Because he's dead. Word on the street was that he asked too many questions and the Body Snatchers arranged his death."

Christy stared at the girl, disbelieving. "Someone had him killed?"

"Yes."

Christy felt goose bumps form on her arms. *The Body Snatchers?* When she got back to her hotel room, she would get on her laptop to see what she could find out about them.

"Look, lady, we've told you enough already," Tiffany snapped. "Probably, more than we should have so just leave us alone."

The door was then slammed shut in Christy's face.

Later that evening Christy checked into her hotel room more confused than ever. After taking a long, leisurely bath she slipped into her bathrobe, put her hair in a ponytail, and decided to check her messages on her mobile phone. She blinked in surprise to find that two were from Alex, and the deep, husky sound of his voice sent shivers through her. It didn't take much to close her eyes and picture him as she'd last seen him, when she was standing in her parents' doorway after he had thoroughly kissed her.

She didn't want to think about all the other things he had done to her that night as well. He had looked so sexy, had smelled so good, and had used his hands, mouth, and fingers like a born expert.

She sighed deeply as she placed her phone back in her purse, deciding not to return his call, although a part of her wanted to. With his connections with the FBI he could check to see if they knew of or were investigating an organization called The Body Snatchers.

But she wanted to do her own research, and tomorrow she would return to Cincinnati and make a few calls to see what she could find out about Detective Mark Tyler.

It was almost eleven o'clock by the time Christy had powered down her laptop and gotten into bed.

A man sat in a dark sedan in the parking lot of the Sheraton Hotel. He pulled out his cell phone and dialed a number. "This is Ford. She's in her room for the night. Do you want me to keep an eye on her to make sure she leaves? He nodded. "OK. I'll keep in touch."

He clicked off the line, then sat back and watched in the darkness.

CHAPTER 12

"Hello, this is Christy. Please leave a message and I will return your call. Thanks!"

Alex hung up the phone. He had already left a couple of messages. When he had arrived in Cincinnati yesterday, he had tried contacting Christy at her office to ask her out to dinner, only to get her voice message that said she was out of town and wouldn't be returning until early Wednesday. Well, it was Wednesday night and she still wasn't back.

He sighed deeply as he paced around his hotel room. Ms. Laverne had made sure he understood that Christy didn't need for him to act as a protector, but hell, he couldn't help but worry about her. Although a part of him knew that, thanks to her brothers, she knew how to take care of herself, he couldn't help but remember what had happened with that guy at the nightclub.

As a way to distract himself he decided to turn on the television and see if anything worthwhile was on. He would wear the carpeting out if he continued to pace. Half an hour later when his mobile phone rang, he quickly picked it up. "Yes?"

"Alex?"

He let out a deep sigh of relief when he recognized Christy's voice. "Where have you been?" He regretted the question the moment it left his mouth.

"Not that it's any of your business, but I've been out of town working on the Patterson case."

He heard the edge in her voice and knew the safest course of action would be to back off. "Any new leads?"

"You wouldn't believe all I've found out."

Her voice was a combination of frustration and excitement. He picked up on both. "You want to talk about it?"

She paused for a brief moment, then said, "Yes, I could use another opinion, but I need to shower first. My return to town was delayed by bad weather in Columbus. Is it OK to call you back later?"

The need to see her was killing him. "I've got an even better idea," he said, checking his watch. It wasn't nine o'clock yet.

"What?"

"How about if I come over?"

He could hear the sudden catch in her voice before she asked, "Where are you?"

"In a hotel room, here in Cincinnati."

"What are you doing here?"

Alex smiled ruefully at her question and could imagine her glaring at him through the phone. "I'm here on a mission."

"What sort of mission?"

"To do whatever I have to do to win back your love."

There was a long pause. "That's not possible. I don't give second chances."

"I'm determined to get one."

He heard her sigh. "Look, Alex, it won't work. And speaking of work, who's running your company while you're here, supposedly winning my love?"

"I left a good man in charge."

Christy frowned. He actually sounded serious. "I meant what I said, Alex. There's no way I'll ever love you again."

"So you've said. Have you eaten anything?"

He could picture her standing with her eyes narrowing, not liking the way he had smoothly switched subjects.

"I stopped at a hamburger place earlier today, around noon," she said.

"Then it's time to eat again. I'll stop and get something for us on my way over there. That way you'll be operating on a full stomach when you tell me everything that you've found out about Bonita Patterson."

Then before she could say something smart about him coming over, he said, "I'll see you in a little while." Not waiting for her to respond, he quickly clicked off the line.

When Christy opened the door half an hour later, and saw Alex's mouth eased into a slow smile, she actually felt her body react. Her breasts tightened, heat pooled between her legs, and her head felt light.

She swallowed the lump that had suddenly formed in her throat, and knowing she needed to do something with her hands—or else she would be tempted to reach out and snatch him inside—she stuffed them deep in the pockets of her skirt. She cleared her throat. "Alex."

"Christy."

She studied him. Boy, did he look good. But Alex had always been a smooth and immaculate dresser. No one else could make jeans and a jacket such professional-looking attire.

But there was something about him tonight, something that made desire shudder up her spine. When she met his gaze, locked on to it, she knew what was different. She had seen wanting and desire in his eyes before. But tonight what she was seeing was fire—fierce, red-hot—burning deep in the depths of his gaze. She shivered at the impact. They had just seen each other Saturday night, four nights ago, but the way he was looking at her, it could have been four years ago.

"Are you going to invite me in?"

His question made her aware of the fact that they had been standing there, as if they had nothing better to do, staring at each other. Her gaze slipped from his eyes to the mouth that had asked the question. He had a sensual mouth that was expert at kissing, and whenever he kissed her, although she had wanted to do otherwise, she had savored each and every moment. And she knew just as surely as her name was Christina Marie Madaris that Alex planned to kiss her at some point tonight, and the thought of him doing so made shivers of excitement and anticipation hum through her body.

"Christy?"

The sound of her name from his lips, lips that she was watching move, intensified the heat that was flowing through her. "Yes, come in," she said softly, taking a step back when she actually wanted to run for the hills. Alex was too much man for her to tackle, but boy, did she want to tackle him, to the floor, and have her way with him.

She watched as he closed the door. Locked it. Then he turned back to her. He set down the bag he was holding on a nearby table and without breaking a stride reached out and his strong, solid, yet gentle fingers clasped her arm. He pulled her to him, timed it perfectly as he lowered his head.

The first touch of his mouth to hers was light, soft. Then when she automatically parted her lips on a breathless sigh, she felt the tip of his tongue ease inside her mouth. And that's when he adjusted the pressure, increased the pleasure, and proficiently and unerringly staked his claim.

OK, she would admit her mouth—for the moment—was his for the taking. And boy, was he taking it. She felt hot, the tips of her breasts that were pressed to his chest felt hard, and coils of intense heat were burning her loins. It seemed every part of her was molded to him. Her mouth, her body, her hands. At some point they had come out of her pockets and were rubbing all over his back and shoulders with an urgency that made small whimpering sounds escape her lips. How that was possible she wasn't sure, since her lips were glued to his and any sound should have been practically nonexistent.

Slowly he lifted his mouth. But that didn't stop her from

darting out her tongue and tracing the outlines of his lips for one more forbidden taste.

"Do you know what I enjoy most about kissing you?" he asked. His voice was low and seductive; the look in his eyes, warm and intimate.

She regretted that her inquisitive mind couldn't resist asking, "What?"

"Knowing the taste I'll get."

He was standing close and his nearness was making her pulse escalate again. "And what taste is that?"

"The taste of my woman."

His woman! Of all the nerve!

Before she could think of some blazing retort to fire back at him, he pulled her to him and kissed her again with the same urgency that she felt, quickly wiping away anger and igniting another type of fire. His hips rocked against her and she felt the solid hardness of him in the jeans he was wearing. His tongue probed deep into her mouth, sending her senses roaring, her breast throbbing, and her nerve endings haywire.

Moments later he slowly pulled back, met her gaze, and calmly said, "I bought Chinese. We'll eat, discuss the Patterson case, and then we'll kiss some more. Just like I know the taste I'll get whenever I kiss you, I want you to know the taste you'll always get whenever you kiss me."

Christy blinked, and then she tried to get the beat of her heart in sync with the racing of her pulse. At that very moment she was forced to admit one very obvious point.

She was in trouble.

Across the street, the man watched as Christy Madaris let the tall, dangerous-looking man into her apartment. He smiled wondering exactly what they were doing right about now. He noted the time, then watched and waited.

CHAPTER 13

Alex finished reading the report Christy had typed into her laptop. A frown marred his forehead. One thing was fact—someone claimed to be an eyewitness to Bonita Patterson's kidnapping. But what was questionable was the assertion that a Detective Mark Tyler, a member of the Philadelphia Police Department, had gotten killed as a result of digging into this so-called kidnapping ring, the Body Snatchers. If that was true Alex was certain that the FBI would have heard about them, and he had no problem using his contacts within the Bureau to find out one way or the other. However, the most important thing at the moment was that under no circumstances would he allow Christy to put her life at risk by asking the right questions of the wrong people.

"Well, what do you think, Alex?"

He glanced up. Christy, who'd been sitting across from him at the table, had stood up. He liked the way her short skirt hugged her curvy figure and the way her blouse fitted perfectly to her firm and full breasts. At the moment what he was thinking was that any other man would be in her bedroom making love to her instead of sitting here discussing some report. But certain things weren't meant to be rushed. When the time came for them to make love, he would have earned that right by reclaiming her heart.

He pushed away from the table, deciding he needed to stay in control no matter how alluring she looked. When it came to Christy he could have the honorable intentions of a saint, but still she was temptation at its finest. "I think there are a lot of unanswered questions. The final one is whether or not there was foul play in Mark Tyler's death when the newspapers claim it was the result of a boating accident."

Christy sighed. "I'm going to see what I can find out about that."

Alex nodded. "And I'll call the Bureau in the morning and see what I can find out about a group called the Body Snatchers."

Christy stiffened at his offer. Bouncing things off of him was one thing, but having him assist in her investigation was another. "No, Alex, I don't want you to do that. I like asking your opinion and I appreciate the feedback. But it's important to me that I handle this investigation without any help from anyone, including you. I want to be the one to follow up my own leads. I need your word you won't interfere with my work."

Alex stared at Christy. He had no problem promising not to interfere with her work as long as nothing she did placed her in any sort of danger. There was no way he would not be concerned about her well-being.

"Alex?"

He sighed. He didn't necessarily have to share with her the fact that her definition of *interfere* was not the same as his. "I told you why I'm here, Christy, and getting involved with your work isn't the reason. I have more personal matters to take care of."

He stood and slowly crossed the room, coming to a halt directly in front of her, allowing no more than a mere foot to separate them. "Now with that out of the way, how about if I acquaint you with the taste you'll get whenever we kiss?"

Christy stared into Alex's eyes, seeing the flare of desire, the heated intent in his gaze. And then there was that arrogant expression he wore like he knew what he wanted and nothing, not even hell freezing over, would stop him from getting it.

She lifted her chin. "I know what you're trying to do, Alex, and it won't work. A few kisses won't jumpstart my heart."

He smiled. "I could never give you just a few kisses, Christy. Besides, I know it will take more than that. You deserve more. I plan on hanging around and dating you properly."

The arrogance of the man! Date her? If that's what he thought, then he had another thought coming. There was no way they would start dating so he could forget that.

"I want you, Christy, the way a man wants a woman."

She drew in a deep breath as his words slid over her entire body like a sensual caress. Almost in spite of herself, desire shivered through her, weakening her defenses, creating a deep longing. His words had been simply stated, so straightforwardly put. She would have given anything to have heard him say those very words that night three years ago. But he hadn't.

And she was hearing clearly what he was saying now. He wanted her, but he didn't love her. "I know all about passion, Alex," she finally said.

He quirked a brow. "And what do you *think* you know?"

"I think you plan to use it to try to seduce me into coming around to your way of thinking. But it won't work."

The curve of his lips deepened. "What won't work? The passion or the seduction?"

"Neither." She watched his smile deepen as he studied her face. It seemed his gaze moved over every angle and curve.

"I like kissing you and you like kissing me," he said huskily. "I also like touching you, seeing your reaction to my touch, seeing the hardness in you soften . . . even if it's only for a little while."

She didn't want to admit that kissing him made her feel connected to him in a way she had never thought possible. While in his arms, she felt surrounded by his strength, every part of his being. Whenever they kissed, she was lured to throw caution to the wind, wrap her arms around him, and indulge.

He reached out and placed his hands at her waist. The shock of his touch sent desire quivering through every bone in her body. The warmth of his hands made her muscles melt. His fingers slowly began caressing her waist, gentle, kneading strokes that began heating her, making her even more aware of him as a man.

There had always been something about his strength, the intensity of him. From the first time she had begun noticing the opposite sex, she had admired it, and from afar she had reveled in it to her heart's content. He had been in so many of her dreams, and as she'd gotten older, the dreams had gotten bolder, more brazen, and definitely more heated. And with each dream came a steadily growing need to become one with him, to feel his muscles beneath her hands while he made love to her, introducing her to lovemaking and becoming the one and only man whom she would ever need or want in her life. Every day, whether distance had kept them apart or not, nothing mattered; her feelings had never wavered or changed.

She swallowed against the sudden pain she felt when she remembered that all it had taken was one night to burst that bubble. He had not hesitated in letting her know that she wasn't his and he most certainly wasn't hers.

"Christy?"

She blinked at the sound of his voice and haughtily lifted her chin. "What?"

As if he'd read her thoughts, he said softly, "Don't let that night continue to stand between us." He dipped his head and brushed his lips to that chin.

She shook her head and held his gaze. "Why shouldn't I? You want me to let go and move on. Why won't you understand that I can't love you again?"

Alex continued to hold her gaze. Oh, he understood things, all right. He fully understood that he was dealing with a Madaris, a member of a family known for its fierce pride, and this was one unforgiving woman. She was stubborn, proud, and defiant. But another thing about a Madaris—something he was banking on—was that they loved forever. If Christy had loved him before, he had to believe a part of her still loved him, although she claimed otherwise. He just needed to unthaw that frozen section of her heart to rekindle the flame.

"I do understand, Christy," he said finally. "Maybe it's time that *you* do."

He lowered his head and captured her next breath. He deepened the kiss and their tongues meshed, entwined, melded. He was intent on her tasting his desire, his claim to her heart and soul. He would ravage her senses until she knew she only belonged to him.

He pulled back slowly and watched as she sucked in a gasping breath, her eyes growing deep with passion. "Taste me, Christy. When we kiss again, I want you to taste everything about me. I want you to feel how my mouth comes alive once it connects to yours, how hungry my tongue gets, its urgency, its need, and its desire so compelling that you're the only woman it wants. I've made myself several promises, and the first one is that no matter how intense the sexual chemistry is between us, I won't make love to you until I know I have recaptured your heart."

Dipping his head, he kissed her again, hungrily, deeply, pulling her closer into his arms, letting her taste him the way he was tasting her. He wanted her to feel what he was feeling.

She pressed closer to him, kissing him back in a way that made him fight hard to control his emotions. He felt her hands on his back, his shoulders. Her fingers moved slowly, sliding over hard muscles, responding to the need she felt in his kiss. She responded to his taste as he drew her into this intimate, profound, and provocative exchange. Deeply. Unhurriedly.

Possessiveness gripped him, adding to his passion, increasing his awareness, and sweeping hold of his senses. She belonged to him whether or not she wanted to accept it.

She might think of herself as an unconquerable force, but he considered himself an immovable object. Intent with purpose, destined to have what he wanted.

And he wanted her.

Moments later he slowly pulled back and watched as she breathed deeply, saw the emotions that rolled through her, the same ones that had fed her with his taste, sharpened her need, and suffused her with full awareness. He refused to acknowledge the sudden quake of raw, primitive hunger that gripped him, that wanted to pull her into his arms and kiss her again, continue to kiss her, sweep her off her feet and take her into the bedroom and make love to her.

Alex forced away the influx of emotions that was tearing through him. He fought the very idea that he wanted her not just for today and tomorrow but for the rest of his life. Panic seized him at the thought that he wanted forever with any woman. He refused to accept the possibility that he was falling in love with Christy. Love had no place in his life. He quickly pushed the very notion from his mind.

He urged her closer, liking the feel of her breasts brushing against his chest. He enjoyed seeing the way her lips were wet from his kiss. "Have dinner with me tomorrow night," he said huskily. His fingers stroked the bare skin on her arm, feeling how she shivered from his touch.

She met his gaze. "I'm going to be too busy to—"

"You have to eat sometime, Christy," he interrupted. The stubborn look she gave him matched his own. "I'll be by around six o'clock tomorrow. We'll have dinner, then go dancing. Our first official date."

He took a step back. He couldn't help recalling how she had danced for him while under the influence. Now he wanted her in his arms, moving on the dance floor with her full senses intact.

He watched her stare at him, felt the sharpness of her gaze cut into him. Penetrating. Stubborn. "I didn't say I would go out with—"

He quickly recovered the distance and pulled her to him and kissed her again; the sigh that escaped his lips was one of impatience. The one that escaped hers was laced with annoyance, but he chose to ignore it; instead he was intent on kissing any of her unpleasant thoughts away.

When he released her moments later she appeared too stunned to say anything. To his way of thinking it was just as well. There was nothing else left to be said. As far as he was concerned, the subject was closed.

But evidently Christy thought otherwise. It appeared she refused to give her mouth a rest. Chin up, she met his gaze. Her eyes bored through him when she said, "You can't assume I'll do whatever you want."

He smiled. "Trust me. You're a Madaris. With you I can't assume anything. But then, I'm a Maxwell, and Maxwells have been dealing with the Madarises for a long time. We understand each other." His smile widened when he thought about his brother and her cousin and how they had constantly bickered most of their lives, but how happy they were now as a married couple. You only had to be in their presence a few minutes to feel the love, as well as the heat and sizzle that generated between them.

He chuckled. "And there is one thing that a Madaris and a Maxwell can't fight."

She narrowed her eyes at him, tilted her head. "Indeed? And just what is that?"

His hand rose to frame her face. "Passion."

He leaned down and brushed a kiss across her lips. "I'm staying at the same hotel if you need me. Otherwise, I'll see you tomorrow evening."

Without saying another word he turned and departed, leaving Christy standing in the middle of the room, struggling to draw in a much-needed breath.

Alex opened his car door, paused a second, and glanced around. He had the sudden feeling that he was being watched.

He frowned, blaming that report Christy had asked him to read for his uneasiness. It had formulated a lot of unanswered questions in his mind, but he would do as she asked and let her solve the puzzle.

As he slipped onto the leather seat of the rental car he was driving, he couldn't help but smile. Christy had his head spinning and had pushed his libido into overdrive. Her mind was on unraveling the case she was working on, but his mind was definitely on unraveling her.

CHAPTER 14

Christy tried concentrating on the report she was reading and not on the huge vase of mixed flowers that had arrived less than an hour ago. To say the delivery had gotten "oohs" and "ahhs" from her co-workers would be an understatement. Since most of them had assumed she wasn't involved with anyone seriously, she had seen a lot of speculation in their eyes. Only Shemell had had the courage to come right out and ask who had sent the flowers.

Alex.

Christy sighed deeply, feeling a quiver in her midsection just thinking about him. After declaring he intended for her to fall back in love with him, and that he wouldn't make love to her until she did, he had stood in her apartment and had kissed her last night for almost a full half hour.

And she had enjoyed every single minute.

She had taken profound pleasure in watching how the angle of his face deepened right before he kissed her, how desire, deep and intense, flamed his eyes, sending a multitude of sensual sensations through her that were similar to the ones she was feeling now.

Something about the way he had kissed her last night was different, and it had taken a full night of tossing and turning to figure out just what the difference was. She had awakened that morning excruciatingly aware that Alex Maxwell had a game plan.

He was trying to possess her.

And he was using the oldest trick known to man: Break down her defenses and her heart would soon follow.

She shook her head and couldn't help but smile. He would discover that when it came to her, pleasure and possession didn't go hand in hand. She'd take great enjoyment in knocking him off that high horse he was riding.

A streak of pure sneaky delight flowed through her. She knew that no matter what, Alex would never intentionally take advantage of her. He had proven it the night he'd refused her advances when she'd been under the influence. But she wondered just how tough his resistance was if she pushed it to the max. He wanted to date her and start off tonight by taking her out to dinner and dancing, believing he was in full control of her eventual seduction. Well, she intended to show him that she was a force to reckon with.

With her decision made, she turned her attention back to the Patterson case. She had reread the article about Detective Mark Tyler and decided it was time for her to fly to Philly and ask questions.

She put down the report when her telephone rang, and quickly picked it up. "Christy Madaris."

"It's Alex."

Her heart began racing. She swallowed. "Hi, and thanks for the flowers."

"You're welcome. I'm just calling to see if you're in the mood for Mexican food tonight."

She quickly decided that two could play his game. "It doesn't matter. I'll be ready to go when you get there."

She waited, knowing she had thrown him a curve. He had expected her to dig in her heels, refuse to go out with him, and because she was now being so agreeable and accommodating, his instincts would push him to act on the side of caution by proceeding carefully.

"All right, I'll see you at six," he finally said.

She chuckled softly to herself. "Good-bye, Alex."

When she hung up the phone, the thrill of predestined

victory surged through her. Her mind began whirling with devious plots.

Alex wouldn't know what hit him.

Alex took a deep breath as he stood in Christy's doorway. He stepped over the threshold and closed the door behind him, his gaze locked on hers. She stood smiling benignly, her eyes filled with total innocence while everything else about her spelled the words "set-up."

He was inclined to go along with whatever plan she had devised just to see how far she would take it . . . and from the looks of things she wouldn't hesitate to take it as far as she deemed necessary.

He allowed his gaze to skim over her from head to toe. She was wearing a dress that was so tight it seemed to have been painted on her body. To say the clingy material was plastered to her curves would be an understatement. He almost swallowed his tongue when he saw no panty line, so he knew she had to be bare under that thing.

Then there was the length of the dress. It was shorter than any other dress he'd ever seen her wear. She definitely had the legs to pull it off. Not every woman could make that claim but Christy Madaris could. And very boldly.

It was the kind of dress she was meant to be stripped out of. It became clear what Christy was trying to do—drive him out of his mind. And the way his body was responding, she was doing just that.

He swallowed. "You look nice tonight, Christy," he finally decided to say, trying to get a grip but finding it hard to do so.

"Thank you," she said, tilting her head to look up at him.

His gaze roamed over the dress again. "That shade of blue. Is there a name for it?"

Christy looked down at herself. Then her gaze lifted to his and she said, "I call it shocking blue."

Alex just nodded dumbly. He could understand why.

Personally, he would call it arousing blue. He decided to shift his concentration to something else, and his gaze moved to the huge vase of flowers on a nearby table. The arrangement did something to the entire room. When he glanced over at Christy and saw her watching him, he thought that she did something to the entire room as well.

Without thinking twice about it, with a slow, purposeful stride he covered the distance separating them, his gaze holding steady on hers. He came to a stop and leaned down and his lips settled warmly, yet firmly on hers.

When her mouth parted beneath his, a groan rumbled from deep within his chest as his tongue swept from one part of her mouth to the next. He fought back a case of raging hormones and could tell from the way she was responding that she was enjoying their kiss. The soft texture of her lips, along with the heated sweetness of her tongue, was making it hard for him to stay in control, but he knew that he had no choice but to do so.

Moments later, forcing himself to pull away, he whispered against the moistness of her lips, "I still want to go dancing after dinner."

"OK."

He lifted a brow. Her capitulation had been too quick, too easy, too unlike a Madaris. He sighed deeply. He wasn't sure just what Christy had up her sleeve but was confident when the time came he would find out.

Alex shifted around in his chair. Christy was taking the phrase "do him before he does me" to great heights. The only problem was that he wasn't *doing* her. He had made it pretty clear last night that he wanted her love before taking care of his lust. She was making him suffer, and if he didn't know better he would swear she had taken the course *How to Torture a Man 101*.

He had to fight back the bout of temporary insanity that invaded his body every time she licked her lips. And if that wasn't bad enough, then there was the way she sipped her drink through her straw, the way her lips moved in such a provocative sucking motion. He could see her applying that same erotic technique to a kiss.

Then there were the other less than subtle things, like intentionally brushing up against him every chance she got, and the way her lush body had deliberately pressed up against his whenever they had danced, actually making his skin burn through the material of his pants. During several slow numbers, her hips had been nearly plastered against his and her hardened nipples had all but dug into his chest, arousing his body even more.

He fought back the memory that it had been over three years since he had slept with a woman. Every once in a while some reminder would creep into his mind, but his intense workload had kept the memory at bay. But now, especially tonight, he was being reminded full force.

He wanted Christy.

And he was very much aware that she knew it and was probably basking in the knowledge that he could want to his heart's content but he would not touch.

He tried to ignore the heat burning within him with the feel of her dallying with his leg under the table, sliding her toe sensuously up and down his pants leg. The thickness of his pants was no barrier to the wantonness of her touch, and he wondered if she had any idea of the fire she was playing with. He glanced across the table at her, raised one brow. She raised two, deliberately letting him know she was fully aware of just what her naughtiness was doing to him.

He shifted in his seat, grounding his restraint even more. "Any new developments in the Patterson case?" he asked after taking a sip of his drink to cool off.

Christy smiled. She knew Alex was fighting his attraction to her. She was playing the role of seductress to the hilt, and although he hadn't broken yet, she figured it would only be a matter of time before he did. He was working too hard not to. But still, she hadn't missed the way he had held her while they had danced. She had been aware of his aroused state the moment he had taken her into his arms. She had deliberately plastered her body against his, and each time she rocked her hips against him she had heard the gritting of his teeth at the same time she had felt the enlargement of his erection.

She had met his gaze and saw the heated look of desire in his eyes, and each breath he had taken had shuddered with need. The woman in her had picked up on all those things, making a mental note of them, determined to use them to her advantage.

First he had taken her to a Mexican restaurant for dinner. Then he had brought her here to this nightclub with a live band. The inside of the place was cozy and intimate and the sexual chemistry that flowed between her and Alex was heated and intense. Deadly combinations.

"Christy?"

She glanced up. "Yes?"

"I asked if there were any new developments in the Patterson case?"

She took a sip of her drink and met his gaze. At the moment, the Patterson case was the last thing she wanted to talk about. Instead she wanted to know how much longer he would be able to handle her bold advances. She had slipped her shoes off and even now her toes were running up the length of his pants leg. She was intent on wearing down his control no matter what it took. She was secure in knowing she could do all the pouncing, but he wouldn't pounce back.

"I'm flying to Philly tomorrow to ask questions," she finally answered.

Alex nodded. "It's been a while since I've been to Philadelphia."

He watched her eyes narrow when what he was alluding to became clear. "Which means?"

He smiled. "I'd like to go with you."

She sat up in her chair, her back ramrod straight; all

thoughts of seduction immediately fled her mind. "Look, Alex, I thought I made it clear that I didn't want you interfering with this investigation."

"And I thought that I made it clear that my wanting to spend time with you has nothing to do with your work. You're the reason I'm here in Cincinnati, and if you take off somewhere, I don't intend to sit around twiddling my thumbs until you return," he said with frustration clear in his tone.

She frowned, sharpened her gaze. "I don't have time for you, Alex. My work is keeping me busy."

"Then I suggest you learn how to multitask so you can deal with me as well as your job, because I don't see either going away any time soon."

She lifted her chin and glared. "Wanna bet?"

He smiled and shot back. "How much?"

Christy frowned. He was as arrogant and conceited as they came and he was deliberately being difficult. She felt her temperature rise in warning degrees, and with their eyes locked, she felt their clashing of wills, their direct opposition. Neither intended to give an inch. He thought he could change her mind about the way she felt about him, and she was just as certain that he could not.

"Besides," he said, interrupting her thoughts, "I can be of assistance by renting a plane to fly us there."

She sighed deeply. She had forgotten that like her brothers, he had his pilot license. "Don't put yourself out on my account."

"I can't think of anything I'd rather do than take you flying with me."

She met his gaze. "This is not a pleasure trip."

"Maybe it won't be for you, but it will for me. I can't think of anything but pleasure whenever I'm with you."

"Tell me," she said softly, her voice filled with the frustration she felt. "How long do you plan to play this game, Alex?"

He leaned in closer over the table and she watched the intensity that was there in his eyes burn in their dark depths.

Her breath caught when the strength of that heat touched her on a primitive level.

"If this appears to be a game, Christy, it's because you've made it one. In all your stubborn, defiant, and unforgiving ways you have deemed that I should suffer for the deeds of that one night. My goal is to show you that all the things you wanted then I will gladly place at your feet now."

The stubbornness, the defiance, and the inability to forgive—the very things he had just addressed, swelled within Christy. "It's too late. I no longer want those things."

A part of Alex refused to believe that. He could not. "I need to show you that you still want them, and so do I, Christy," he said softly.

His heart clenched at the hurt and pain he still saw in her eyes whenever they discussed that night. "I made mistakes but I'm willing to do whatever I have to do to correct them," he said, softer still. "I refuse to give up on you and what we can have together. Please open your heart and meet me halfway."

Christy's jaw tightened. "No. Like I said, it's too late." She placed her napkin aside. "I'm ready for you to take me home, Alex," she said as she stood.

He got to his feet and signaled the waiter for their check. "And I'm ready to take you home as well."

And he doubted that she was prepared for what he intended to do when they got there.

CHAPTER 15

The moment Alex entered her apartment and closed the door behind him, Christy could feel the mounting tension in the air. She had tried talking him out of walking her to the door, and when that failed she had told him there was no need for him to come inside, since they had said enough already.

But he had ignored her words, taking the key from her hand and opening the door. Now he stood in the middle of her living room, with his eyes glued on her and looking so elementally male that she felt flames, hot and intense, stirring up her insides.

"We need to talk."

Christy's brows rose upon her hearing he was back to that again. "We have nothing to talk about, Alex."

"Oh, I think we do."

She watched, one heartbeat at a time, as he crossed the room. And when he stopped in front of her, his gaze moved all over her. The heat of that gaze burned her senses and caused a cascade of sensations to flood through her. "Do you want to tell me what this shocking blue dress was about tonight?" he asked in a deep, husky, sensuous tone.

Trying to hold on to her sanity, Christy narrowed her eyes at him. "I have no idea what you're talking about."

His eyes held hers in a penetrating stare and didn't even blink when he said, "I believe that you do. You've done your best to get me hot and bothered, and you have succeeded."

He took a step closer and she saw the edginess in his

gaze, felt the ravenousness in the heat he was generating. "Now my question to you is what you plan to do about it."

His question pulled at her nerve endings, made her feel suddenly light-headed to the point where she had to pull in her next breath. He was right. She had deliberately baited him tonight with the full intent of breaking through his control. But now every muscle in her body felt tense at the thought that he'd known what she was up to, had been privy to her every move. Deciding to play it safe, she said, "You indicated we won't make love until I fall back in love with you. Since I don't see that happening, I don't plan on doing anything about it."

For a little while neither said anything, but Christy could feel the tension between them mounting even more, almost consuming them, making the electrified air they were breathing almost unbearable. "I care to differ," Alex said with seemingly calm remoteness.

She lifted a brow. "You can differ all you like, since there's nothing you can do about it."

Alex smiled. "Oh, there's plenty I can do about it. I can get you as hot and bothered as you've gotten me."

With that simple statement she saw the intent in his eyes and took a step back. Her mind raced as she tried figuring a way out of the mess she had gotten herself into. "I want you to leave, Alex."

His eyes held hers in deep concentration, entrenched penetration. "No. I don't think that you do."

Glaring, she glanced up at him. "Oh, you're into mind reading these days?" She tried to ignore his manly scent, which was gripping her senses, escalating her desires.

"No, I can't read your mind, but I can read your heat. I can feel it radiating all through me and I've felt it all evening," he said, removing his jacket. "You're a little annoyed with me right now, but you don't want me to leave until . . ."

She lifted a brow. "Until what?"

"Until I make it possible for both of us to sleep tonight.

I doubt that we'd get a good night's rest in our present state."

His words made her acutely aware of just what that present state was, and it was getting more defined with every second he stood in front of her. Sensations she'd tried holding at bay slipped through her and made her skin tingle. A part of her wanted to believe her desire for him was sheer madness, but she knew no matter how insane it might be, he was right. She wouldn't get much sleep tonight without thoughts of him invading her unconsciousness. The big question of the hour was what he had in mind when his options were limited.

She hadn't broken his control like she had wanted, and although he said he was hot and bothered, he was doing a good job of holding himself in check. Even now it was evident that his emotions were smoothly controlled, and the magnitude of everything male about him was disturbingly underscored by the way he was standing there, towering over her, looking at her like he was a hungry cat and she was a bowl of cream that he intended to lick all over.

Summoning up all the composure she could muster, she made a move to walk past him, and he reached out and touched her arm. She drew in a deep, sharp breath the same exact moment he did. The contact reverberated through their bodies simultaneously with the ferocity of a hot, powerful storm and she looked up at him as he looked down at her. Sound suddenly ceased to exist. Even the breath they expelled died a sudden death the moment it left their lips. Both individuals were locked in an exchange of mesmerizing gazes.

The moment stretched, and when Alex slowly lifted his hand and let his fingertips slide across her jaw Christy found her eyes caught, held, in a sharp and penetrating stare.

Trying hard not to cave in, she lifted her chin and continued to hold his gaze, determinedly fighting the emotions rolling around inside of her. But when he moved his fingertips from her chin to frame her face with his hand, she knew she couldn't fight him tonight if she wanted to. She had set out to bait him, yet she had been the one captured, ensnared in her own trap.

When he slowly lowered his head she readily offered him her lips. He took them, hungrily, greedily, as desire racked their bodies, ravenously stole their minds, leaving them totally aware of nothing but each other.

Alex's arms tightened around Christy and she inched closer, returning the kiss with the same ardent participation that he was. Tongues mingled and mated, intimately, unhurriedly. Senses reeled, passion ignited, groans became moans as they vigorously contributed to this intimate exchange, both determined to get what they wanted and needed.

But it wasn't enough and they both knew it.

Raising his head, he swept her into his arms and crossed the room to the sofa, sat down, and cradled her in his lap. He kissed her again deeply, hungrily, stealing the very sigh she moaned from her lips. Moments later when he broke the kiss, he stared down at her, noted the way her hair flowed across his arms, saw the glazed look in her eyes from beneath long lashes, and watched her slowly draw in shuddering breaths.

He waited patiently until her eyes held his again, and then in a voice that was drenched in the deep desire he felt while his fingertips boldly slid beneath the neckline of her clothing he said, "Now about this dress . . ."

Christy's eyes locked with Alex's as every part of her came to full awareness. Heat burned through her as his fingers slowly caressed her bare skin beneath the neckline of her dress, making it difficult for her to breathe. And the hard, firm, muscular thighs beneath her body made her acknowledge that he was a man with a whole lot of experience. Definitely more than she had.

She would have given an in-depth analysis to that reflection if he hadn't slid his fingers farther into her bodice to brush against her bare breasts. She wasn't wearing a bra and knew the exact moment he had verified that fact.

Immediately he captured her mouth with his, slow, deliberate, like a magnet, drawing her tongue into his mouth, sucking on it, claiming it, at the same time his fingertips inched even lower beneath her neckline, caressing one breast and then the other. She arched in his lap, automatically responding to the intimate touch.

He pulled back and traced the lining of her lips with his tongue before asking in a husky voice, "Why did you wear this dress tonight?"

Christy sighed, unable to do anything but tell him the truth. "I wanted to make you lose it."

He lifted a brow. "Lose what?"

"Control. You're always cool and calm, and for once I wanted to see you not hold back."

He frowned. Years of training had taught him how to maintain control of his emotions, which was something he'd always prided himself on. However, she would never know just how hard it was for him to maintain that control around her. If he ever let her push him completely over the edge, that would be the end of it, because he wanted her just that much. "I have to stay in control," he said quietly.

"Why?"

"Because it's a part of who I am," he said, deciding that was all he would tell her.

"Well, I don't like it," she said, glaring at him.

"Then maybe I should give you something you'd like." He then leaned down and kissed her as his hand resumed stroking her breasts.

Christy moaned as Alex kissed her deeply, angling his mouth in various ways for better contact.

He slowly lifted his head and met her gaze. "I want to see your breasts. May I?"

Just the thought of him asking sent hot, molten liquid flowing through her. Her pulse began racing and her heartbeat increased. She met his gaze. "Yes," she said softly, barely able to get out the single word. "You can see my breasts if you let me see your bare chest."

Thoughts of everything fled from her mind when he shifted his body to slowly ease his shirt from the waistband of his pants and began unbuttoning it. Turning in his arms, she watched, mesmerized, as each button slowly slipped free. The moment she saw his bare chest, she reached out and let her fingers trace the firm, hard planes of his muscles. Her fingers, of their own accord, slowly caressed the flat nipples on his chest, and the instant she did so she heard his sharp intake of breath. She couldn't help but marvel at the fact that she was responsible for the forced way he was breathing, the increase of his heart rate beneath her hand, and the look of heated desire in his eyes. She found herself drawn into a bevy of emotions that booked no barriers and had little tolerance for restraints. She may not have the ability to make him lose control, but even he had admitted that she could turn him on.

"It's my time to see you," he whispered in a voice that increased the passion simmering between them. He shifted her on her back in his lap and slowly eased the dress from her shoulders, baring her nakedness to the waist. She felt the cool air touch her skin, but the heat of his gaze soothed it, making the puckered darkened tips throb with a need she didn't understand.

Evidently Alex understood, and he lowered his head and drew a firm tip into his mouth. She gasped at the sensations that suddenly ravaged her body when his tongue licked, sucked, tortured, claiming one breast thoroughly before moving to the other. She closed her eyes and surrendered to the sensuous thrill his mouth was stirring as his hand cupped her breast, holding it hostage while his mouth feasted.

"Alex."

His name was whispered from her lips in first an indrawn breath, followed by an uncontrollable gasp. She felt intense heat settle in her midsection at a degree that threatened to burn her to a cinder, and she felt herself being pushed over the edge where the only thing awaiting her was satisfying, earth-shattering sensations destined to explode in a million pieces.

Bur Alex refused to let it happen just yet. She had tortured him all evening, and now it was time to show her that payback wasn't a bitch but was a man with very strong and deliberate intentions.

He pulled back and stood with her in his arms, then placed her on her feet. She'd said she hadn't remembered him removing her panty hose that night she'd been under the influence; well, there was no way she wouldn't remember it this time.

He knelt down in front of her and removed the high-heeled shoes from her feet. He knew she watched him as he reached beneath her short shocking blue dress and began skimming her panty hose down her legs, deliberately caressing the curves of her hips and the inner parts of her thighs while he did so. He tossed the panty hose aside.

Then when she stood bare legged in front of him, in a very bold move he pushed her short dress up to her waist, leaving her completely bare except for the black lace thong she was wearing. Then in one smooth motion he slid his fingers beneath the skimpy material and tugged the thong down her hips as well.

Still on his knees before her, he raised his head and met her gaze at the same moment his hands tightened about her hips. "Enjoy," he whispered, just seconds before his mouth latched on to the most intimate part of her.

Christy's heart stopped when in smooth and easy motions Alex's tongue swept into her while his hands curved about her hips, holding her in place. Of their own accord, her thighs parted as he intimately stroked her time and time again, refusing to let up or let go.

She trembled and moaned out words whose meaning she

didn't know, but he pressed on, making heat flare through every part of her body and enticing the type of throbbing passion she'd only heard others whisper about. Now she was experiencing for herself such an intimate personal caress as his tongue went deeper and deeper still. Her senses raged out of control; nothing mattered but the way he was making her feel.

"Alex!"

Then it happened; pleasure streaked through her, made her shiver uncontrollably. She struggled to breathe and found it difficult when he increased the pressure of his mouth on her and expanded the deep stroking of his tongue. She felt the shudder that rocked through her, and would have sunk down to the carpeted floor had he not held her immobile, refusing to let her tumble into anything other than pleasure.

It was only when Christy's shudders subsided that Alex pulled back. He got to his feet and wrapped his arms tightly around her, just as overwhelmed by what had taken place as she was. Even now the passion between them still simmered, and he knew of only one way to put out the flame. But it was a way they would not share until she admitted to loving him.

He straightened her dress to cover her, then eased her down to sit on the sofa while he rebuttoned his shirt and tucked it neatly back inside his pants.

Christy sat and watched him, her gaze following his every movement. Satiated, her head fell back against the sofa cushions and discovered the heat of him was still surrounding her. "You're dangerous, Alex."

He looked over at her. "In what way?"

Without meeting his gaze she whispered, "In every way. What are you doing to me?"

"Convincing you to love me."

She lifted her head up, met his gaze, held it for the longest time, then let her head fall back against the sofa cushions again.

He sighed, knowing that a war was taking place within her, a vortex of feelings, an overabundance of emotions. And he would continue to ply her with passion, make her see that she was his. With each and every intimate act they shared, he felt he was reaching that goal, laying down the foundation, breaking through her defenses, and destroying the walls of stubbornness that threatened to keep them at odds no matter what progress they made. He wouldn't be completely satisfied until she told him she loved him and spoke from her heart.

"I should have things finalized so we can fly out by seven in the morning," he said, breaking into the silence that had encompassed the room.

Christy lifted her head off the back of the sofa and met his gaze. She knew it wouldn't do any good to ask him not to go, since he was hell-bent on going. "I'll be ready."

Walking back over to the sofa, he leaned down and placed a kiss on her lips and the area beneath her ear. "Think about me tonight."

After what had happened just moments ago, she knew there was no way she could not think of him. But still, she said, "Only if you think about me."

He straightened, locked in on her gaze. "I always think of you, Christy." And then he pulled her to her feet and into his arms, plastering her body against his while he took her mouth in unhurried, sensuous strokes. Moments later when he finally released her, he whispered, "You're mine."

When she opened her mouth to deny his words, he placed a finger to her lips. "Even if you don't agree, how about just humoring me tonight?"

She hesitated a moment, thought about what they had done moments ago, and then relented as a small smile touched her lips. "All right, just for tonight. But tomorrow is another day."

"And another battle," he added, chuckling. "But I find that I'm beginning to enjoy the fight. Good night, sweetheart."

Christy watched as he grabbed his jacket off the back of the chair before walking out the door.

• • •

Alex inhaled deeply when he stepped out on the breezeway of Christy's apartment. All thoughts fled his mind when he suddenly felt uneasy. This was the second time this had happened. He narrowed his gaze and glanced around. Usually his instincts were sharp, keen . . . and they were seldom wrong. There were several parked cars, but none appeared occupied. But still . . .

A number of possibilities crossed his mind, and he didn't like any of them. He didn't want to believe that Kevin what's-his-name would take to stalking Christy after getting his ass kicked at that nightclub that night. But then, Alex couldn't discount anything. Then there was the Patterson case she was working on. Also, he couldn't overlook the off chance that it had nothing to do with Christy but concerned mainly him. When you handled as many cases as he did, sooner or later you were bound to piss someone off.

He scanned the parking lot one more time before walking down the steps to his car. Something wasn't right. He could sense it and he intended to keep his eyes open. The one thing he didn't like was surprises.

Although he was dressed in all black, moonlight illuminated the man who slipped from behind one of the apartment buildings. Albert Ford breathed deeply, grateful he had gotten out of his car to walk around and stretch his legs. Otherwise, he would have been seen. He didn't know what was going on between the man and the woman but was experienced enough to recognize him as someone who possessed some type of background in law enforcement. It was there in his stance, the way his brows had risen at the slightest sound and movement as if either was a personal invasion.

With a muttered curse Ford threw down the cigarette he was smoking, promising himself, like he always did, that it would be his last one.

He would check in tomorrow; curious about the man's

identity. The woman's snooping around was bad enough. The last thing they needed was someone who could possibly be an ex-cop doing likewise.

Houston, Texas

"Where the hell is Alex?" Dex Madaris asked, glancing around. "It's not like him to miss a poker game."

The three Madaris brothers, Justin, Dex, and Clayton, along with their friends Trevor Grant and Trask Maxwell, sat around the table in Dex's home, getting ready to play cards. Justin and his family had arrived in town earlier that day, and as was the norm whenever the brothers and their friends got together, a game of cards was in order.

It was Trask who answered Dex's question by saying, "Alex decided he needed a vacation."

That statement got the attention of the other men. They all knew Alex well enough to know he lived for work and didn't know the meaning of relaxation.

"Alex is actually taking some time off?" Justin Madaris asked, after throwing out a card. Like everyone else, he was totally surprised.

Trask nodded. "Yes. He said he won't be back for a couple of weeks or so."

"Damn, he must have finally gotten burned out. He couldn't continue working at the pace he's been going at for the last few years," Clayton Madaris said, shaking his head. "All work and no play can be the death of a man. No matter how hard I worked, I always made time to play. When I was his age I was—"

"We all know what you were doing when you were his age," Trevor Grant said, grinning. "That was before your Syneda days. Your notch was probably on every single woman in Houston's bedpost."

Clayton grinned, not ashamed of his past. He *had* been a player of the third degree when he was younger. But he'd had no problem turning in his player's card after falling in love with Syneda. And a few years ago he had passed the case of condoms that he'd kept in his closet to his younger cousins, Blade, Slade, and Lucas. Clayton hoped they were getting as much use out of the condoms as he had.

"Did Alex go to visit your mom in Waco?" Justin asked, pulling another card off the deck.

"No, he deliberately avoided telling me where he was going and said if I needed to reach him to contact him on his mobile phone."

Clayton lifted a brow. "Umm, sounds like there's a woman involved. That's good and it's about time. I was beginning to worry about him."

Dex raised a brow as he threw out a card. "Not everybody strives to match your former reputation, Clayton. I didn't meet Caitlin and fall in love until I was thirty-two. Before I met her, just like Alex, work and not women dominated my time. I went out on occasion, but nothing serious."

"Well, I'm happy for him if he's finally met someone," Justin said, smiling. "Alex is a fine young man and a hard worker. Whatever woman catches his eye will be pretty lucky."

Everybody at the table nodded, agreeing with Justin's assessment.

"Well, his being missing in action means he's not available to let us know how Christy is doing," Dex said.

Trevor lifted a dark brow. "I thought the three of you promised Christy not to interfere in her life."

Dex shrugged. "We're doing it to keep our parents from worrying."

Trask chuckled as he shook his head. "Yeah, right." He then glanced over at the brothers. "And what does Alex have to do with the three of you keeping tabs on Christy?"

Clayton was amused when he said, "It seems we had the same idea and contacted Alex after finding out he had a business interest in Cincinnati, and asked him to check on her whenever he was out that way. He was there a few weeks ago and reported she was doing fine. And of course we checked things out for ourselves when she came to town for the twins' party."

Trevor shook his head. "She's not a kid any longer. Isn't it time for the three of you to let Christy live her own life?"

"No," the Madaris brothers said simultaneously.

It was Clayton, the one known to enjoy a good argument, who spoke up to elaborate. "Although we agree that Christy's not a kid any longer, she's pretty much lived a sheltered life. We've tried to prepare her for the players out there—men who will break her heart without a moment's glance, men like I used to be, who only want one thing. The thought of her getting involved with someone like that bothers us. We want to spare her any unnecessary misery."

Trask raised his eyes to the ceiling. "So what would happen if she met a really nice guy?"

Justin grinned. "We'll have Alex investigate him to make sure he's as nice as he seems. We've done it before and have sent several supposedly nice guys packing."

"Don't you think that's a little extreme?" Trevor asked, shaking his head.

"No," Dex answered quickly. "I plan to handle Jordan and Ashley the same way. Any man who comes within ten feet of my daughters better have something positive on his mind. Hey, you just wait until Phoenix gets older," he said to Trevor about his newborn daughter. "I bet you'll feel the same way." He then glanced over at Trask. "And so will you when Madaris starts dating."

"So with Alex's being missing, what are we going to do about Christy?" Clayton then asked. "Since we saw her last week we know she's OK and doing fine, but Alex never said whether or not she was seeing anyone."

Dex rubbed his chin. "Yeah, and come to think of it, he really didn't say much of anything. In fact, he seemed somewhat evasive. Maybe he's beginning to feel guilty about checking up on her for us."

Trevor chuckled. "Or maybe he's smart enough to know he doesn't want to deal with Christy's wrath when she finds out what the three of you are up to. Personally, I wouldn't want her mad with me."

Justin shrugged. "We can handle Christy's anger," he said softly. "But we couldn't handle her getting hurt because someone broke her heart."

"Yeah," Clayton and Dex agreed concurrently.

"Umm, maybe it's time for us to check out things in Cincinnati for ourselves," Dex said, throwing out another card.

"Yes, maybe you're right," Clayton said, agreeing. He glanced over at Justin. "What do you think?"

Justin smiled. "I think the Cessna is fueled and ready to fly whenever the two of you are."

Dex leaned back in his chair grinning. "Then it's final. Since Alex hasn't really told us much of anything, let's make plans to drop in on her unexpectedly next week to see what's really going on."

Caitlin Madaris eased away from the doorway without being seen. She had intended to interrupt the game to find out if the guys needed anything like more beer or chips when she overheard their conversation.

Backing away, she quickly walked toward the room where the other women were sitting. "There's trouble brewing."

Syneda, Lorren, Corinthians, and Felicia met her gaze. "What kind of trouble?" Syneda asked, coming to her feet. They had been sitting on the floor playing with the babies; her and Clayton's daughter, Remington; Caitlin and Dex's son, Gregory; Corinthians and Trevor's two, Rio and Phoenix; and Trask and Felicia's daughter, Madaris.

"It seems the brothers are planning a trip to Cincinnati sometime next week to surprise Christy."

Felicia frowned. "That's not good news, especially if that's where Alex has gone."

The other women nodded.

"That means it's up to us to ditch whatever plans they are making and do everything within our power to keep them busy. The last thing Christy and Alex need is for the brothers to show up unexpectedly in Cincinnati," Syneda said, not believing the nerve of those Madaris brothers, although she really wasn't surprised.

She and Clayton had had this conversation several times, and he knew just how she felt about his overprotectiveness of Christy. And Syneda had told him in no uncertain terms that she would not let him raise their daughter that way. Their difference of opinion on that issue had led to one of their worst arguments. But then, arguing was second nature to them, just like making up afterward—and boy, did she enjoy making up with her husband after an argument. It took a lot to cool her down, but he was so darn good at it.

"So it's agreed. Our job is to keep our husbands extremely busy over the next week, right?" Lorren asked, reclaiming Syneda's thoughts.

"Yes," Syneda said, smiling. "And frankly, I'm looking forward to doing it."

CHAPTER 16

Christy tried ignoring the shivers that touched her body as she watched Alex's hands at the controls of the Cessna. Although she could tell he was an expert at what he was doing, she was studying his hands for another reason. She couldn't look at them without remembering how he had touched her breasts last night, fondled them, kissed them, tongued them all over. Nor could she look at his mouth and not remember what he had done with it as well. The pleasure he had given her still made her entire body tingle just thinking about it. She had slept well last night thanks to him. It was the best rest she had gotten in a long time.

She shifted in her seat when a pool of heat invaded her midsection. And it wasn't helping matters that the cockpit of the plane was small, cozy, and intimate; it was a two-seater and nothing like the roomy Cessna her brothers had purchased together, which could hold up to ten people. And of course it was no comparison to the huge Cessna jet her uncle Jake owned, which was too beautiful for words. She had tried to talk her brothers into giving her flying lessons, but it had been her uncle who had eventually taken the time to show her how to operate an airplane.

"You look nice today, Christy."

Alex's words nearly startled her. They were both wearing a set of headphones, which made communication easier in a plane this size. She slanted a glance over at him. They had kept conversation to a minimum since taking off. She hadn't wanted to distract him in any way. "Thank you," she said, although she didn't see anything spectacular about the outfit she was wearing, a chocolate-colored pantsuit she had chosen to wear for comfort.

"You look nice yourself," she said, deciding to return the compliment. And she meant it. He always looked nice.

"Thanks."

She tried not to remember how he had greeted her when she had opened the door to him that morning. As soon as he stepped over the threshold, he had pulled her into his arms and kissed her like a starving man, and of course she had immediately responded, kissing him like a starving woman, which had set off intense hunger and desire within the both of them.

She had heard herself moan—although she wasn't sure how that had been possible when he'd been sucking the air right out of her lungs, but she had remembered the exact moment he had cupped her bottom, bringing her closer to the fit of him, as if he wanted her to feel his hardness, to know what she could do to him in the arousal department. She had definitely gotten a *firm* idea.

Last night she had wanted him. In the state she'd been in, if he'd suggested that they sleep together, she would have gone along with it. She knew they had slept together before—or, more correctly stated, had shared the same bed for a while that night she had been under the influence. Her memory denied her the ability to recall any details, and she would give just about anything to know how it felt to have his entire hard body pressed to hers, limb to limb.

"So what do you want to accomplish today with this trip?" he asked, again bringing her concentration back around to the business at hand. She was grateful, since the thoughts she was having could get her in trouble.

She glanced over at him. "To find out all I can about Detective Mark Tyler's death, to see if perhaps there was foul play and he was killed investigating that kidnapping ring."

She released a deep sigh. "And while I'm busy doing that, what will you be doing?" She deliberately asked the question as a reminder that although he had insisted on coming along, she didn't intend for him to become involved in her investigation.

He looked over at her and smiled. "Umm, I can think of a number of things I'll be doing. Like I said, I haven't been to Philadelphia in a while, so I intend to check out the sights."

Christy nodded. That sounded like a workable plan and one where he wouldn't get in her way.

"How about dinner tonight when we return to Cincinnati? And I thought we could do the zoo this weekend. I heard the Cincinnati Zoo is one of the best in the nation."

Christy sighed. "She wasn't sure about it being one of the best in the nation, but she knew it was one of the oldest. In fact, it was the second-oldest zoo in the United States. Unfortunately, she hadn't had the chance to visit since moving to town. Going there with Alex would be nice if she didn't know what he was trying to do—break down her defenses. All she had to do was remember what happened last night in her apartment to recall just how close he'd come to doing that very thing. Her defenses hadn't stood a chance and she couldn't handle a repeat of last night anytime soon. It was hard to fight his killer charm and blatant seductiveness.

She met his gaze as she raked her fingers through her hair. "Dinner tonight and the zoo on Saturday? I'll think about it," she said, deciding not to commit to either.

She watched as Alex slanted an irresistible grin before saying, "Yeah, you do that."

Alex couldn't help but smile inwardly. Christy wasn't giving him an inch, but then like he had told her last night, he was beginning to enjoy the fight. The battle would make the victory that much sweeter.

He still couldn't erase from his mind the sight of her last night in that shocking blue dress. He had thought about it all night as well as first thing this morning. Nor could he get out of his mind the taste of her on his tongue.

"How long before we land?"

He glanced over at her and grinned. "It won't be long. Don't you like my company?"

"It's OK."

He grinned a little wider. "Just OK, huh? Well, later I'm going to have to make you think it's more than just OK."

Christy got a heated feeling in her stomach just thinking about how he might go about accomplishing that. Deciding to ignore him for a while, she glanced out the window only to shield her eyes from the brightness of the sun. She had forgotten to bring her sunglasses.

"You want to use mine?"

She glanced over at him. She was beginning to wonder if he was into mind reading like she'd suggested last night. "What will you use? Doesn't the sun bother you, too?"

"I'm used to it," he said, handing her the pair of sunglasses that was sitting on the console between them.

"Thanks," she said, putting them on. "Nice fit."

He looked over at her. "When it comes to us, Christy, there will always be a nice fit."

She inhaled, slowly and deliberately, trying not to imagine another nice fit they would make . . . in bed together.

"Make sure your seat belt is fastened," Alex said, snagging back her attention. "It's time to take this baby down."

Christy nodded. She was becoming a lost cause. In spite of her resolve to remain unaffected by Alex's presence, the truth of the matter was that she *was* affected. A part of her knew that this plane wasn't the only thing going in for a landing.

Christy frowned as she looked across the desk at the man sitting behind it. "And you're sure there isn't anything else you can tell me, Lieutenant Jones?"

"Unfortunately, that's it. According to our report, Detective Tyler's death was an accident."

Christy nodded. "And you weren't aware of any type of investigation he was doing regarding a ring that's kidnapping teenage girls and shipping them out of the country to use as part of a slave trade?"

The man shrugged. "No, I can't say that I was."

He wasn't telling her the truth; Christy could feel it. Lieutenant Jones had been completely taken aback by the questions she had begun asking him, and she saw how cautious he had been to answer each and every one. She could tell that there was a lot he wasn't telling her. Why?

"Did Detective Tyler have any family?" She asked the question although she knew he hadn't. According to the obituary, Mark Tyler was thirty-four and single. She had seen a picture of him. He was a very nice-looking man, so chances were he had a girlfriend.

The lieutenant's eyes narrowed. "Why do you want to know if he had a family?"

With him being a cop she would have thought it was obvious but decided to answer anyway. "I'd like to talk to them."

She watched as he snagged a paper clip off his desk and began toying with it. "I'd prefer if you didn't bother them."

"Why?"

"They've been through enough already. Losing him was hard on them." He held her gaze. "Losing Mark was hard on all of us. He was a valued member of this force."

She let out a weary sigh. "I only want to ask them a few questions."

"And like I said, I'd prefer that you didn't bother them."

Christy leaned forward in her chair. The man had gotten on her last nerve. "And I really don't care what you prefer. There's someone claiming that young girls are being kidnapped and taken out of the country. That might not mean anything to you, but it means a hell of a lot to me, especially if it's true."

The man shifted his gaze from her to glance out the

window. Moments later his glance returned full force, pinning her to her chair. "You can't believe everything you hear, Ms. Madaris."

She lifted a haughty brow. "No, but as a reporter, I have a right to deliver news based on facts I've obtained after a thorough investigation. And that's what I intend to do." She stood. "Thanks for your time, Lieutenant."

Lieutenant Jones released a deep, troubled sigh after the woman walked out of his office. He picked up the phone and dialed a number he had memorized. As soon as a voice came on the line, Jones spoke rapidly and angrily: "I think you guys have a problem."

Fifteen minutes later Christy was sitting in the coffee shop that was across the street from the police station, sipping her coffee. Her next stop would be the dock where Mark Tyler kept his boat and question the person in charge there. Perhaps he could describe what he saw before the detective took the boat out.

Christy lifted her brows in surprise when the waitress slid a small plate containing a pastry in front of her. She was about to open her mouth and let the woman know she hadn't ordered anything when she noticed the folded slip of paper that had been placed beside the plate.

She studied the woman, someone who appeared to be in her late sixties, smiled, and said, "Thanks."

The woman merely nodded and walked off. Christy glanced around, making sure she wasn't being watched, then picked up the note and quickly read it:

> *I understand you're asking questions about Mark Tyler's death. Meet me in the lobby of the Marriott Hotel in thirty minutes so we can talk.*

Christy refolded the paper and glanced over at the waitress who had delivered the note. She was busy taking the order from a group of police officers who had just walked in.

Slipping the note into her purse Christy wondered who had sent it. She knew where the beautiful hotel was located, and she intended to be there to find out what they had to say to her.

She glanced down at her watch. She was supposed to meet Alex for lunch in a couple of hours. She dismissed the idea of calling him on his cell phone to tell him of her meeting with this mystery person at the hotel. Like her brothers, Alex had an inherent protective streak and wouldn't hesitate to interfere. The less he knew about what she was doing, the better.

Taking a last sip of her coffee, she left enough bills on the table to pay for the coffee and the pastry she hadn't eaten before walking out of the café.

A frown marred Alex's features as he watched Christy leave the café at a hurried pace and cross the street to her car. They had rented separate vehicles and had planned to meet up later.

She thought he was sightseeing. Little did she know, he had intended from the very beginning to stick to her like glue. And it was a good thing he did because she looked like she was hurrying off to meet up with trouble. And how did he know it was trouble? Because Christy and trouble seemed to go together like apples and pie.

Another reason he intended to stick to Christy was that his suspicions of last night had been proven true when he'd noticed a car following them from her apartment to the airport this morning. That observation prompted him to consider that the reason they were followed had something to do with this case she was investigating.

Yes, no matter where she went, he would be right on her tail and he actually felt his body react from the vision that very thought provoked.

• • •

Christy glanced around the elegant lobby of the Marriott hotel and didn't see anyone other than members of the hotel staff. She was about to walk up to the desk to see if a message had been left for her when she noted this young woman who seemingly appeared out of nowhere to come stand beside her.

"You've been asking questions about Mark."

Christy lifted a brow. The attractive young woman with long red hair and beautiful green eyes appeared to be just a year or so older than she was—if that. She hadn't referred to him as "Detective Tyler" but had used his given name, which indicated she'd known him on a personal basis. "Yes, I'm Christy Madaris, a reporter for a newspaper in Cincinnati and I've been asking questions. How did you know?"

Instead of answering, the woman nervously glanced over her shoulder and looked around. "I suggest we go sit in the hotel's cafe and talk. It's better than us standing in the middle of the lobby conversing."

Christy nodded in agreement and followed the woman to the cafe that was located not far from a bank of elevators. They bought coffee at the counter, grabbed a table in the back, and sat down.

"Now where was I?" the young woman asked after taking a quick sip.

Christy lifted a brow. "You were about to tell me how you knew I'd been asking questions about Detective Tyler."

She saw the bout of pain and sadness that appeared in the woman's eyes and knew that her earlier assessment had been correct. This woman had known Mark Tyler in a deeply personal way.

"I still have friends on the force."

Christy's brow lifted higher. "Friends on the force?"

"Yes. I used to be a beat officer. My name is Mariah Long. Mark and I were lovers."

For a moment Christy couldn't say anything. She was

struck by the ease with which the woman had defined her relationship with Mark Tyler. She had spoken without any sign of regret or shame. Christy wondered how she would define her relationship with Alex if anyone were to ask. They most certainly weren't lovers, although she had given him more liberties than she had given any other man. Just thinking of those particular liberties made her blush.

Christy cleared her throat. "What about the woman in the coffee shop? Another friend of yours?"

"Yes. Mark and I used to go there often for coffee before reporting to work."

"And you used to be a police officer?"

"Yes. Mark and I met on the force. I had been a rookie. We connected right away, and dated exclusively for six months."

"Why did you leave the force?"

"Because I believed there was a cover-up involving Mark's death."

Christy slowly nodded upon hearing her suspicions actually put into words. "The reason I'm asking questions about Mark's death is because I met a runaway who also believes his death wasn't an accident. She thinks the reason he was killed was because he was investigating a kidnapping ring that sent runaways out of the country as part of a slave trade. Do you know anything about it?"

"Not much, but I told that FBI agent all that I knew."

Christy raised a brow. "An FBI agent questioned you?"

"Yes. He questioned Lieutenant Jones as well. The lieutenant knew what Mark was investigating. I know for a fact that Mark reported everything to him."

"Umm, that's strange. I specifically asked Jones if he knew anything about it and he said he didn't."

"Then he's hiding something. I used to think Lieutenant Jones was one of the most honest men I knew, but since Mark's death I've seen another side of him."

"What do you mean?"

"He refused to entertain the possibility that Mark's death wasn't an accident. In fact, he was the one to suggest that I take an extended leave from the force to get myself together. But I quit instead."

Christy nodded. "So what do you do now?"

"I work here, at this hotel as a special security agent."

Christy leaned back in her chair. "Why do you think Mark's death wasn't an accident?"

"Because I know he was working on something big that involved some high-powered people in this city. Although this kidnapping ring seems to have expanded nationally, Mark was convinced he was putting together proof that the ringleader was someone well-known from this area."

Christy leaned forward. "Did he say who?"

Mariah shook her head. "No. There were certain aspects of the investigation that he kept me in the dark about. He figured what I didn't know couldn't hurt me. He wanted to protect me."

Christy nodded again. "Do you know if he was in touch with any runaways during this investigation?"

Mariah took a deep breath. "Yes, there were a couple. That's how he first found out that the ring existed."

"Do you recall any names?"

"No. But I do recall he got a call from one living in Columbus, Ohio. He believed the kidnappers had expanded there. Some girl living there verified that theory, but I don't recall her name. I know it started with a B, though."

Bonita? Christy lifted a brow. "And how do you know that?"

"Because she called one day, and he was about to write her name down and remembered I was there beside him, and the letter B was the only thing he jotted down before tossing the paper aside." She paused for a brief moment, then said, "Again, he was trying to protect me."

Christy swallowed, hearing the break in the woman's voice. "Tell me about the boating accident."

Mariah inhaled deeply. "That wasn't an accident. Mark was killed."

"The authorities are saying otherwise."

Mariah met her gaze and leaned forward. "And like I told you, they are trying to hide something. If you ask me, they are all in this together."

Christy stared into eyes that actually believed what she was saying. "Were you around when Mark was killed?" she decided to ask.

Mariah shook her head sadly. "No, that weekend he had convinced me to visit my mother in Arizona. I think he knew something was about to go down and wanted me out of harm's way, especially after he purchased that plane ticket."

Christy paused with the coffee cup halfway to her lips. "A plane ticket to where?"

"I don't remember, but I know it was a place located on an island. Mark was convinced he had discovered the name of the place that was being used as a drop-off point for the kidnapped teenagers before they were split up and sent elsewhere."

Christy wished Mariah could remember the name of the island. "What about the boating accident? Did Mark own a boat?"

Mariah shook her head. "No. Although he would go fishing occasionally with friends and knew how to operate one, he only became interested in boating recently. Personally, I think there was something going on at the docks that was connected to his investigation. He would go out on a boat practically every weekend. What he was looking for, I'm not sure."

"How did he die?"

She watched as the woman took deep breaths before answering. "There was an explosion. There was nothing left of Mark . . . except for a few items that were used to positively identify him."

Christy studied the woman, watched the tears that flowed down her eyes to drench her cheeks. Mariah was having a hard time dealing with her loss, and Christy couldn't help but wonder how she would feel if anything were ever to happen to Alex.

She suddenly felt a deep punch in her gut, a sudden invasion of emotions she had tried holding at bay, keeping under lock and key for three years. They were trying to return and she was determined not to let them.

"Christy?"

Breathing deeply, Christy met Mariah's gaze. "Mark's death wasn't an accident."

Christy felt a lump thicken in her throat. "If it wasn't an accident, then I intend to do everything within my power to prove it." She refused to think about the time limit that Malcolm had given her. First thing in the morning when she returned to work, she would meet with him and convince him of the necessity of her having more time.

Mariah released a deep sigh. "Thanks. I owe it to Mark for everyone to know the truth about what happened to him, and his son has a right to know what really happened to his father."

Christy lifted a surprised brow. "His son?"

A smile touched Mariah's lips. "Yes, I found out I was pregnant with Mark's child a few weeks after he had died. He's all I have left of Mark, and I want the people responsible for taking him away from us brought to justice, but more than anything I think Mark deserves for everyone to know just what a heroic man he was."

A half hour later, Christy parked her car at the entrance to the docks. She checked her watch. She had another hour before she needed to meet Alex for lunch.

Moments later, she was walking up the entry ramp and saw all the boats lining the water. It was a nice day and people were taking advantage of it. She immediately headed toward the building that indicated the manager's office. After a couple of knocks on the door, she was gruffly ordered to come in.

"What can I help you with, lady?" a huge man with a beard asked from behind a desk.

"Are you the manager?"

He stood and came around his desk. "It depends on why you want to know."

Already she had a feeling he would be difficult. "I'm Christy Madaris, a reporter from Cincinnati, and I need to ask you a couple of questions about Mark Tyler's accident."

She sensed him tense. A cautious shadow that appeared in his eyes as well as the straightening of his shoulders gave him away. He stuck out his hand. "I'm Hank Adams, and yes, I'm the manager. I told the cops everything I know."

Christy shook hands with him. "Perhaps there's something you might have forgotten."

He frowned as he walked back to his desk and sat down. "There's no perhaps about it. I didn't forget anything. Mark started hanging around here a month or so before his accident. He was a nice guy, kept to himself. It was a shame he died that way."

"Yes, it was, wasn't it? Did you see him that last day?"

"Yeah, and talked with him too. Briefly though. He was eager to get out on the water."

Christy nodded. "Did he say why?"

"Nope, and I didn't ask."

"Did he ever seem particularly interested in any of the other boats docked here?"

The man shrugged huge shoulders. "No, not particularly."

"Did he ever ask you about any of your other customers who used this dock frequently?" The man wrinkled his eyebrow, which was a sure sign of irritation. "No. Like I said, he minded his own business." He then attempted an easy grin which became a forced smile and said, "I wish others were like him."

A part of Christy wondered if the man was giving her a warning. "Is it okay if I take a look around?"

The man rubbed his hairy chin and stared at her. His forced smile had vanished. "Suit yourself."

"Thanks."

She then walked out of the office.

CHAPTER 17

"Sorry I'm late," Christy said, slipping into the chair across the table from Alex. "Were you waiting long?"

He glanced up from the menu. "No, actually, I just got here myself."

"Did you enjoy the sights?"

He smiled. "The sights were great."

He wondered just how much she would tell him if he were to ask how her investigation had gone. He had sat in the hotel's cafe, unobserved, while she talked for almost an hour to the woman she had met there. He had no idea what they'd discussed, but it was obvious Christy had hung on to the woman's every word. He'd also hung in the background while she had strolled around the Philadelphia port. A call he got on his way to meet her for lunch, had been from a friend at the Bureau who indicated he'd run into a snag getting information about a group called the Body Snatchers, but that he would continue to do his research.

"Did you find out anything that might help you in your investigation?" Alex decided to go ahead and ask.

"Possibly." Refusing to meet his gaze, she pulled a menu out of the rack and began studying it. "Umm, everything looks good. What are you having?"

"I haven't ordered yet," he decided to say, feeling somewhat disappointed she wasn't telling him anything. "But a hamburger and French fries sounds good."

She glanced up at him and smiled. "I think that's what I'll have, too."

Heavy rain kept them from leaving Philadelphia until later and they got back in Cincinnati past the evening hours. Alex suggested they do takeout instead of going out to dinner, and on the way stopped by a soul food restaurant.

Together they set the table, the smell of fried chicken, crème corn, rice pilaf, and corn bread filling Christy's kitchen. After sitting down and saying grace she and Alex wasted no time digging in, enjoying each other and the food.

They hadn't done a lot of talking on the flight back and now their conversation focused on how everyone was taking bets on whether Clayton and Syneda would have another child, since Remington, who would be celebrating her third birthday in a few months, was quite a handful, and how well Blade and Slade were doing with the construction company and the big projects they were getting.

They were finishing up their slices of peach cobbler when Christy looked up. "The Philadelphia Police Department is standing behind their report that Mark Tyler's death was an accident, but . . ."

Alex waited for her to continue, and when he saw the indecisive look on her face he asked, "But what?"

She breathed deeply, then said, "I met with his girlfriend and she provided some interesting information."

Alex lifted a brow. "Such as?"

"Such as the fact that Mark was assigned to the investigation so there's no way Lieutenant Jones didn't know about it. And Mark was operating on the premise that some high-powered individuals were behind the Body Snatchers, and that the ringleader was from the Philly area."

Alex took a sip of his iced tea. "That is interesting. Does she have any proof of this?"

Christy leaned back in her chair and laced her hands together. "No, but I have a feeling that Bonita contacted him about what was going down in Columbus. I plan on tracing phone records tomorrow since Bonita owned a cell phone. I also went to the docks to check out the place where Mark rented that boat. The guy wasn't helpful, but he did mention Mark was eager to take a boat out that day."

"Umm, I wonder why?"

"So do I. I'm going to spend my time on the Internet tonight to see if I can find information as to what other boats went out that day as well."

Alex released an indrawn breath and leaned back in his chair. "Well, considering how it appears things are going with this, I think it's best that you pull out and let the federal authorities come in and do an in-depth investigation. In fact, I know someone within the Bureau, a good friend by the name of Leon Hughes, who will—"

"No, Alex, I thought I made myself clear in the beginning. I'm going to see this investigation through until the end."

He fiercely frowned at her. "Think about what you're involving yourself in, Christy. Mark Tyler had good intentions, but good intentions got him killed. You need to turn whatever information you have over to people who can handle the—"

"No," Christy said, straightening in her seat and glaring at him. "I don't care what you say, Alex, the answer is still no. The FBI had their chance, and they blew it. According to Mariah, they questioned her after Mark Tyler's death and did nothing. As far as I'm concerned, they might be as corrupt as the police department seems to be. Why didn't Lieutenant Jones admit Mark was involved in an investigation?"

Anger flitted through Alex's eyes. "I have no idea, and if the Bureau didn't take action on Mariah Long's information, there's a good reason for it."

"Yeah, you would say that, ready to defend them at any

cost. After all the corruption that was discovered within the CIA and FBI during that episode with Drake and Tori, I won't discount anything," she said refusing to back down.

Alex held Christy's gaze steadily. "You're taking things to the extreme."

She lifted a defiant chin. "It's my right to take it wherever I want to take it, Alex Maxwell, and as far as I'm concerned this conversation is over. And don't expect me to discuss the Patterson case with you again."

He stood and glared at her. "The hell you won't."

She stood and glared right back. "The hell I will."

Alex walked around the table. He had reached his limit with her stubbornness. When he came to a stop in front of her, he narrowed her eyes and said, "You enjoy being difficult, don't you?"

"If that's what you think, then yes, I enjoy it," she said, holding her ground.

"In that case, you won't be satisfied until you get yourself killed," he said in a growl, leaning over and bringing his face within inches of hers.

"It's my life to do just what I please with, and you can't tell me how to live it or what to do with it."

Alex glared through darkened slits. "The hell I can't!"

"The hell you can!"

Alex's face hardened even more; his chest felt tight, convulsed; anger locked his jaw; and his hands tightened into fists at his sides. He drew in a deep breath, and for one heart-stopping moment he felt he was losing it, actually losing control, which was something he thought could never happen to him again. He wanted to snatch her in his arms and show her just what he could do. She was his and her life wasn't hers alone; it was also his. The thought of losing her was more than he could bear at the moment. He took a step back away from her and dragged in another deep breath, knowing he could not lose control now. He could not allow her to push him into doing that.

"I'm leaving," he said, walking out of the kitchen and through the living room as he headed for the front door.

An angry Christy was right on his heels. "Good, I'm glad you're leaving. You want my love but not once have you said anything about giving me yours. So go and don't bother coming back."

He stopped with his hand on the doorknob, his gaze angrily locked with hers. "I'll be back, Christy. You can count on it. And when I return we'll settle things between us once and for all."

And then he left, slamming the door behind him.

The sound of the door slamming woke Albert Ford. He watched as the big hulk of a man angrily walked away from the woman's apartment, got in his car, and drove off. *Umm, evidently there's trouble in paradise,* Ford thought as he leaned back in his car seat, shaking his head.

He still hadn't gotten word on the man's identity. Ford had followed the couple to the airport that morning, and after checking their flight plans he had discovered they had taken a trip to Philadelphia.

Ford sighed, thinking it was time to stretch his legs. Opening the car door, he got out and had turned to walk around it when suddenly, "What the hell!"

"Don't move!"

Ford suddenly found himself face-to-face with the barrel of a small but deadly revolver that was aimed directly at the area between his eyes. He stilled, too startled to move. He met the man's gaze. It was the same man who had stormed out of the woman's apartment just moments ago. Damn! How in the hell had he circled around and come back without being seen?

From the look on the man's face it was obvious he was still angry, and he was all but growling when he said, "Who are you and why have you been keeping tabs on my woman?"

• • •

An angry Christy paced the confines of her living room. Alex thought she was being difficult and she thought he was being controlling. How dare he tell her what she could and could not do? Just who did he think he was? He wouldn't like it if someone were to dictate rules to him regarding his job, so why was he trying to do so for hers?

No matter what he thought, she could take care of herself. She was just as capable of facing danger as he was. OK, so he had been there to get her out of a rather sticky situation with Kevin that night at the club, but that had been one isolated incident. Just when she'd felt herself mellowing toward him a little, he would do or say something that ticked her off.

And then he had the nerve to say he would be coming back and they would settle things between them once and for all. Ha! There was nothing for them to settle. It wouldn't bother her in the least if she never saw him again. If he thought she would give him her undying love when she didn't have his, he was stone crazy.

She snapped her head around when she heard the ringing of the telephone. If that was him calling, she would let him know in no uncertain terms that they had nothing else to say to each other.

Crossing the room, she snatched up the receiver. "What!"

"Christy? Christy Madaris?"

Christy frowned, not recognizing the voice at first, and then she drew in a deep breath when she did, her anger momentarily forgotten. "Mariah? Yes, this is Christy."

"You told me to call you if I found out anything else or if I remembered something."

"Yes, and have you?"

"I think I have. I'd forgotten that the last time Mark came over to my place he woke up in the middle of the night to use my computer. I just noticed that he flagged something in the '*Favorite Places*' of my Internet."

"What?"

"Information on a place called Vanuatu. Have you ever heard of it?"

Christy shook her head. "No. But I'm going to look up information about it. Do you think that's where he planned to go before he was killed?"

"I believe so."

"Well, I'm going to see what I can find out and I'll get back to you."

"OK."

After hanging up the phone Christy walked across the room to her office, intent on finding out all she could about this place called Vanuatu.

Sweat popped out on Albert Ford's forehead. The man staring at him had dark eyes, almost filled with glacial ice. For some reason Ford had a feeling he wouldn't hesitate to use the weapon if he had to.

"You have less than a second to start talking or I will put a bullet in your ass."

Ford swallowed. "I'm a federal agent. I'm here on government business," he quickly said.

"Bullshit."

Ford sighed. "Look, I'm telling the truth. If you give me a second I can get my badge and show it to you."

Holding his gaze while still aiming his revolver between his eyes, Alex took a step back. As soon as he'd walked out of Christy's apartment he had experienced that uneasy feeling again. He had gotten into his car and circled around the complex and parked, returning on foot to check things out. He had recognized the car as the one that had followed them to the airport that morning. And now this guy claiming to be a federal agent was a bit too much. If there was a chance he was telling the truth, then why would the FBI have a tail on Christy?

"Remove it slowly," Alex said.

Ford nodded. He carefully eased his badge out of the top pocket of his shirt and carefully flipped it open.

Alex studied the badge. Then he drew in a deep breath and said, "Damn."

CHAPTER 18

Christy leaned forward in her chair as she read the information on her computer screen. Vanuatu was a small island in the South Pacific located three-quarters of the way from Hawaii to Australia. The land area was slightly larger than Connecticut and had the natural hazards that were associated with islands in that region, namely, cyclones and typhoons. The terrain was mainly mountainous islands. The legal system was a unified one created under both French and British rule, and the three official languages were English, French, and Bislama.

She continued reading and lifted a brow when she read that a large amount of the island's money was made from imports. She couldn't help but wonder if perhaps some of those imports were human beings being shipped illegally.

She turned from her desk and picked up the information she had printed out of her computer earlier. It was a list containing the ships that had left the port the same morning Mark had gotten killed. What she'd found interesting was that there was a huge shipping vessel owned by Dove Distributors, and the destination had been Vanuatu.

A chill crept up Christy's spine, but she refused to shake off the feeling. It didn't take much to be convinced that a ship headed for Vanuatu the same day Mark was killed was more than just a coincidence.

Switching her attention back to the computer, she checked to see what ships were due in the Vanuatu port within the coming weeks. She scanned the list, murmuring the names aloud. Her breath caught after saying one particular name. The ship owned by Dove Distributors was on the list and was due in port in two days.

She wondered if the ship was linked to any Philly high-rollers or politicians. After an entire hour of checking several sites on the Internet and coming up with nothing, she decided to make a call to a college friend who worked for the governor of Pennsylvania. Judith Akins did some checking and called her back within an hour with some very interesting information. Pennsylvania's Senator John Harris's family owned Dove Distributors. Judith indicated that fact had been a bit hidden, since the senator was not involved in any activities relating to that particular business.

Christy ended her conversation with Judith and shouted, "Bingo!"

She glanced back at the computer screen and again read the information that the ship was due into the Vanuatu port in two days. What she was thinking about doing was pretty damn risky, but she intended to do it anyway. Her passport was up to date, and this was the break she had been waiting for. If there was human cargo on that ship, then she intended to expose them.

A part of her wanted to call Alex and ask him to go with her, but after tonight she knew how he felt about her involvement in the Patterson case. If he had any idea what she planned to do, he would probably try and stop her. She wouldn't put it past him to call her brothers and get them involved.

No, she couldn't tell Alex what she planned to do under any circumstances. The less he knew of her travel plans, the better.

"Now that you know I'm a federal agent, will you put that gun away?" Ford asked in a somewhat shaky voice. He was twenty-eight and had been with the Bureau for a couple of years. Recently he had begun thinking that this wasn't the type of job he was suited for. Returning to Iowa and going back to work for a police department sounded real nice, especially now.

"Not until you tell me what's the Bureau's interest in Christy Madaris."

Ford sighed. "I can't divulge that information, and if you continue to hold that gun on me you'll find yourself in real serious trouble."

Alex's eyes narrowed. "No offense, but I don't give a damn. It's you who owe me an explanation, and I want one."

Ford frowned. "I can't give you one. I'm merely following orders."

"From who?"

"My boss."

"Then let's get him on the phone."

Alex stepped back as Ford walked back to the car, opened the door, then eased slowly into the seat. He punched some numbers into a phone that was installed in the car's console.

"Put it on speaker," Alex ordered, keeping his gun leveled on the man.

Within seconds a voice came on the phone. "Baker here."

"This is Ford."

"Yeah, Ford?"

"It's about the woman I've been ordered to watch."

"I'm glad you checked back in," the deep masculine voice said. "I ran the license number of that car through the system, and it's rented to an Alexander J. Maxwell. Your suspicions were correct. Maxwell does have a background in law enforcement. It seems that he used to be an agent with us before leaving to start his own detective agency a few years ago. I'm pulling contacts now to determine his involvement in all of this. If your guess is right and he *is* the woman's boyfriend, we might have problems. From what I understand from someone who used to work with Maxwell, he's a boy wonder when it comes to solving cases. And I've also heard that he isn't someone you want to tangle with."

Without taking his eyes off Ford, Alex leaned forward and reached out and pushed the talk button. "Baker, this is Alexander Maxwell. Your advice came too late. Ford *has* tangled with me and I suggest someone come up with some answers real quick to get him untangled."

A couple of hours later, back in his hotel room, Alex poured coffee into four mugs, then turned to the three men standing in his hotel room and handed each a cup.

It had been an hour since the two agents had arrived and had identified themselves as Oran Baker and Stan Coulter. But still, Alex hadn't been told what he wanted to know. He didn't need a sixth sense to figure out when someone was leading him in circles. One thing about a circle: there wasn't a point in it.

He stared at Oran Baker, who was evidently the boss, and said, "Don't you think it's time you leveled with me and let me know what's going on?"

Baker slowly poured cream into his coffee. "Like I told you, this is a highly confidential investigation and—"

"And like I told you, I don't give a royal damn about that when my fiancée is involved."

Baker lifted a brow. "Fiancée?"

Alex's gaze didn't waver. Christy wasn't his fiancée but she was *his* and he wasn't going to apologize for staking his claim. Besides, what they didn't know wouldn't hurt them. "Either you tell me what's going on or I'll find out for myself."

Alex watched as the three men exchanged glances before Baker sighed deeply. "Your involvement might impede our investigation."

Alex lifted his dark brow. "Frankly, I don't give a shit."

Baker took a sip of coffee before saying, "You should, unless you want to place your life in danger."

Alex shrugged. "It's been there before. Danger doesn't bother me any."

"Then are you willing to place your fiancée's life in danger?"

Alex moved around the bed and sat down, leaving the three men standing. "The way I see it, her life could be in danger anyway, but I really don't know, since the three of you seem to have locked jaws."

Baker drew in a deep breath. "You're making this rather difficult, Maxwell."

"Good."

Baker took another sip of coffee and Alex exhaled slowly. He knew what the man was doing—trying his patience, toying with his control. But he refused to back down.

It took a few minutes for the reality to dawn on Baker that Alex's position wouldn't change. "The street name is the Body Snatchers, but the official name of the organization that stretches over several countries and continents is the Kantar Cartel," he said finally. "Have you heard of them?"

Alex shook his head. "No."

Baker nodded slowly. "Then let me tell you about them," he said, taking a wingback chair in the room. "Three years ago an informant working a drug bust brought to our attention that teenage girls—mostly runaways—were being snatched off the streets in Philly and shipped out of the country to be part of a slave trade. It started out as a small operation, but now it has escalated into a billion-dollar business and expanded worldwide."

Alex released a long whistle. "That's some business."

Baker stared into his coffee and said, "Yes, which equates to a lot of young girls being sexually abused and exploited, most between the ages of fourteen and eighteen."

He lifted his head and met Alex's gaze. "It took the Bureau a solid two years to piece together information, follow up on leads, and plant informants in the right places before we discovered a growing network behind this operation that included the involvement of wealthy businessmen from all over the world and highly respected leaders and politicians from various countries."

After taking a sip of coffee, he continued, "The girls, and oftentimes young boys, are exploited as sex slaves for tourists who consist of both Western and Eastern males traveling to specific countries for the sole purpose of fulfilling their sexual fantasies. Within the past eighteen months, we have tightened our investigation, and it's just a matter of time before we close in on the operation. We would have done so sooner, but Mark Tyler's death set us back. Somehow he found out about the kidnappings, and it was brought to our attention. Since the runaways felt comfortable talking to Mark, he was assigned to the investigation on a local level. Once he began asking questions, the cartel didn't hesitate to take him out. Luckily for Morganna Patterson, no one took her seriously, until your fiancée came along. If word gets out that she's snooping—if it isn't out already—it could mean bad news for Miss Madaris as well as bad news for us. It will set us back again, which means more girls will be taken against their will. So it's imperative that Christina Madaris stop her investigation."

Alex inhaled deeply at the thought of the danger Christy was now in. "What about Cincinnati's FBI Agent Horace Mansfield and Lieutenant Jones of the Philadelphia Police Department? Christy got stonewalled when she questioned them."

"They're working with us and were operating under our direct orders. We couldn't let anything or anyone impede our investigation when we were so close to ending this nightmare for those young teens."

Alex leaned forward. "What about the guy who manages the dock in Philly?"

Baker's lips drew in a serious line. "Hank Adams is definitely tied in with the cartel, and we have more than enough evidence to prove he was involved in Mark Tyler's death. And if the cartel knows about your fiancée's meddling, it's because Adams tipped them off."

Baker sighed deeply. "As a former agent, I think you can understand how important it is for us to do whatever we can to bring an end to this cartel."

Alex nodded. He did understand and Christy would understand, too, if he could give her the same facts he'd just been given, but he couldn't. He knew how the FBI operated. There was a trust factor involved, and men's lives—namely those of their agents and informants—were at stake. Baker didn't know Christy like Alex did. To Baker she was a reporter, and reporters went after stories. She might agree to stop her investigation, but they couldn't take the chance that she wouldn't decide to publish the story at the least opportune time.

"We know the players in this sick game and the names that head the list are of a number of well-respected politicians in this country. But there are more. Fortunately, we have been able to get two respected world leaders to assist us by joining the cartel and becoming informants."

"Who are they?" Alex asked.

"One is a high-ranking official within the French government, and the other is a wealthy sheikh from the Middle East. Both men have proven to be resourceful and trustworthy and have provided us with a ton of valuable information while placing their lives in danger."

Alex knew how important trusted informants were in any undercover operation.

"Now that I've told you everything," Baker was saying, "I'm sure you can understand the importance of Ms. Madaris ending her investigation as soon as possible, and we need to count on you to make sure that happens."

Alex inhaled, thinking of the argument that he and Christy had had earlier that night, and knew meeting Baker's request wouldn't be an easy task. But then, the man was right. Until the Bureau brought an end to things, innocent girls would continue to be sexually exploited.

"Can we count on you, Maxwell?"

Alex shifted his gaze from Baker and fixed an unblinking stare on a flashing sign that could be seen outside his hotel room window. Christy's snooping could get her killed, and Alex couldn't let that happen. The thought of losing her that way was too much for him to bear.

He looked back at Baker. "Yes, you can count on me."

Knowing that Malcolm arrived in the office early, Christy was at her desk before dawn waiting for him. It took less than an hour to convince him that she needed more time. He gave her an additional week. She wished it could be more, but she was grateful for what she got.

By ten that morning she was packed and ready to go. She had called and spoken to her parents. Without divulging the nature of her trip, she had told them she was on her way out of town on business.

A couple of times she had been tempted to call and talk to Alex, but something had held her back. She was still upset with him. She hadn't planned to be gone but a few days and would deal with Alex when she got back.

Right now, she had a story to go after.

Alex woke upon hearing the phone. He immediately glanced over to the clock that sat on his nightstand. It was nearly noon. It had been close to six that morning before the three agents had left and he'd finally been able to go to bed to try to get some sleep.

He snatched up the phone on the third ring. "Yes?"

"This is Baker. You need to keep up with your fiancée. I just got word that she boarded a plane for Vanuatu."

Any traces of sleep left Alex and he quickly sat up in bed. "What!"

"I said Christina Madaris has boarded a plane for Vanuatu."

Alex was out of the bed in a flash. He placed the call on the speakerphone. "Is she traveling alone?"

"Yes."

Damn. Double damn. He found himself losing it at the thought of where Christy was headed. Vanuatu had come up last night in his discussion with the agents. It seemed that was the country where the kidnapped girls were being taken before being shipped to other parts of the world, and it was the last place Christy needed to go snooping around.

Alex pulled his luggage from the closet. The thought of anything happening to Christy was unbearable, and he felt his control starting to shatter as anger consumed him. Vanuatu was a place that wasn't tourist-friendly. There had been documented reports of several serious attacks on foreigners when the victims had been alone. It was a place a woman should avoid traveling, and especially by herself. Hell, the United States didn't have an embassy over there anymore, which meant all Americans traveling in that country were on their own.

"So what do you plan to do?" Baker inquired in an agitated voice.

Alex drew in a deep angry breath. "Go after her."

"And I hope you find her before she causes problems. We just received word from one of our informants that the Kantar Cartel is having a major summit in Vanuatu in a few days. This is just what we've been waiting for and might be the break we need to close them down permanently. I can't risk Ms. Madaris screwing up things with this investigation, Maxwell, especially now."

Without giving Alex a chance to respond, Baker disconnected the call. Alex fumed as he continued to throw things into his luggage. He had to find Christy, and when he did, she would regret the day she had made him come this damn close to losing control.

Book Three

The Capture

CHAPTER 19

After embarking off the plane, Christy glanced around the small airport and sighed. She was glad she had finally reached her destination. After leaving Cincinnati she had caught four connecting flights and hoped whatever information she got from this trip was well worth the entire day she'd lost in the air.

She couldn't help but feel tired, but then at the same time another part of her was excited that she was following up on another lead in Bonita Patterson's disappearance. The first thing Christy intended to do was go to the hotel and freshen up. Afterward, she would visit the docks and see what information she could find out there. She hoped she wouldn't be in Vanuatu but a couple of days at the most and planned to make good use of her time.

By now Alex would know she had left town, but what he wouldn't know was where she had gone. And she had made Shemell promise not to tell him anything on the off chance that he sought her out.

Christy turned and looked for the exit, since she didn't have any baggage to claim. She'd figured that with four connecting flights the chance of her luggage getting lost would increase, so she had decided to carry everything on the plane with her. Taking a firm grip of her carry-on as well as her briefcase, she began walking toward the airport's exit.

The airport was crowded with both arriving and departing passengers and wasn't as empty as she'd assumed it would be. She hadn't heard of Vanuatu until Mariah had mentioned it, and now she wished she'd made time to stay longer to visit its beaches.

The first thing she noticed walking out of the airport was that traffic was driving on the right. She intended to rent a car so she could have her own transportation around the island. She'd never been in a place where they drove on what she considered the wrong side of the road and knew it would be something she would have to get used to.

She glanced at her watch. It was almost six in the morning and there were a few cars on the road. The island was still asleep and there wasn't much activity going on. Her travel agent had promised that a rental car would be waiting at the airport for her and that the hotel was a few miles away. Everything was in the main hub of the city and nothing was in any isolated areas, which her travel agent had cautioned her to avoid.

She saw a movement out of the corner of her eye and in a split second she turned to stare into the unshaven face of a huge man with dark, mean-looking eyes. When he reached out and grabbed her arm she immediately thought of screaming, but he quickly reached out and placed a large hand over her mouth.

She'd been taught by her brothers how to fight, and she put everything she knew into action, grateful for the freedom of her jeans. He gasped in pain when she kicked him in the midsection, and when her carry-on gave him a hard whack to the shoulder, making him stagger, he released his grip on her somewhat. However, it wasn't enough for her to get away.

She frantically glanced around. People were passing by watching the commotion, but instead of anyone coming to her rescue it was as if they were deliberately trying to avoid getting involved. Where was a Good Samaritan when she needed one?

She tried getting away and figured a loud scream would

scare him off if nothing else. But she never got the chance. The man, now angrier than ever, snatched her to him. She went for his face, determined to scratch his eyes out, when she felt it, a sharp sting to her thigh. It only took seconds for her to realize she'd been given a shot of something with a hypodermic needle.

She fought frantically, but the fight was useless. She felt her head begin to spin, and the legs holding her up suddenly felt weak. She glanced into the man's face and saw the look of triumph, and the last word she remembered speaking was the name of the one person she would give anything to see right now: "Alex."

Ennis, Texas

"Lorren? Justina said you wanted to see me."

Lorren Madaris turned to meet her husband's gaze. She caught her breath, thinking that she found Justin just as handsome today as she had when they first met nearly eight years ago. She would never forget the night she'd been at a party and had an eerie feeling of being watched, only to turn and find him doing exactly what he was doing now—casually leaning against a wall and watching her with the most beautiful pair of eyes she'd ever seen. And just like then, her pulse increased and her breathing was becoming erratic.

"Lorren?"

She blinked at him and remembered she had sent their daughter for him. "Hi," she said in a breathless greeting. "Do you have a few minutes?"

As he was the only doctor in the rural area where they lived, she knew that he had been busy with patients all day. But a phone call she had received from her sister-in-law and best friend, Syneda, made this conversation necessary. Evidently the brothers had set a date next week to drop in unexpectedly on Christy. Lorren and Syneda agreed that Christy and Alex needed uninterrupted time together to work out their problems.

"I'll give you all the minutes you want, sweetheart," Justin said huskily, crossing the room to her, with long, purposeful strides. "What's up?"

For a moment while looking into the chocolate chip coloring of his eyes, she almost forgot her plan. But feeling the deep emotion of her love for him, she was reminded that Christy and Alex deserved a chance to share that same kind of love, and they wouldn't get it with the brothers' interference.

"I was thinking that it's been a while since the two of us have gotten away alone and was wondering if you're interested," she said, smiling up at him. "Your parents have offered to watch the kids and I thought next week would be a wonderful time to for us to go somewhere."

He lifted his brow. "Where do you have in mind?"

Her smile widened seductively. "Any place would be nice as long as I'm with you, Justin."

She could tell her words pleased him, and although she was setting him up, she meant every word she was saying. She wanted the two of them to spend time together, so she was effectively killing two birds with one stone.

"And you want to go somewhere next week?"

"Yes." She knew that he would have to make a choice between going away with his brothers to unexpectedly drop in on Christy and going somewhere and engaging in all kinds of irresistible passion with her.

He pulled her into his arms. "Dex, Clayton, and I had planned on flying to Cincinnati to see Christy next week, but I'm sure they'll understand if I bail out."

Lorren reached out and placed her arms around his neck, gazing lovingly into the handsomeness of his chestnut-colored face. He still had an aura of masculinity that could turn her on like nobody's business. "Yes, I'm sure they will," she whispered moments before pulling his mouth down to hers for a deep, lingering kiss.

* * *

Taking heed of the blinking sign, Alex snapped his seat belt in place. The next time the plane landed, he would be in Vanuatu. He had been cooped up in airports all day and was exhausted and irritable. He would no longer waste his time being Mister Nice Guy. This was it for Christy. His insides felt shredded at the thought of the danger she had placed her life in. If anything were to happen to her, there was no way he could go on.

He covered his eyes with his hands when the intensity of his emotions hit him solidly in the face. For years he had believed that the pain of his father's desertion had kept him from taking a chance on love, when in fact he had been in love.

With Christy Madaris.

Alex's gut clenched, and his thoughts suddenly swirled back in time to all the memories they'd ever shared, and there had been many. Memories of her as a kid as he taught her to ride her first bike; memories of her as an eleven-year-old declaring he wasn't just Alexander, but he was her *Alexander the Great* after studying about the fierce Macedonian king in one of her classes; memories of her as a teenager in high school when he'd tried not to notice the beautiful young woman she was becoming; and memories of her in college when he couldn't help but notice the stunning beauty she had grown into.

But the memory that he held closer to his heart than any other was the night of that charity auction when they had kissed for the first time. Amidst all the hurt and anger that shrouded them that night, he had been left shaken by a wisp of a girl who had somehow thawed out a section of his heart, and it had been slowly melting ever since.

Removing his hand from his face, he drew in a long, deep shuddering breath. His desire for her was one thing, but the love he felt, what he could finally acknowledge and accept, was another. It was elemental, highly potent, and substantially significant.

Christy was more than just his woman. She was his life, his very reason for living, and no matter what it took, he was determined that she would love him just as much as he loved her.

He leaned back in the seat and closed his eyes, determined to get things settled with her once and for all when he saw her.

CHAPTER 20

Still feeling somewhat groggy, Christy opened her eyes and slowly glanced around the room at the same exact moment she heard the sound of the door opening and several footsteps entering the room.

She braced herself, not knowing what to expect if one of them was the huge, mean-looking man who had abducted her. Her stomach clenched as she tried not to be frightened. She had gotten herself into this mess, and no matter what she had to do, she would get herself out. After all, she was a Madaris, and nobody pushed a Madaris around.

She wondered if she should pretend to be asleep, then thought that was the coward's way out. She wanted to look directly into the faces of the people responsible for snatching her off the streets of Vanuatu in broad daylight. She pulled herself up in the bed and met four pair of eyes.

Christy took a deep breath. Two of the men were Americans, and one she immediately recognized from the research she had done on the Internet before coming to Vanuatu. He was Pennsylvania Senator John Harris. The second American she didn't know, and the third man appeared to be a Frenchman. The fourth . . .

She swallowed, suddenly hit with a whammy as she studied his features. He had to be the most handsome man she had ever seen—or at least, he came in second to Alex. He was tall, extremely good-looking with piercing dark eyes, skin the same color as hers, and straight black hair that flowed loosely around his shoulders. It was obvious he was someone from the Middle East, and dressed in his native garb, he looked the epitome of a dashing Arab prince.

"So, Miss Madaris, it seems you've been busy."

Her attention was drawn back to Senator Harris. He was a heavy-set, balding man who she knew to be in his early sixties. "I have no idea what you're talking about," she said, meeting his gaze.

Senator Harris stared at her with heated anger in his eyes. "Don't play games with me. I received a call that you've been asking questions, and we can't have that. And then to think you had the nerve to travel all the way here by yourself. Just what did you expect to accomplish doing that?"

Neither the sound of her heart pounding like a jackhammer nor the way her stomach was tightening in fear stopped Christy's anger from rising. "To expose you and your group for being the sick persons that you are," she snapped.

She watched a slow smile spread on the senator's face. "Too bad you won't be accomplishing your goal. However, my friends and I appreciate your visit." She then saw the glint of lust appear in his eyes when he added, "We're going to make sure it's rather useful."

Christy backed up on the bed. "You can't hold me here against my will. I am an American citizen."

"One who unfortunately is in the wrong place at the wrong time. I know who you are, Miss Madaris. After I got a call from Hank Adams, I did a little checking, and I know all about your family. You are Jake Madaris's niece, aren't you? How charming. The bad news for you is that I never have liked your uncle because of his friendship with a fellow lawmaker of mine, a person who I detest by the name of Senator Nedwyn Lansing. Over the past couple of years, I've tried to destroy Lansing's political career, but because he has friends in such high places, like Jake Madaris, I've been deterred each time."

Senator Harris leaned back against the wall, laced his

fingers together, and smiled triumphantly as he continued, "As far as I'm concerned, it's time for me to get even since there's no way you can return to your former life. This cartel has too much to lose if you were to disclose our activities. So now it seems that your fate has been sealed. At some point in time, my dear, you will be killed."

Christy swallowed the lump in her throat. How could this man who was highly respected in her country speak so callously of ending her life? But then, she had to remember he was the one behind Mark Tyler's death as well as the exploitation of young girls and boys, teenagers who were young enough to be his grandkids. She also couldn't forget what Morganna Patterson had described as Bonita's fate. That thought made Christy rub her neck. A beheading wasn't the way she'd figured her life would end one day.

There was a silence in the room, and then another voice began speaking. It belonged to the second American, who appeared to be in his late forties.

"Hank Adams was right, John. She's a beauty and I want her," he said, actually licking his lips. The gesture made Christy's stomach turn. His words also sent chills up her spine. Senator Harris's laugh made it worse. "Let's not be greedy, Congressman Blair. There's enough of her to go around. I have no problem in sharing," the senator said, amused.

"I have a problem with it."

All eyes, including Christy's, shifted to the Middle-Easterner. He met the other men's gazes. The look he gave them was dark and penetrating. "I don't share."

Congressman Blair didn't seem at all happy with the man's statement and said, "Now, look here, Sheik Valdemon, you can't make any demands here. We share and share alike."

The sheik's eyes suddenly became darker. "No, I want her."

The congressman's face set into a hard, deep frown. "I said I wanted her first."

Senator Harris felt the need to step in. "Gentlemen, let's not lose our friendship over this woman. Remember, we're gathered together in this place for a more important reason, which is to discuss the cartel's expansion. Let's not let our lust come between us."

The sheik's eyes darkened, and anger lined his brow. "Do you deny me the chance to negotiate for her?"

At the mention of what he knew to be money, Senator Harris's smile widened. "And just what are you offering, Your Highness?"

The sheik turned and gazed at her, and Christy felt her fear shudder all the way through her bones. She saw ruthlessness in his gaze, and she shrank back even more in the bed under the scrutiny of his direct, unwavering stare. He then turned his attention back to the other men, including the Frenchman who hadn't uttered a single word through the entire thing.

"A million dollars."

Christy sagged back against the wall next to the bed for support. This man was willing to pay a million dollars for a night with her before she lost her head, literally?

Senator Harris seemed rather shocked, yet pleased as he stuttered, "A-a million d-dollars? Umm, I think that amount will be sufficient to satisfy the three of us since another ship filled with young tasty delights will be arriving at port tonight." The senator's expression then turned serious. "Just remember after your night with her, she goes to the gallows."

"No," the sheik said vehemently. "For a million dollars, she becomes my possession to do what I please with for whatever length of time I want. You have no say in the matter."

Senator Harris stared hard at the sheik. "That's impossible. We can't risk her escaping and—"

"She won't," Sheik Valdemon cut in. "Once she becomes part of my harem, there is no escape. Nothing changes in the plans you had for her except that her life will be spared. She will never return to her country, and if anyone ever tries to find her, she will be tucked way too deep to ever be found."

Oh, God, Christy thought, as she heard the sheik's words. He meant every word he said.

Senator Harris thought so as well. He laughed and looked over at her. "I can imagine how your family will suffer not knowing if you are alive or dead. Tsk, tsk, what a shame." He then met the sheik's gaze. "All right, Sheik Valdemon, she's all yours."

He then turned to the other gentlemen and chuckled. "Come on, let's leave them alone to get better acquainted."

Before the men walked out the door, Sheik Valdemon said, "I'm taking her away from here, to my own villa."

Before opening the door, Senator Harris said over his shoulder, "Suit yourself and enjoy her."

Sheik Rasheed Valdemon gazed across the room at the beautiful young woman whom he had just purchased for a million dollars. "I am Sheik Rasheed Valdemon, and I suggest we leave here as soon as possible. My manservant will be coming for you soon."

Before Christy could open her mouth to utter a single word, the man turned and walked out of the room.

A couple of hours later back at his villa, Sheik Rasheed Valdemon turned to his top adviser and trusted friend, Terek Ahmadi, who was standing across the room looking at him. "How is she, Your Highness?" Terek asked.

Rasheed's lips lifted into a smile. "Christy Madaris seems to be in better shape than Ishaq," he said, thinking of the scratches on the face of his trusted servant. "She assumed he meant to harm her and she put up a good fight."

Rasheed walked over to the window and looked out. His good friend Jake Madaris would certainly owe him for this. What on earth could the woman have been thinking to come to Vanuatu alone, and of all things to take on the Kantar Cartel?

The organization's ruthlessness knew no bounds, and Rasheed had gladly accepted the United States' top law enforcement agency's offer to be a part of the sting operation that would finally put an end to the cartel.

Because of his wealth and strong influence, he had easily been accepted as a member of the cartel, and he passed on whatever information he could to tighten the net around the men who thought they were above the law and who further thought it was their God-given right to establish a business that exploited young women for their pleasure.

"Is the Madaris woman beautiful, Your Highness?"

Rasheed sighed deeply. He turned and said, "Yes, she is definitely beautiful, but her timing is lousy. Her unexpected appearance could destroy two years of carefully laid-out plans to bring the members of the Kantar Cartel to justice."

"Are you going to tell her that she's safe here with you and has nothing to fear?"

"Not at the moment. The less she knows, the better." Back in Mowaiti, he had a harem full of women—and all of them were there of their own free will, since he didn't believe in forced enslavement. At the age of thirty-seven, he was very experienced when it came to women.

He sighed deeply and glanced back out of the window. Since Vanuatu was the stronghold of the cartel's operation, he and several other businessmen, all connected in some way to the Kantar Cartel, had purchased luxurious private villas along the beach. Because of the entourage that usually traveled with him, Rasheed's villa was large and isolated, which was a good thing. If he had to hold a woman hostage for a while, it was best that his neighbors knew nothing about what was happening under his roof.

He had arrived on the island a few days ago to take part in an important meeting of the cartel. He looked forward to gathering whatever information he could pass on. He knew the price he would pay if the cartel ever found out he was a traitor. But then, placing his life at risk was a small way he could repay the American government for allowing the joint venture between the government of Mowaiti and a private corporation, Remington Oil.

It had been the first type of agreement ever made between an American-owned oil company and a foreign nation. And it had been a union that had been successful when an oil basin had been found in Mowaiti two years ago, saving his people from living impoverished lives. And for that reason he felt a special kinship to his Texan friends who had helped to make such a union possible; especially Corinthians Avery Grant, the geologist whose tireless efforts had resulted in not only the basin but the location of several oil reserves in his country as well.

And because of his association with Corinthians and her husband, Trevor, Rasheed had become well acquainted with the members of the Madaris family and their close friends. In fact, he and Jake Madaris stayed in constant contact, and Jake and his beautiful wife, Diamond, had visited Mowaiti on several occasions. Likewise, Rasheed had been a guest at Whispering Pines, Jake's sprawling ranch in Texas, a few times.

"I'm surprised Senator Harris doesn't recall your association with the Texas oil company," Terek was saying.

Rasheed couldn't help but smile. "He's too busy trying to decide how he's going to spend his share of my million dollars."

"Do you remember her? Christy Madaris?"

Rasheed shook his head. Christy Madaris was not a woman a man could easily forget meeting. "No, but then, I do remember the Madaris brothers mentioning they had a sister who was away at college. Given the young woman's age, it must have been her."

Terek sighed deeply. "I'm surprised they would let her travel alone, especially to a country like Vanuatu."

Rasheed understood what Terek meant. Vanuatu was one of those countries still stuck in a time warp where men ruled and women were meant to be ruled. It wasn't safe for a female to travel alone. That was the reason no one had stopped to help when she had been abducted in broad daylight. In this country, women literally had no rights and any unmarried woman who was not in the care, custody, and control of a husband was fair game.

"Knowing what I do about those brothers, it's my guess that they don't know about it," Rasheed said. After finding out the woman was Jake's niece, Rasheed had been committed to do whatever was within his power to assure her safety. Once he was sure it was safe to do so, he would notify his contacts at the FBI to let them know what had happened and that Christy Madaris was safe and now in his possession.

"When will it all end, Rasheed? The exploitation of innocent young women's lives?"

Rasheed turned and met the gaze of his childhood friend. "Very soon, Terek. It's only a matter of time before they are brought to justice."

Christy angrily paced around the room she had been given, trying hard to ignore just how beautiful it was; a bedroom fit for a princess. Earlier she had tried opening the door only to find it locked. She hadn't been surprised.

She jerked her head around when she heard the door opening, only for her gaze to collide with same man who had paid a million dollars for her. Sheik Rasheed Valdemon.

She blinked, seeing she hadn't imagined things. He was as tall as her brothers and Alex and was simply gorgeous. She tilted her head back and lifted her chin. Gorgeous or not, this sheik had no right to take her anywhere and make her his sex slave. She backed up when he entered the room. If he thought he would have her willingly, then he had another thought coming. She would fight him until there wasn't any more breath left in her body.

"I see you are moving about," he said after coming to a stop in front of her.

"Let me go," she said, gazing into the piercing dark eyes looking down at her. She thought there was a possibility that he was well-versed in American ways since he spoke the English language so well. "If you let me go, I won't implicate you in any of this. It will be my silence in exchange for my freedom."

Sheik Valdemon sighed deeply. "I'm sorry, you are my guest and as such, I can't allow you to leave," he said, deciding to be as truthful with her as he could.

His guest? Christy thought to herself. *What a laugh. Did he think she didn't know of his plans for her when he had pretty much spelled them out to Senator Harris in front of her?* "Where am I?" she decided, already planning her escape.

"You are at my villa on the beach."

He watched as she then lifted a haughty brow. "You might as well know that someone will be coming for me."

Rasheed lifted a brow. She seemed pretty confident about that. Without saying anything, he moved to stand next to the window and looked out. Below he could see the beach and how the water was hitting the sea wall mercilessly. His villa sat high on a cliff, with the fortitude of a fortress.

Anyone who tried invading his estates would have to first make it over the seawall and then tackle the job of climbing over the huge wrought-iron gate that surrounded the perimeters of his property. Not an easy task. The villa's original owner had lived a reclusive lifestyle, but Rasheed had fallen in love with it for an entirely different reason. It had been an architectural dream, and the view that was outside every window on the east side was breathtaking. It was a magnificent view that oftentimes brought a tranquil calm when his life became somewhat turbulent.

"Did you hear what I said?"

Rasheed sighed deeply as he turned around. "Yes, I heard you," he finally said when her eyes narrowed at him like sharp spears. "And who is coming for you?"

Christy sighed deeply. She didn't know when or how, but

she believed in her heart that Alex wouldn't hesitate to tear this country apart if he discovered her missing. He was good at finding people, and she refused to consider that the odds weren't in her favor since she hadn't left him any information as to her whereabouts.

Alex, wherever you are, please come and find me, she inwardly pleaded.

"I'm waiting for your response," Rasheed said, interrupting her thoughts and staring at her with curious dark eyes. "I asked who you thought would be coming for you?" If there would be another untimely visitor to the island who could impair the sting operation, then he needed to know about it.

Christy sighed and allowed herself a moment of silent, deep thought. This was probably the worst situation she'd ever found herself in, but with a keen sense of spirit and a strong sense of will she knew she would get through it. She lifted her chin and glared at him. "The person who's coming for me is Alexander Maxwell."

Rasheed's brow lifted, wondering if the Alexander Maxwell she had just named was the same one that he knew. He walked back to where Christy was standing and decided that yes, they were discussing the same Alexander Maxwell. And given Alex's association with the Madaris family, Rasheed really wasn't surprised. He could see how this woman could have captured Alex's heart.

"And you believe this Alexander Maxwell will actually come for you?"

She continued to glare at him. "Yes, I believe it."

Christy watched as the man stared at her for several long moments without saying anything; the expression on his face was unreadable. Then he turned and left the room, leaving her wondering if she had made a mistake by removing what would have been the element of surprise. They knew Alex was coming and would be ready and prepared. She had unintentionally placed his life in danger.

She crossed the room and collapsed on the bed. *Oh, God, how could she have done such a thing?*

"The woman belongs to Alex Maxwell?" Terek asked in shock while watching Rasheed pace the wood floor.

Rasheed stopped his pacing and met his friend's gaze. "It seems that way. And she is certain that he is coming for her."

The two men had met Alexander Maxwell, as well as a number of the members of the Madaris family and their close friends, four years ago when Mowaiti had hosted a huge gala at the palace to thank Remington Oil and its associates for what they had done to improve life in his country. Rasheed's jets had flown the entourage of Americans from Texas to spend a week in his homeland.

Rasheed chuckled as he crossed the room to pour two glasses of wine. "I find Alex coming here to rescue her as she claims rather interesting."

"So what do you plan to do?" Terek asked, crossing the room to take the glass of wine that Rasheed was offering him.

Rasheed met Terek's gaze. "Nothing. If Alex is coming for her, then that's a good thing. Within the next day, members of the Kantar Cartel will be arriving for an important meeting. The FBI will seize the opportunity to finally bring the organization to an end when everyone is nestled under one roof. My concentration needs to be placed on that happening and not on our houseguest. The sooner she leaves, the better."

Terek took a leisurely sip of his wine and then asked, "So will you get word to Alex where the Madaris woman is being held?"

A mischievous smile touched the corners of Rasheed's lips. "And take the fun out of him putting his well-honed skills to work? Jake Madaris once mentioned how proficient Alex Maxwell is as a private investigator. According to Jake, Alex unraveled the plans of a madman determined to take Jake's life."

Rasheed shook his head, grinning. "No, I think Alex Maxwell is capable of tracking down Christy Madaris without my help. The only thing we should do is get prepared for his arrival."

Houston, Texas

Moving with a stealthy grace that was unusual for a man of his size and height, Dex Madaris crossed the room to where his wife was standing with her back to him as she looked out of the window.

"Caitlin?"

Caitlin turned and smiled as a shiver automatically passed through her. Although they had been married for a number of years, her body never failed to respond to the strength and power that seemed to emanate from her husband.

The years had been good to him. Even now, his nut-brown features were still those of a very handsome man. It was hard to believe there was an eleven-year difference in their ages, but she could proudly boast that Dex Madaris had taught her everything she knew, and she wouldn't have it any other way. And she of all people knew how hard it was in the beginning stages of a love affair for any couple. She and Dex had gotten married within weeks of their initial meeting, and because of a lack of understanding and communication, they had separated and had lived apart for four years before reuniting.

She wanted to spare Christy and Alex the pain she and Dex had endured during that time they had been apart. The last thing the couple needed was to deal with three overprotective brothers. That was the main reason Caitlin had agreed to go along with Syneda's plan to stop the brothers from interfering, no matter what it took.

"Caitlin?"

When Dex said her name a second time and pulled her into his arms, she smiled up at him. "Yes?"

"My secretary said you called and wanted me to come home for lunch."

Her smile widened as the corners of her lips tilted. "Yes. The girls are still at school and it's Gregory's naptime, so I thought we could spend some time together."

"Oh," Dex said, staring down at her. His charcoal-gray eyes were dark and piercing. "And what do you have in mind?"

A ripple of excitement combined with anticipation surged through Caitlin's body. Dex could turn her on with a mere look, touch, and sensual suggestion. "A number of things, but I wanted to get your opinion about something first."

He lifted a brow. "OK, what?"

"I think it would be nice if the two of us got away for a few days alone next week. I need a break and so do you."

Dex gazed lovingly down at his wife. "Alone for a few days, huh?"

Caitlin grinned, knowing the thoughts that were probably going through his mind and looking forward to acting on all of them. "Yes, I thought it would be nice if we took a short trip to Galveston. You do remember our last trip there, don't you?"

From the look in his eyes she knew that he did. They had spent a week on the beach and been saturated in the beautiful waters of the Gulf. They had gone there to be alone with the sole intent of making a baby. And they had. Gregory—named after Dex's best friend from childhood, who had committed suicide when the two had been in college—had been born nine months after that trip.

Although they didn't plan on any additions to their family, Caitlin thought it would be nice if they revisited the place that held so many special memories for them. Because of the opening of the Madaris Building and a number of work projects for Dex's company, Madaris Explorations, they hadn't taken the time to go away together. Usually they did group things with Dex's brothers and their close friends.

"And you want us to go next week?"

She nodded, knowing of the plans he and his brothers had

made for next week. She snuggled closer into his arms. "Yes. Next week will be perfect. Will you agree to go away with me?"

He pulled her even closer, and she found herself ensnarled in his seductive masculine heat. "There's no way I can resist such an offer," he said as his warm lips moved across her forehead before unerringly claiming her lips in a deep and thorough kiss.

CHAPTER 21

What the hotel clerk was saying didn't make much sense, or maybe he just wasn't hearing the man correctly, Alex thought. He was well versed in several foreign languages, and the man was speaking words that were a combination of butchered English and chopped-up French and was definitely putting a killing on the art of conjugating verbs.

Alex decided to start over and take things slow. "I want to know the number to Christina Madaris's room."

The man shook his head and spoke rapidly. "She was to be our guest but never arrived."

Alex lifted a brow. "She never arrived?" he repeated to make sure he had heard the man correctly.

"Oui."

Alex wondered how that could be when Christy's plane had landed a good six hours before his. "Are you sure?"

"*Oui,* sir."

Alex immediately became troubled by that information. If Christy hadn't made it to the hotel from the airport, then where was she? He opened his wallet and pulled out a recent photograph he had of Christy, one that was taken the year she graduated from college. She had sent it to his mother and he had made a copy of it. "Do you remember seeing this woman?" he asked the man.

The man studied the photograph and then shook his head. "No, she didn't come to this hotel. We have her room waiting, but she didn't come."

Alex's jaw clenched as he returned the photograph to his wallet. If Christy was missing he would turn this island upside down to find her.

She was planning her escape.

Christy stood at the window and studied the scenery outside of it. The villa sat high on a hill and below, all she could see were cliffs and water, but she refused to be held hostage. The first chance she got she intended to escape and take her chances on the outside rather than the inside.

"Would you like to take a bath before dinner?"

Christy quickly turned around. A middle-aged woman stood in the middle of her room. Just like Rasheed, the woman was dressed in mideastern attire, and from her accent Christy could tell she spoke just enough English to get by. "Who are you?" she asked the woman curiously.

The woman smiled. "I am Hajji, a servant of the sheik. He has asked that I take care of you."

It was on the tip of Christy's tongue to tell the woman that she didn't need anyone taking care of her; then she thought better of it when she heard the grumbling of her stomach. She was hungry, and a bath and change of clothes sounded rather nice. "Yes, I would like to take a bath before dinner. Do you know what the sheik did with my carry-on and purse?"

The woman's forehead bunched in confusion. "Carry-on?"

"Yes, my luggage. I'm going to need clothes to put on after my bath."

When understanding dawned the woman smiled. "Yes, I will bring you clothes."

Christy nodded. "Thanks." She then watched as the woman left the room. Christy turned back to the window. If this sheik thought she would remain here he had another thought coming. The first chance she got, she intended to blow this place.

• • •

Alex returned to the hotel four hours later and checked into his own room. He had met an island man who owned a fruit stand across the street from the airport. The man claimed that he had seen the abduction of an American woman taking place that morning in front of the airport. The man swore the woman had been Christy after taking a look at the photograph Alex had shown him. But that was where the information had ended. Everyone else Alex questioned seemed to have seen or heard nothing, or they had refused to get involved by saying anything.

Alex had tried calling Baker at the FBI headquarters to see if he knew anything, but all he'd gotten was the man's secretary, who was evidently screening the man's calls. Pulling his shirt off, Alex tossed it across a chair. He wasn't ready to notify the Madaris brothers that their sister was missing. All hell would break loose when he did. Besides, Christy was his, and he would find her no matter what.

He was about to remove his pants when he heard a knock on his door. He quickly put his shirt back on and picked up his revolver. Easing over to the door, he looked out the peephole. It was the man he'd talked with earlier that day and he was with a woman who Alex assumed was his wife.

Alex slowly cracked the door open a little. "Yes?"

"My woman has information. She thinks she has seen your wife."

Hope flared through Alex's tired body. He hadn't gotten any sleep in the past twenty-six hours, but he refused to think of rest until he found Christy. He told everyone he'd talked with that she was his wife, since he was well aware of the care, custody, and control rule these islanders lived by. An unmarried woman roaming around without the protection of a husband was fair game, but the abduction of a married woman was not acceptable.

"Please come in," he said, moving aside to let the couple

enter. The woman, he noticed, waited for her husband to go first and then walked in meekly behind him.

Alex closed the door behind them. "When did she see her?"

The woman began talking in Bislama, a language Alex did not know. The man translated his wife's words. "My wife says when she delivered fruit to the sheik who that lives on the hill, a woman who looks like your wife was being taken inside the villa."

Alex lifted a brow. "A sheik lives on this island?"

"Yes. He recently purchased the villa and only comes here occasionally, and when he travels he does so with a lot of servants."

Alex nodded. "And you say that he lives on a hill?"

The man shook his head. "Yes. His house is big and looks down at the beach. It's the only one that's on the private road leading up the hill and is surrounded by a huge black iron gate."

Alex breathed in deeply. Just the thought of Christy being held somewhere against her will amplified his anger. If she was harmed in any way, he would kill the bastard who'd had the nerve. "How far is it from here?"

"Around five miles. He has a bodyguard who looks mean and dangerous."

It was on the tip of Alex's tongue to tell the man that he was mean and dangerous as well. Instead, he thanked the couple for the information and escorted them to the door.

"I hope you get her back," the man said with sincerity in his eyes.

Alex met the man's gaze and said, "I will." And there was no doubt in his mind that he would. Getting Christy back was the most monumental thing he'd ever had to do, and it would take all of his skill, control, and discipline to accomplish the task. But he would master all three because at that very moment he could not imagine his life without the woman he loved in it.

After the couple left, Alex was suddenly filled with a new

burst of energy. He couldn't depend on the local authorities to help him, so he began making plans to go in and rescue Christy. Besides, he worked best alone. He knew he needed to wait until night, when everything was dark and the chance of being seen would decrease.

Alex didn't know who this sheik was but planned to snatch Christy back from beneath the man's arrogant nose.

Houston, Texas

"Remington, read Daddy's lips. It's bedtime."

The two-and-a-half-year-old little girl with sea green eyes and a mop of golden-bronze curls on her head glared at her father, stuck out her bottom lip, and said, "No. I don't want to go to bed."

Clayton inhaled deeply. He didn't have to wonder where his daughter got her temperament. She was a clone of her mother in both looks and attitude. He inhaled again as he glanced at his watch. Syneda had called an hour ago and said she was on her way home after a long day in court. Since the day care that kept Remington was located in the Madaris Building, he had brought his daughter home, fed her dinner, given her a bath, and put her PJs on her. It was past nine o'clock and he had promised Syneda he would have Remington in bed even if she didn't go to sleep. Their daughter tended to be a real grouch in the mornings without her proper rest—another thing she had inherited from her mother.

"I want ice cream."

Clayton lifted his brow. "Don't hold your breath for that one, kiddo," he said, thinking of how he'd been told when he had picked her up that once again she had spent most of her day in "time-out."

He picked her up into his arms. "I hate to be the bearer of bad news, sweetheart, but there won't be any ice cream for you tonight or any night until you learn not to argue so much with the other children." He sighed, knowing she had inherited her argumentative nature from both him and Syneda.

He sat down on the sofa with Remington cuddled in his lap. He cherished this child who was a product of his and Syneda's deep love for each other. He knew they had spoiled her rotten, but the way they saw it, she was theirs to spoil. Besides, he knew when to get firm with her. "Do you want Daddy to read you a story?"

She shook her head. "No. I want Daddy to give me ice cream."

He was about to tell his daughter once again that she wouldn't be getting any ice cream when he heard the sound of the front door opening and closing.

A smile touched his lips. "Mommy's home."

"Mommy!"

Before he could catch her quick enough, Remington had scattered out of his lap and raced out of the living room toward the front door.

A smile captured Syneda's lips as she took her daughter into her arms. Clayton thought Remington favored her, but Syneda knew that except for her daughter's hair, eyes, and skin coloring, she looked like her father. She had Clayton's nose, forehead, and mouth. "Where's Daddy, sweetheart?" Syneda glanced around knowing he wasn't far.

When he walked into the room from around the corner her breath caught as their eyes met. She wondered if it would always be this way with them—that instant surge of stimulating sexual chemistry that enticed them to tear each other's clothes off no matter where they were or, better yet, sneak off someplace private and just get it on.

"Hi," she said, finding it almost hard to swallow as she watched him lean against the staircase. Another thing that amazed her was how much her husband still attracted her. He had changed out of the business suit he had worn to the office and was dressed in a pair of jeans and a T-shirt. In her book he was one good-looking man with a body that he definitely kept in shape. It always made her feel good to know that she was the one he had chosen to love unconditionally and spend the rest of his life with.

"Hi, sweetheart, how did things go in court?" he asked.

She beamed. "I won!"

He returned her smile and crossed the room to her. Angling his face around their daughter, he kissed his wife, immediately feeling desire flow through all parts of his body. Moments later he reluctantly pulled back and held her gaze and whispered, "I know a wonderful way we can celebrate after we put Remington to bed."

"I don't want to go to bed, Daddy."

Clayton smiled as he tousled his daughter's curls. "Sorry, sweetheart, but the sooner I can you get you in your bed, the sooner I can get your mother in mine."

He took Remington out of Syneda's arms and kissed her little rounded cheek. When she had been born the media had tagged her the *Remington Princess,* since millionaire oil magnate S. T. Remington was her grandfather and S.T. had been quick to let everyone know that he intended for his granddaughter to run Remington Oil one day.

An hour or so later, Clayton lay in bed and watched as Syneda disrobed. Remington had finally gone to sleep. His heart began pounding when he saw what Syneda had changed into after her bath—a very skimpy nightgown. She turned to him and smiled, placing her hands on her very shapely hips. "I've been thinking, Clayton."

He nodded. Yeah, he'd been thinking, too. Just the thought of making love to her was causing his body to throb. "What about?" he asked when all he wanted to know was how soon she was going to get into bed with him.

"I want to celebrate today's win in court. I mean really celebrate. I've been so busy working on that case and now that it's over I need a break. I think it would be a wonderful idea if we took off next week."

"Take off to where?" he asked when at the moment his

total concentration was on the fullness of her breasts as she slowly lowered her nightgown.

"Clayton . . ."

He blinked and quickly glanced up at her face. "Huh?"

"Are you listening? I said I want to go somewhere special to celebrate for an entire week."

Clayton swallowed deeply, fighting the urge to get out of the bed and drag her into it. "An entire week? What about Remington?"

Syneda smiled. She'd known he would ask that. "Dad has been anxious to have her stay at his ranch with him again, and I think it would be a perfect time for her to do so. And you know how much Remington adores Dad's housekeeper, Emilie. She'll be there to help him take care of her. I talked to Dad on the cell phone on my way home and he loves the idea."

Clayton frowned. "Yeah, and when we pick her up she'll be spoiled rotten."

Syneda grinned as she walked over to the bed, naked. "She's already spoiled rotten."

She stood next to the bed and gazed down at him. "I thought we could really make it special if we took a trip to Saint Augustine Beach, Florida, where it all began for us."

Clayton couldn't help but remember that time. They had gone on vacation together as friends and eventually had become lovers. "Saint Augustine Beach?"

"Yes. Just think, one week alone, just the two of us."

He *was* thinking. He then remembered he had another trip planned for next week. "Oops, I almost forgot," he said disappointedly. "Justin, Dex, and I have a trip planned for next week. There's a business matter we need to check on."

Syneda nodded, knowing full well just what business matter he was talking about. She lowered her lashes. "Oh, I understand. I just thought it would be nice for us to spend some time together. Maybe we can do it some other time."

Clayton inhaled deeply. He knew she was disappointed.

Hell, he wanted to go to Florida as much as she did. They hadn't taken a trip anywhere alone since Remington had been born. They loved their daughter, but every once in a while parents needed playtime, too. And as far as his trip with Justin and Dex to check on Christy went, he would have to bail out and check out things with her another time.

He reached out and tumbled Syneda down into the bed with him. "Make plans for us to go to Florida," he whispered against her lips.

A huge smile touched both corners of her mouth. "Really? You mean it?" she asked excitedly.

He loved making his woman happy. "Yes, I mean it," he said, smiling.

She began raining kisses all over his face and throat. "Thank you, Clayton," she said softly as her hand moved seductively over the solid muscles of his chest.

He pulled her into his arms, straddling her body over his. "I can think of another way you can thank me, sweetheart."

She quirked a brow and looked down at him. "Would you like to demonstrate?"

He laughed throatily as he cupped her face into his hands. "With pleasure," he whispered just seconds before he gave her a long kiss, which was only a prelude to what else he had in mind.

Christy's gaze narrowed speculatively at the outfit Hajji had placed on the bed. "Surely I'm not expected to wear this," she said, picking up the garment, whose material was pretty much on the thin and flimsy side. She had to admit it was beautiful, but she could picture herself playing the starring role on *I Dream of Jeannie* while wearing it.

"You don't like it?"

Christy turned, not wanting to hurt the woman's feelings, but it was hardly a practical outfit that she could escape in. "Yes, I like it," she said, "but I prefer wearing my own things. If you will bring my luggage then I will—"

"Sheik Valdemon has put your things away and says while you're a guest we will provide everything for you."

Christy sighed deeply. It was hard to appreciate kindness from the man who planned to induct her into his harem. She wrapped the bathrobe she was wearing tightly around her and dropped into a nearby chair.

She had just taken a bath in the biggest tub she had ever seen. To her amazement, the bathroom had a one-way wall-to-wall window that looked out at the ocean. Although Christy could see out, no one could see in, which had been a good thing, since she had stayed in the tub for more than an hour. Part of that time she had relaxed her body deep in the bubbly waters to ease out her aches. The rest of the time she had stood by the window looking out, taking stock of her surroundings and trying to figure out an escape route. All she saw was water. Although she was a good swimmer, the thought of diving into a shark-infested ocean was a definite turnoff.

She looked up at Hajji. "The view outside the window is beautiful. Is this place completely surrounded by water?" she asked innocently, fishing for information.

The woman shook her head and smiled. "No, not completely. There is land on the other side of the woods, as well as the cleared path down the hill to the main road, which is the way we go into town."

Christy nodded. She hadn't been sure if she'd been brought to a small island or something. It was good to know that part of the place she was being held was connected to land. Now all she needed to do was find a way to get out of here and make it to town. Once there she would find the local police and tell them everything.

"Sheik Valdemon would like you to join him for dinner."

Hajji's words interrupted Christy's thoughts. She frowned. "Tell him thanks but no thanks. I prefer eating alone in my room."

The woman nodded and then quickly left, closing the door behind her. Christy moved over to the door and tried it and she wasn't surprised to find it locked.

She sighed deeply. No matter what, she was determined to leave this place. She glanced over to the bed and gazed at the outfit Hajji had left and hoped she wouldn't have to wear that when she did so.

Her gaze moved to look out the window. It was getting dark and she knew night would be the best time to make her move.

Alex, dressed completely in black, hid behind a huge boulder. He rubbed his chin, feeling the stubble there. He was past having a shave, but that was the least of his problems, he thought, looking at the wrought-iron gate that surrounded the villa. There was no doubt in his mind that this place was highly secured and there were probably security cameras on the ground.

He glanced at the backpack he had placed by his feet. It contained a small arsenal of firearms as well as the tools he would need to go in and get Christy. No matter where you were, you could always depend on finding out where to purchase illegal goods if you asked the right questions and were willing to pay the right price.

As soon as it had gotten dark, he had carefully prowled around the outskirts of the property, and to his surprise he hadn't seen any guards lurking around. Evidently this sheik felt pretty safe behind a strong gate and security cameras.

Before leaving the hotel Alex had been able to pull up the structural design of the villa on his computer. He had viewed a number of high-quality photographs of nearly every room in the house that had been displayed during the time the villa had been up for sale.

He knew that the best angle to penetrate this villa was by crossing over the seawall on the eastern side of the house.

That meant becoming a rock climber, which was pretty risky business at night, and the only light he would have was the illumination from the moon and stars.

But when it involved the woman he loved, a man had to do what a man had to do.

As Christy had requested, dinner was brought to her room, and she had eaten alone. She had expected the sheik to show up and insist upon eating with her, and she was glad that he hadn't.

Thankfully Hajji had brought Christy's carry-on. She hadn't wasted any time changing out of the *I Dream of Jeannie* outfit into a pair of jeans and a top.

She knew since she couldn't just march down the stairs and out of the front door, that in order to escape she would have to create some type of diversion when Hajji returned. With all the attention the woman had been giving her, Christy knew she would probably return in a few hours to check on her.

That meant that she had to come up with a plan, and a darn good one.

Grateful for his unique night vision, Alex glanced around. When he was certain that all was silent he came out of hiding and glanced around the beach. He had taken time to smear his face with camouflage paint. Usually he wore gloves, but this time he needed his bare hands for climbing. Once he reached the top of the cliff he would use his gloves. Fingerprints were the last thing he wanted to leave behind.

Moving with the fluid ease of a man well skilled in this type of clandestine activity, he pulled out the rope, then went about anchoring it to a nearby tree. Moments later he was ready for the climb and hoped he hadn't miscalculated and the sheik's men would be able to spot him.

Although it had been strenuous, definitely no easy task,

he'd scaled the seawall, and an hour or so later he had found himself at the top of the cliff, right on the sheik's property. With the patience of a man who knew the pitfalls of being overanxious, he glanced around. He was surprised at the lack of security at the east side of the house, and the only reason Alex could come up for it was that a mistake had been made by the owner in assuming no one in his right mind would attempt to invade the property by risking a climb over the seawall.

Adrenaline was pumping through Alex's veins as he circled around the servants' quarters while making his way to the main house. He was desperate to get in and find Christy but knew he had to channel his desperation, since desperate people made mistakes and at this point any wrong move might cost Christy's life.

Upon reaching the house he checked the back door and was surprised to find it unlocked. A sense of unease suddenly knotted his gut. Either the sheik was extremely lax in security or it was a setup and someone was expecting him.

Tightening his hold on the gun he held in his hand, he slowly opened the door, thinking this was not the time for him to become paranoid. He eased inside the house knowing a step in the wrong direction might trigger an alarm. He sank back into the shadows when a big hulk of a man crossed the hall ahead of him after he came down the stairs to go into a room and close the door behind him.

A few moments later, with silent efficiency, Alex eased out of the shadows and slowly made his way up the stairs. Other than the man he'd just seen, there was no sign of anyone in the house. When Alex reached the second floor he noted all the room doors were closed. He knew the one Christy was probably in was the one that he would find locked.

Christy crouched behind the dresser in the room, waiting for Hajji to come check on her for the night. She had made up the bed to appear like a body was lying in it, all covered up.

It was her hope that when the woman came and saw she was asleep she would leave quietly, but that would be only after Christy had slipped out of the opened door.

Her breath caught when she heard the sound of someone toying with the lock on her bedroom door. She wondered if it was the sheik or, worse yet, the big, mean man who had brought her here.

She watched as the door eased open, and felt a prickling at the base of her neck. From the brevity of the sunlight that poured into the room, she could tell that the shadowy figure was not Hajji. It was a man, and she watched as he softly pushed the door shut behind him before slowly moving toward the bed.

Deciding she wasn't about to wait around for an introduction, when he passed her she made her way out of her hiding place and inched quietly to the door. Suddenly the intruder turned in her direction and a big strong hand reached out and grabbed her. Before she could let out a scream, a hand clamped over her mouth and she was snatched to a hard, muscled body.

"Don't fight, baby. It's me," a deep, husky voice said in a mere whisper close to her ear.

Upon recognizing the voice, Christy sagged against him. Tears filled her eyes. Alex had come for her.

"I'm going to remove my hand, but I need you to remain quiet until I can get us out of here. Understand?"

She nodded. Then, driven with a need to let him know how glad she was to see him, when he removed his hand from over her mouth she turned in his arms and, dismissing the danger surrounding them, unerringly found his lips. Fire swept through her veins the moment their mouths connected, and the way he was kissing her back indicated he was as glad to see her as she was to see him.

One minute Alex's mind had been on the best route to get the two of them out of here alive and the next he was kissing Christy like they had all the time in the world. Now was not the time and definitely not the place, but there was no way he could not take a part in this. A part of him wanted to say, *Damn the danger,* and sweep her up into his arms and take her over to the bed. The way she was kissing him was steadily stoking flames through his entire body.

Suddenly the room was filled with a bright light. Alex broke the kiss and pushed Christy behind him as he raised his gun.

"Welcome, Alex. You're earlier than I expected."

Alex's gaze collided with the man who strolled past an armed guard as he entered the room. Alex lifted a dark surprised brow. "Rasheed?"

CHAPTER 22

"So as you can see, Ms. Madaris, there was no way I could tell you that being kept here was for your safety without explaining everything. And at the time I couldn't do that."

Christy nodded. She and Alex were sitting in Sheik Valdemon's study and had listened while he told them everything. She had thought their lives had come to an end when the light came on and she and Alex stood in the middle of the room caught like deer in a headlight. Even now she had a hard time believing that Alex and the sheik knew each other and not only that, but the man also was very familiar with her entire family.

She could see Alex out of the corner of her eye. He was conversing openly and freely with the sheik but hadn't said a whole lot to her. Although Alex might have been glad to see her—his kiss had certainly shown that—it didn't take much to tell that it didn't erase the fact that he was pretty pissed with her.

"Well, I for one will be glad to leave here and return to the United States and will do so after I find out what happened to all those girls who arrived on that ship last night," she said.

Alex leaned forward and pinned Christy with a fierce glare. "Did you not hear everything Rasheed said? A summit of the Kantar Cartel will take place on this island in less than twenty-four hours, at which time all hell is going to break loose when the FBI storms in and makes arrests. It's over, Christy; I'm sure the federal government will release information to the families on all the young women who were abducted."

Christy breathed deeply, in and out, as she tried to hold on to her temper. She stared him straight in the eye. "I heard what Rasheed said, Alex, but I'm a reporter and I happen to be in an excellent position to be the first to get the story. Surely you don't think that I'm leaving here now."

He leaned closer to where his nose was just mere inches from hers. "I don't think it, sweetheart; I know it."

Christy glared right back. "Then I hate to inform you, but you're wrong."

"Excuse me, Ms. Madaris, but there's something else you might not know about this island," Rasheed said, interrupting the two.

Christy's head snapped around. "What?"

"A woman may enter this country single, but she can't leave here unless she's married. So in order for you to leave here you and Alex must get married."

Christy frowned. "That's the craziest thing I've ever heard."

"Yes, that may be true," Rasheed was saying, "but it's a fact, an ingrained custom, and is part of the care, custody, and control policy these islanders live by. The only single women who can move around freely are nuns; otherwise unmarried women are considered fair game. That's why Senator Harris's man could abduct you in broad daylight and nothing was done. Even if you had made it to the local authorities they would have returned you to the person who'd abducted you."

"And it's the reason I had to tell anyone I questioned that you were my wife," Alex tacked on. "Otherwise, no one would have given me any information about your abduction."

"And," Rasheed decided to add upon seeing how the color was draining from Christy's face; he needed her to understand just how serious her position as a single woman in this country was; "even if the authorities would have gotten you back, any one of the senior officers could take you as his wife or mistress, regardless of how you felt about it. Beautiful American women in these parts are trophies to some. Even with you married to Alex we still have to be careful that you don't catch the eye of anyone who may decide to get rid of him to have free and clear access to you."

Christy was aghast. "That's barbaric, simply crazy."

"That might be true but that's the way it is. Americans aren't popular here. I suggest the two of you leave as soon as possible, and if getting a story is that important to you, then I'll be glad to give you . . . how they say it in your country . . . *the inside scoop, an exclusive* . . . when everything is over. But we've come too far for anything to go wrong now, and if you remain and start asking questions, it can place many lives, including my own, at risk. And I strongly suggest the two of you avoid the airport. As you recall I'm supposed to be holding you as hostage for my harem. We can't take the chance of someone seeing you leave and reporting that information back to the cartel."

"What other way do we have to leave if not by air?" Alex asked Rasheed.

"By sea. Once you reach an island called Kiribati, adjacent to the port there's a private airfield where I keep a plane. You can use it to fly out from there to Hawaii. Then you'll be home free. But even in Kiribati you'll need to be careful. It's a republic that's headed by a president about to be ousted, so there might be a bit of unrest and tension there."

Rasheed leaned back in his chair and continued. "I have a mini-yacht you can use to get to Kiribati, and it's fairly easy to operate. It's my understanding that very few people are stopped by the sea border patrol between here and Kiribati. However, since there's a possibility that you might be, the two of you will need to have papers showing you're married. Otherwise, if you're stopped they can take Ms. Madaris and there won't be anything that Alex can do."

Christy stood. "Marrying Alex just to leave this country is

out of the question. I refuse to be forced into marriage by anyone."

"You don't have a choice," Alex said through clenched teeth. "We can get the marriage annulled as soon as we hit the States, but for now we need to do whatever is necessary to get the hell out of here." He turned to Rasheed. "The last thing we want to do is place you at risk with the cartel."

Rasheed smiled. "Thanks."

Christy glared at both men. "I don't like it."

Alex stood. He didn't particularly like it, either; especially when it was apparent that she still didn't love him. Although he wanted to marry Christy, he wanted her to come to him of her own free will and not because she was forced to do it. "Whether you like it or not, Christy, that's the way it's going to be."

He watched her raise furious brows before she angrily walked out of the room. He then turned to Rasheed. "Do you know of anyone who can perform a quick ceremony?"

Rasheed nodded. "Yes. There's an English church in town. I'll have one of my men bring the priest right away."

"Thank you for coming, Father," Alex said to the Englishman who he'd learned had been a missionary in Vanuatu for a number of years.

The priest nodded. He glanced across the room to where Christy was sitting on the sofa. With a pout on her lips a mile long, it was apparent to everyone that she wanted no part of what was about to take place.

When the priest met Alex's gaze again, he knew exactly what the man was thinking and spoke up, saying, "I agree that we need counseling, but there isn't time. We have to leave here as soon as arrangements are made."

The priest nodded again. "Are you ready for the ceremony to begin?"

Alex rubbed a hand down his face and said, "Yes, as ready as I'll ever be."

• • •

Christy was fuming. This was not how she had always envisioned her wedding day would be. Yes, in her mind Alex had always been the groom, but she'd always dreamed of a big wedding, surrounded by those she loved and who loved her. Today the only people present beside the priest were Rasheed and his top adviser, named Terek. She shook her head and glanced down at herself. She wasn't even wearing a dress. She hadn't been given time to change out of the jeans and top she'd had on earlier, and Alex was still wearing all black and looking excruciatingly male.

She frowned as she watched that same male body make its way toward her. She tried to read Alex's expression and found his features unreadable. It was evident that he didn't like this any more than she did. She stood as he got closer.

"The priest is ready," he said when he came to a stop in front of her.

"And there's no way we can leave here without doing this?" she decided to ask one more time. After living in a free country all her life, hearing how women were treated in this third-world nation was too much to stomach.

A frown deepened Alex's features. "Look, Christy, you heard what Rasheed said, just like I did."

"I could always pretend to be a nun."

His gaze roved over her from top to bottom. "Forget it. Nuns don't look like you. This is the only way, and like I said, we can get the marriage annulled as soon as we get to the States."

She looked away. She'd felt the intensity of his gaze as if it had been an intimate stroke. Sighing, she tried to take in everything the two of them were about to do. She had always wanted to marry Alex, but not this way.

"Let's not think of ourselves for a moment, Christy."

Alex's words, spoken in a rather unusual soft and gentle tone, made her return her gaze to him. "Let's think of all those helpless innocent teenage victims and what they have gone through, which makes our sacrifices appear as nothing," he said. "The nightmare for them is about to come to an end. The FBI has done a good job by infiltrating the cartel. Now it's time they close down shop and arrest every damn person involved. They need to put Senator Harris, Congressman Blair, and any others who are involved *under* the jail and not in jail. Hell, as far as I'm concerned, why waste a good cell? Just take the bastards out back somewhere and blow them away."

The harshness of Alex's words floated all around her. She understood his anger and bitterness. He was right; the world would definitely be a better place without those evil men in it. And what he'd said was true. What had been forced on those young teenagers was a lot more than what was being forced on her right now. She could get back her freedom with an annulment, but there was no way any of those teens could ever get back their innocence.

Sighing faintly, she said, "You're right, Alex."

"Then you're ready?"

She slowly nodded. "Yes, I'm ready."

Taking her hand in his, he walked her over to where the priest was waiting for the ceremony to begin.

"Is there a ring?" the priest asked when they got to that particular part of the ceremony.

Alex blinked. He had totally forgotten about a ring. But then when he glanced down at their joined hands he immediately knew the ring that would be perfect. "Yes, there is a ring," he said quietly, then proceeded to remove the one off his pinkie, the one that had always been hers.

Christy stared at Alex. He was giving her back the ring. A part of her wanted to snatch her hand back and declare that, since their marriage wouldn't last past the time it took them to reach the States, a ring wasn't necessary. But the moment he slid the ring onto her finger and she lifted her head to meet his gaze, her breath caught. And suddenly their nuptials had special meaning.

"Now repeat after me, Mr. Maxwell. 'With this ring I thee wed.' "

Alex's face rigid, he continued to hold her gaze as he repeated the priest's words in a somewhat trembling voice. "With this ring I thee wed." Then he was holding her hands tight in his again.

"I now pronounce you man and wife. You may kiss your bride, Mr. Maxwell."

The priest's words, spoken in a heavily British-accented voice, made a knot form in Christy's throat that extended all the way to her stomach. And when she glanced up and met Alex's eyes, the knot tightened and she suddenly felt hot all over. Considering everything, she knew this kind of effect he was having on her was not good, but she was having it nonetheless.

And then she felt herself being gently pulled into his arms and engulfed by the manly scent of him. Her heartbeat increased as their gazes met. "No matter what happens tomorrow, Christy, this is now." His low murmur as well as the deep intensity in his eyes sent a bank of shivers all the way through her body. And then he kissed her, eliciting a response with the first stroke of his tongue, and she gladly gave him more.

He tasted powerful and made her feel ravenous. The breasts pressed against his chest ached, and the need to deepen the kiss gripped her. But like him, she heard the sound of three male throats clearing and knew Alex had done more than just kiss the bride. He had literally devoured her.

He pulled back and she stepped out of his arms. She could barely acknowledge the customary words of congratulations Rasheed, Terek, and the priest were giving. She felt Alex's tenseness. The eyes holding her steadily were ablaze, and the hard planes of his face looked unyielding. He took her hand in his and led her over to the desk to sign the papers that would legally bind them as man and wife.

"I will have this document sent to your country by overnight express so an official record can be made," the priest was saying. "And I will give you the necessary papers to carry with you so the two of you can leave this place without any hassles."

Alex looked down at Christy and then back at the priest and said, "Thank you."

"And I'm going to have to leave," Rasheed said in a thick mideastern accent. "I have business to take care of and probably won't be here when the two of you leave tomorrow. Ishaq has been instructed to have the yacht ready for your departure." Rasheed then smiled charmingly. "Terek will be coming with me, which means the two of you will have the villa to yourselves tonight."

Alex nodded, then gave the man his hand. "Thanks for everything, Rasheed, and do whatever you have to do to stay safe."

The light in the sheikh's eyes faded somewhat. "I knew the risk involved when I decided on this venture, my friend, but it was something that I had to do for all other young women who were used against their will."

He then turned to Christy and regally inclined his head. "And to you, Christina Madaris Maxwell, it has been a pleasure, and if it's Allah's will, I shall contact you soon for your exclusive story. But for now I bid you farewell."

"Thank you for everything." And because she felt, considering all he had done for her, that he was truly a special person, she added, "Your Highness," and then curtsied as best she could in jeans.

She watched him grin before he turned and, with an arrogance that was definitely connected to royalty, left the room.

"The food is delicious, don't you think?"

Alex glanced up. "Yes." He then looked down and resumed eating.

Christy frowned. She personally didn't like his attitude since the marriage ceremony. He'd barely said two words to her, and since all the servants—except for those such as Ishaq who lived in the villa but in the west wing—had left for their private quarters out back, the place had an eerie silence. Alex's lack of conversation wasn't helping matters.

"Using the yacht, how long will it take us to reach Kiribati?"

He lifted his head again and she saw the slight frown that agitated the arch of his dark brow. "Probably six to eight hours. According to Rasheed this mini-yacht we'll be using is rather fast, with speeds that can get us there in a fairly good amount of time. Once we get to Kiribati we'll use Rasheed's private plane to fly to Honolulu." He hadn't told her, but he had spoken with her uncle Jake Madaris. Alex had told Jake everything and the older man had agreed to be in Honolulu when they got there.

Moments later, after Alex and Christy had finished eating, the servants removed the remnants of their meal. Alex stood, his expression distant, reserved, and unapproachable. "Ishaq has indicated if the weather cooperates, we can set sail first thing in the morning. I suggest you go to bed and get a good night's sleep."

Christy stared at him, her chin tilted. If he could be that way, then so could she. "I will."

With nothing else left to be said, she watched as he walked out of the room.

CHAPTER 23

Once Alex made it to the guest room that he'd been given, he shut the door, closed his eyes, and swore beneath his breath. Christy could push a man's control to the limit. The fury he felt for her having placed her life in so much danger kept him from doing the one thing he wanted to do with a vengeance: lock his arms around her like unyielding steel, kiss her senseless, and drag her to the nearest bed, tell her how much he loved her, and make love to her, lose himself in passion—the kind that only she could ignite within him.

For the past thirty-four hours he had been in a state of sheer panic, not knowing if he would find her on this hell-hole of an island where lawlessness was a way of life. And then after he found her and discovered that she was safe, thanks to Rasheed, her having the nerve to declare she wasn't ready to leave Vanuatu had been the last straw. It had taken every ounce of control Alex could muster to not throw her over his shoulder and play the role of a Neanderthal. To not lose control.

Twice now since finding her he had kissed her, momentarily losing grip on his fury: the time when he'd found her safe and then when the priest had pronounced that they were married.

Christina Madaris Maxwell.

When Rasheed had called her by that name the sound had played on Alex's senses, sent a possessive thrill shooting through him, and made him feel elementally male. It was as if the woman he loved and wanted as his mate had finally become his, and the sheer thought of her belonging to him had sent mind-whirling sensations through every part of his body.

He drew himself up and walked away from the door. He couldn't continue to go on like this, he would lose his sanity. As much as he loved her, it was plain to see that she still didn't love him, and he refused to hold her in a loveless marriage. As soon as they returned to the States, he would make sure they did whatever was needed to end their farce of a marriage. That shouldn't be hard to do since they had no plans to consummate the damn thing. He still meant what he had told her. He would not make love to her until she loved him.

And from the way things looked, that would not happen.

Christy angrily paced the guest room she'd been given. How dare Alex ignore her! OK, so she *was* the reason they were in this mess, but that was beside the point. Nobody had asked him to make it his goal in life to keep her safe.

Yet he had.

She stopped pacing when that realization mentally halted her steps. That night three years ago that was exactly what he'd been doing. She had actually expected him to walk out of her dreams and straight into her arms. But because of her inexperience he had done what he thought was the right thing, which was to discourage her by walking away.

Yet at the point when he had finally realized that the two of them were meant to be together, he had been man enough to seek out her forgiveness and ask for another chance to win her heart. And although she had continuously rebuffed his advances and had told him countless times it was a waste of his time, he hadn't given up. On more than one occasion he had been there for her—keeping her safe and proving with his actions instead of with words that somewhere deep down in his heart he did love her.

But her Madaris pride had kept her from clearly seeing that love.

And now she was losing him. That thought sent fear worse than any she'd ever known slithering up her spine. She had done a lot of thinking when she'd assumed she was Rasheed's hostage, and the one thing she could not deny was that she loved Alex, had always loved him, and would always love him. It was time to tell her pride to take a hike before she completely lost the most important person in her life.

The sensible thing to do would be to demand a talk with him first thing in the morning before they set sail. But a part of her didn't want to wait that long. Nor did she want to be sensible. Tonight was her wedding night, and despite what she'd insinuated, she didn't want to get their marriage annulled. She wanted to be with him for better or for worse, in sickness and in health, forever.

She glanced down at her hand and gazed at the ring he had placed there, and she felt tears spring into her eyes and reaffirmed in her heart that she loved him, had always loved him, and would always love him. And tonight more than anything she wanted to be held by him, loved by him; a part of her craved to be in his arms.

She remembered what Lorren, Caitlin, and Syneda had told her about how they were the ones to bring her brothers around. Men, her sisters-in-law had said, sometimes didn't know what was good for them, and oftentimes it took a woman to show them.

It was time she showed Alex.

Christy glanced across the room to the bed. Before taking her leave for the night, Hajji had left several beautiful nightgowns for Christy. All of them were fit for a bride to wear when she presented herself to her husband on their wedding night. At first when she had entered the room and seen them she dismissed them from her mind. Now she was grateful for the older woman's insight.

Just maybe, Christy thought, she had been given a second chance.

• • •

Alex heard the sound of his door slowly opening and was about to lean over and reach for his revolver off the nightstand when his night vision stopped him.

Christy.

Inwardly cursing, he swung his legs out of the bed and stood wondering what the hell she was doing creeping into his room. He reached out and switched on a bedside lamp.

Then wished that he hadn't.

She was standing in the middle of the floor wearing . . . hell, he didn't know exactly what she was wearing . . . but he couldn't help the way his gaze automatically became glued to it. Nor could he help the way the outfit was stealing his very breath.

It was sheer black and stopped midway down her thigh. There were splits on the sides and in the center, and the top portion was transparent. The tips of her nipples were hard and had puckered against the sheer fabric. Desire, potent and turbulent, suddenly engulfed him, and he took a step forward. Then just as quickly, he reined in his control and brusquely took a step back.

"What are you doing in here?" he asked, his voice husky, his gaze still transfixed on her.

She paused near the foot of the bed. "I would think that would be obvious."

Alex frowned. Obvious, hell. Nothing was obvious when it came to her. "Well, it's not, and I would appreciate it if you told me what's going on."

"It's our wedding night."

Alex tilted his head. She had spoken those four words like they explained everything. He drew in a deep breath. Didn't she know what he was going through? There was no way things could be like they'd been before. In the past he'd had enough control to take her into his arms, kiss her, and give her pleasure while denying his own. That was then. Now he wasn't strong enough to do that. He loved her and wanted her so bad it hurt, and he was afraid that if she pushed too much, he would push back and lose control.

"I want you to leave, Christy. Go back to your room."

"No."

He lifted a brow. "No?"

She lifted one back. "No. I'm staying."

Alex breathed in deeply. This was sheer, unadulterated madness. "Have you lost your mind?" he asked her, clenching his hands by his sides.

She lifted a chin. "No, I have all my senses."

"Then use them, dammit."

She frowned and lifted her chin another notch. "I am."

"Apparently not. You shouldn't be in here."

"Why? Are you afraid I might tempt you to do the very thing you vowed not to do?"

Alex's hand reached out and clenched the bedpost. He needed to hold tightly on to something. "I don't have time to play games with you."

"And I don't have time to play games with you," she countered.

Alex drew in a deep, furious breath. He watched as she made a move toward him, and when she did, her outfit parted in the center, deeply underscoring the darkened area between her legs. "Stop! Don't move!" he all but shouted. If she took another step and exposed herself any more his control would snap.

She followed his command and went still, remaining where she was. A taunting smile touched her lips. "Are you sure you don't want me to move?"

Alex's jaw hardened. From somewhere deep down he was losing his ability to think straight, and she wasn't helping matters. He reached out and snagged his shirt off the back of the chair and tossed it to her. "Dammit, cover yourself."

She caught his shirt and defiantly threw it down on the floor and met his gaze. "How about uncovering yours?"

Alex's eyes flashed fire. Christy's chin lifted yet another

notch. "You're the one who claimed we had unfinished business between us, Alex," she said, reminding him in an irritated voice.

His glare sharpened. "I was wrong."

His tone made it perfectly clear that he actually believed that. He stood by the bed wearing nothing but a pair of loose-fitting black shorts. Her gaze fixed on his chest and how a thick line of hair tapered off beneath the waistline of those shorts. Taking a deep breath, she forced her eyes upward to his face and studied the stony lines that were etched there. "Well, I happen to think you were right," she said, trapping his gaze.

"It's too late now."

His bold declaration, the same one she'd made to him several times, made Christy's heart thud heavily in her chest, but she refused to give up or back down. And more than anything she wanted to break through his control. "I'm glad you told me there's nothing between us, Alex. Now I have no qualms in remaining here," she lied, ignoring his frown and strolling around the foot of the bed to stand on the opposite side of it from him.

She watched him raise a brow as he tried to keep his gaze steady on her face and not on her nightgown. "Remaining where?" he asked in a deep, husky voice.

"Remaining here. I've decided that waiting for Rasheed to give me an exclusive isn't good enough. My boss expects me to have a story when I return to work. You can go on ahead in the morning without me. I promise to be careful and not put Rasheed at risk and—"

"Dammit, Christy, you aren't staying!"

She hadn't seen him move, but in a blink he had dived across the bed and pulled her down, tumbling her into the bed with him. In one smooth sweep she was on her back and he was looming over her. The fury in the eyes staring down at her blazed through her. "You don't tell me what to do, Alex Maxwell."

As she had hoped, her words made him angrier. Steam was all but coming out of his ears. "I said you aren't staying, Christy," he growled.

She met his gaze levelly, all the while tasting the victory that was within her reach. "And I say that I am staying."

"I won't let you."

"There's nothing you can do about it."

"The hell there isn't."

And then in another blink, a mere fraction of a heartbeat, he leaned down and devoured her mouth in one frantic sweep. Her lips parted under the onslaught of his and he began lapping her up like a hungry man.

His control broke and need overtook Alex's senses and ripped his mind to shreds. He locked his arms around Christy and brought her breasts fully against his chest, molding her thighs to his and enduring the softness of her belly pressed against the hardness of his aroused body.

Intense desire, he was discovering, was a hell of a lot stronger than mind control. And her tongue was tangling with his in a frenzy that was eating away at his restraints and increasing his desperation to know her as no other man had known her. He wanted to brand her. Claim her. Make love to her all night.

He thought about lifting his head, to get a moment of air, but all he could do was change the angle of the kiss, deepen it, duel with her tongue some more as he felt a pool of desire slide through every vein in his body as they succumbed deeper and deeper to passion. His hands on her hips urged her closer. He could feel her and knew she could feel him. Urgency tore at him. It was a compulsion, an aching, spiraling need.

When it registered that breathing was no longer an option but a necessity, Alex pulled back, his breath coming out in deep, hard gulps. He looked down at Christy; the rate of her breathing wasn't much better. For a moment they just stared at each other. He was fully aware of her, everything about her—especially her skimpy nightgown—and fought an urge to draw her back into his arms, reclaim her mouth in another scorching kiss. Instead he reached out and framed her face with his hands. She had stripped away every vestige of control that he had, and there wasn't a thing he could do about it. He was defenseless to fight it.

"I can't let you stay here in Vanuatu, Christy," he said huskily, gazing deep into her eyes. "If anything were to happen to you I couldn't survive the loss."

She searched his dark eyes and a warm feeling rushed through her, overwhelming her, enthralling her. "And I couldn't take it if anything were to happen to you, either, Alex."

It was as if her words sent a sudden surge through him. A groan erupted deep in his throat and he leaned down and captured her lips, kissing her like he was addicted to her taste. She returned his kiss as if she was addicted to his. She felt his hardness even more against her stomach. Heat seared through her, and she knew it had to be affecting him, too. Her senses were reeling and sooner rather than later he would discover what she already had: kissing wasn't enough.

The moment he made that discovery the tenor of their kiss changed and he pressed her closer to the fit of him. She felt his palms open, and his fingers began a slow, seductive movement on her, arousing her even more. The thin material of her gown was no match for the heat of his touch.

He pulled back slightly and captured her gaze in his. "I want you," he said as the sound of desire rumbled from deep within his throat. "But if we make love there's no turning back, which means there won't be an annulment. Do you understand?"

Christy couldn't stop the shiver that raced through her as she nodded her head. "And if we make love," she countered, sliding her hands over his chest and noticing that his breathing was as ragged as hers, "I'll be a woman sharing the highest degree of intimacy possible with the man she loves. Do *you* understand?"

It was as if her declaration of love unfurled an explosively powerful reaction from him. The planes of his face shed their hardness, and the desire that had been glowing in his eyes intensified. Alex drew in a deep, shuddering breath. He thought he understood what Christy had said but wanted to make doubly sure that he had.

He searched her eyes. "Are you saying that you love me?"

She tilted her chin. "Yes."

Alex raised a brow. "Since when?"

"Since always. I never stopped loving you, Alex, and I understand why you did what you did that night. I had unrealistic expectations, for you to feel the same way about me that I felt about you. But that night doesn't matter anymore, because although it took me a little longer than planned, I am what I've always wanted to be."

"And what did you always want to be?"

"Your wife."

Her words, uttered softly but with so much meaning, seized the last of Alex's control and ripped it. He had wanted her love, had fought for it, and now to know he had it back was almost too much. "I love you," he whispered, overwhelmed and overfilled.

She smiled up at him. "And I love you, too, Alex."

He met her gaze and saw the love she claimed shining within their depths and his heart broke free. They still had a lot to work out, a lot to deal with—her brothers, for one thing—but they would deal with it. Together they would deal with anything.

Leaning down, he buried his face in her neck, needing to breathe in the scent he had begun associating with her. She pulled his face up and held his gaze. "Alex, make me yours," she said quietly.

Her words unleashed an explosion of need and desire and he pulled back enough to remove her gown, tossing it aside. And then his hands were all over her, sliding over her nakedness.

"Do you know what I'm going to do to you?" he asked as he stood and removed his shorts, not taking his gaze off her naked body. She was so incredibly beautiful.

"No, tell me," she whispered.

"What we're going to do goes beyond sex, Christy. It will be lovemaking in its purest form. It will be perfection."

Then he was back on the bed and his own naked body stretched out beside her. And before Christy could utter a single word, he began using his mouth and his hands all over her, loving every part of her body, getting reacquainted with the taste of her breasts, his tongue tormenting as well as providing pleasure.

Their legs intertwined and he wanted her to feel him, know how much he wanted her, needed her. And then he moved atop her, bracing his weight on his elbows, and looked down into her face. "I promise you won't regret loving me again," he whispered.

He leaned down and gently kissed her lips before moving lower to kiss her neck. Then he was back to her chest, tasting her breasts, wreaking torment of the sweetest kind, and making her cry out.

"Alex!"

But he didn't stop there and she felt his mouth moving lower, his breath hot against her skin, his lips and tongue drawing circles around her navel, tasting her, nearly pushing her over the edge. She whimpered and felt her inner muscles crave the pleasure he had given her time and time again.

"Not yet," he whispered, lifting up his head to meet her eyes. "I want to cherish you here," he said, reaching down and touching the most intimate part of her.

Christy writhed under the significance of his words and felt him nudge her legs apart just moments before his mouth settled intimately on her as his tongue penetrated her feminine folds. He used his finger to part them as he sought out the swollen, throbbing flesh tucked behind them.

Of its own accord, her body lifted off the bed, and his

mouth clung to her; his tongue pressed deep inside of her, drawing circles, stroking, claiming, and filling his mouth with the taste of her. She gasped out his name. Her hands clutched the side of his head; one part of her wanted to make him stop, but then another thought if he did stop she would die.

Just like before, worshipping Christy with his mouth was touching him deeply, and as he continued to taste the fruit of her desire, inciting passion of the most tantalizing kind between them, heat was igniting within every part of his body.

"Alex!"

He felt her body explode, he tasted it, and it was only when the last shudder had ripped through her that he lifted his head and looked at her. Her eyes were closed, her breathing ragged, her face filled with the sweetest signs of passion that he'd ever seen. He leaned up and kissed her rounded belly again and knew one day his child would expand it, a child who would be created from their love.

He pulled himself up, settled his weight on her still-trembling body, adjusting to the fit of her. "Open your eyes, sweetheart. Look at me."

And when her eyes opened and her gaze met his, held it, he said, "Open yourself to me. Take me inside." Then remembering the request she had made of him earlier, he needed to make that same appeal to her: "Make me yours."

His breath caught when she reached down and gathered him in her hand, directed his throbbing hard shaft to her opening, which was slick and wet. And when she slowly guided him to the mark, letting the tip of him probe, stroke, and caress the bud of her desire, over and over again, his senses raged out of control.

"Christy . . ."

Reaching down and pulling her hands away, he proceeded to hold them above her head while he kissed her mouth furiously at the same time he eased his body into hers. She was tight, wet, and ready.

He pulled his mouth away, looked down, and met her gaze at the same time he entered her, hesitating when he found her too tight to go any further. He wanted her but didn't want to hurt her.

"Do it, Alex," she said, wrapping her legs around him just in case he changed his mind. "I'm your wife. I'm the woman who loves you more than life itself. Do it."

"Christy."

He said her name the moment his body thrust instinctively. He suddenly went still when he heard her cry of pain. He was about to pull out, but she tightened her legs around him. "No, don't stop," she whispered. "I'm OK. Honest."

He looked down at her and saw her tears and he knew at that moment that he loved her more than he thought humanly possible. This beautiful twenty-four-year old woman hadn't bowed to what everyone else was doing. She hadn't let a man touch her this way until now. Until she was certain. She had saved herself for this moment. She had saved herself for him.

"You sure?" he asked, not wanting to cause her any more pain. He kept his lower body immobile, giving her time to adjust to the size of him.

"I'm positive," she assured him, smoothing her hands over the hard muscles of his chest. She smiled at the heat she saw in his gaze.

He smiled back, and feeling the depth of himself in her hot, wet body he began to move, slowly, and felt her opening herself to him more, completely, compelling him to rock deep into her, mate with her, give her a special brand of body-to-body passion, soul-to-soul connection, and a heart-to-heart commitment.

And as they continued to make love, the process becoming as natural as breathing, he made her his, totally, irrevocably. He took everything she had to give and then gave her everything he had to share only with her, his wife, his lady, the heart of his desire.

His strokes were long. They were hard. He went in and pulled out, stroking her over and over again. Then she was shuddering again, heading for the cliff, and that same shudder touched his body, and he joined her as they both went over the edge and the world crashed down on them. Incredible sensations claimed their minds and bodies, spreading fire as explosions after explosions ripped around them.

He heard himself cry out her name. He heard her cry out his. This kind of pleasure had been a long time coming but had been worth the wait. His lips returned to hers, sealing their fate, interlocking their minds, and firmly bonding their marriage.

Love mingled with desire and passion and they knew what they were sharing was just the beginning.

CHAPTER 24

The sun was rising in the sky when Christy slowly opened her eyes. Her gaze was instinctively drawn to the man lying at her side, whose legs were intertwined with hers. Although his eyes were closed, she knew he wasn't asleep.

She studied his features. Dark shadows from the shave he needed accentuated his chin and gave him a rugged look. He had worried about leaving marks on her body, but she had assured him that she considered any marks left behind as his brand.

Memories of what they had shared last night and during the wee hours of the early morning sent shivers invading her. She closed her eyes as she remembered the passion, the heat, and the sexual fulfillment. Everything had been just as she had dreamed so many times. He had been gentle, attentive, and his ardor had been simply breathtaking, carrying her to heights she had never journeyed before.

Suddenly she felt an electrical current spark the air and slowly opened her eyes to stare into his face. His eyes were opened and he was watching her. She felt her body respond automatically, spontaneously, to the darkness of his gaze. The heat of it sent blood simmering through her veins, and without him saying a word she knew what he wanted.

She slid over to him, filled with love and desire, and he pulled her closer to him. "Let's capture the moment," he whispered huskily as he encapsulated her mouth with a passionate hunger that she returned.

They had captured a lot of moments since last night. After making love to her that first time he had lovingly swept her into his arms and taken her into the connecting garden bathroom, where they shared the huge sunken Jacuzzi tub.

He had lathered her body in the warm bubbly water, massaged her sore limbs, and held her in his arms until the water had cooled. Then he had wrapped her in a towel and carried her back into the bedroom, where he had sat in the love seat and held her like she was the most precious thing to him. And while holding her, he had painstakingly explained how his father's desertion had affected him, making him lose faith in love and its true meaning, and why he'd vowed never to lose control. But that thanks to her, love had new meaning for him. His words had touched her heart, and she'd vowed never to let him lose faith in love again.

She must have fallen asleep in his arms, because all she remembered after that was being kissed awake by him and making love again. Hours later when all he had to do was touch her and she would respond, he had swept her away on the wings of passion all over again.

Now it was a new day and she moaned his name as she melted into his kiss, was seeped into another existence where all her thoughts, desires, and wants were centered on him. The urgency of the kiss propelled her to arch more into the strong arms that gently and protectively held her, giving her all she desired and more. And when, without breaking the kiss, he reached out and filled his hands with her breasts, softly stroking the hardened tips, she released a groan of pure pleasure.

Then he broke off the kiss. "Look at me, sweetheart," he murmured huskily.

She lifted her gaze to him and felt the heat of him flow through her. "Always know that I love you," he said; the tremor in his voice was deep and vividly clear. She heard the love, the passion, and the sincere emotion in his words and her heart swelled.

She tilted her head back and nodded, her eyes steady on his. "And always know that I love you, too."

He kissed her again, moving her under him, holding her hips and lifting her to him, joining their bodies in one smooth entry and establishing a rhythm that was intimately familiar. The movement of his tongue matched the tempo of their bodies, and each stroke promised an even deeper penetration. He filled her, withdrew, and filled her again, and she writhed beneath him, continuously moaning out his name. And then it happened, and gloriously so. Sensations tore through them, sending their senses escalating.

Alex sank deeper into the warmth of the woman he loved, giving her all and knowing she had a place in the deepest recess of his heart. They pleasured each other to the sweetest oblivion while locked together in a mindless state of endless release. All existence became nonexistent and when the final wave crushed down on them they went under, drowning uncontrollably in a sea of passion.

"I talked to your uncle yesterday before the ceremony."

Christy forced her eyes open to look into Alex's face. "Uncle Jake?"

"Yes."

She rolled over on her stomach and propped her face up with the palms of her hands and lifted a curious brow. "Why?"

Alex reached out and gently stroked her bare back, loving the feel of her soft skin. "Rasheed felt that I should, and he was right. Considering everything, leaving this place may not be easy, and I wanted Jake to know where we were in case something goes wrong."

Christy nodded. "Did you tell him we had to get married?"

He shook his head. "Yes, but I asked him not to mention it to anyone for now. I also asked that he be at the Honolulu airport when we got there."

She flipped on her back. "I bet he has a lot of questions."

Alex chuckled. "Yes, but Jake trusts me enough to know that when I'm ready, I'll give him answers. And I asked that he not mention anything to your brothers, but now I think I'll call him back and suggest that he bring them with him." Alex leaned forward to trail a kiss across her cheek and down to the base of her throat.

Christy fought to keep her mind on their conversation; however, the sensations that were beginning to flow through her made it nearly impossible. "Why would you want to do that?" she whispered, barely able to get the question out.

"Because I think it's time they knew the truth and we should be the ones to tell them." His lips licked the corner of her mouth and slowly moved toward the lower portion of her ear.

Christy knew he was right, but she didn't look forward to telling her brothers anything. She didn't even want to think of how they might react.

Alex read her mind and his arms went tight around her. "We're married, sweetheart, and no one, not even your brothers, will change that."

She leaned up and placed a kiss on his lips. "Thanks for not giving up on me, Alex."

When she tried to pull back Alex didn't let her. He pulled her closer and kissed her in a way that made her feel even more special.

A few hours later
Houston, Texas

"No disrespect, Jake, but what the hell do you mean, Christy's in trouble? What's going on?" Dex Madaris asked, firing the questions one behind the other.

Jake Madaris rubbed a hand down his face as he recalled the phone call he had received from Alex that morning. The call yesterday had asked Jake not to tell his nephews. Now it seemed that Alex had changed his mind and wanted them to know what was going on and wanted Jake to bring them to Honolulu with him.

Jake glanced at the three men. Why now of all times did his nephews have to be difficult? At least Dex and Clayton were. Justin, being Justin, had the calmness of a seasoned politician. Jake knew Justin was just as concerned as his brothers; however, in situations such as this, he took the role of a diplomat.

"I'm sure Jake will tell us if we calm down and give him the chance," Justin said in a composed voice as he leaned in the door frame.

With three pairs of eyes on him Jake shrugged. "Right now I don't have a lot to tell other than Christy flew to some island in the South Pacific chasing after a story. Alex called and—"

"Alex?" Clayton asked, his gaze going from intensity to confusion. "What does Alex have to do with this?"

"He's the one who discovered Christy had gone to this island and he went after her."

"I thought Alex was somewhere on vacation," Dex piped in. He was just as confused as Clayton.

"He was, but apparently he got wind that the situation Christy was walking into was a FBI sting operation and went after her."

"Thank God for that," Justin said as relief shot through him.

"I bet Alex wasn't on vacation like we assumed but was working somewhere undercover and found out about Christy that way," Clayton said as his analytical mind went to work.

"So when do we leave?" Dex asked with a stormy look on his face. "If Alex called and asked that you bring us, then he might suspect trouble. I'll give Trev and Trask a call, as well as Ashton and Sir Drake."

Jake shook his head and shoved his hands into the pockets of his jeans. He knew it would be a waste of time to tell Dex there wasn't a need to assemble what Jake considered a three-man hit squad. Trevor, Ashton, and Sir Drake were former members of the Marines Special Forces. It didn't take much to give them an excuse to reenact those roles.

"Fine," Jake said, looking at his watch. "We take off in less than an hour."

"How are you holding up, Captain?"

Alex looked over at Christy and smiled. Her beauty took his breath away. Even now, when his concentration should be on operating the boat, he couldn't keep his eyes off her. Her hair, gloriously wind tossed, hung loose around her shoulders. She had tried pinning it up, but that hadn't worked. Personally, he liked it down. And early this morning when he had placed her atop him in bed, her hair had cascaded over his face when she leaned down to kiss him.

"I'd hold up a lot better if you come over here a moment," he said huskily. He glanced out at the blue-green waters and thought he couldn't wait until they got to Hawaii. But then he couldn't forget the call he'd made to Jake before they'd set sail asking that he bring the Madaris brothers with him, which meant there wouldn't be any private time for him and Christy. He glanced over at her again and decided he would make time.

Christy, who had been standing at the rail looking out over the beautiful Pacific Ocean, smiled as her gaze met Alex's. The flapping of the waves against the boat, along with the sound of the motor running, was reassuring. They were on their way back to the States, and she was happy about it.

Turning, she walked over to where her husband was standing and wondered if there was any task the man could not do. Rasheed's mini-yacht was a beauty, and Alex was handling the boat like a born sea captain. They had been onboard for over six hours, and according to Alex, the Kiribati island was less than a couple of hours away.

When she reached Alex he pulled her into his arms and they stood that way for the longest time with his arms holding her protectively and snugly in their embrace. Christy then turned in his arms to face him. "You know Mom is going to want to plan another wedding."

Alex smiled. "That's fine."

"And Gramma Laverne might come up with some traditional reason why we'll need to remain apart until after the wedding."

Alex frowned. "Now that's not fine. Baby, you and I are married and I have no intentions of spending one night anywhere without you. And just as soon as I can, I plan to take you shopping for a real wedding ring."

She glanced down at her hand and smiled quickly. "I happen to like this one." She looked up when she felt his body suddenly stiffen and saw the deep frown on his face. "What is it, Alex?"

His eyes were staring straight ahead. "Looks like we have company."

Christy's gaze followed the direction of his and she saw a boat that carried the flag of the Vanuatu government approaching them. A nervous jolt went through her body when she remembered Rasheed saying the Vanuatu authorities could be just as ruthless as the cutthroats they arrested.

"Relax, sweetheart," Alex whispered in her ear. "For them to check out things is just a formality, and then we'll be on our way."

Christy nodded, hoping Alex was right. She was wearing a pair of jeans and a cotton blouse. Alex was wearing jeans, a pullover shirt, and a Houston Texans jacket. "But just in case, I want you to have this," Alex said softly, slipping his small revolver into her hand.

He didn't bother asking her if she knew how to use it, since it was a known fact that her brothers had taught her how to handle a gun at an early age. He used to think it was ludicrous when Dex would take a teenage Christy to the gun range with him on Saturday mornings, but now Alex was grateful that Dex had.

Alex smiled faintly when she lifted a questioning gaze to him. "I'm just taking every precaution," he said quietly.

The two grizzled men whose vessel came alongside of theirs looked mean and spoke in rapid French. Christy stood close to Alex but began getting nervous when one of the men's gazes kept coming back to her.

Alex noticed it, too, and placed an arm around Christy's middle. He knew that thanks to Rasheed all their papers were in order and wondered why the men were hesitant about leaving. When the men suddenly stopped speaking French, a language Alex understood, and began conversing in Bislama, a language that he did not, his sense of danger kicked in. Some things went beyond language, and the two men's attention to Christy was way too obvious. He eased her closer to him.

"If there's nothing else, we need to be on our way," Alex said in French, watching the two men cautiously. The larger of the two men nodded but instead of handing the papers back to Alex, tossed them over the boat into the water.

And then suddenly both men lunged for him, one with the blade of a knife. Alex quickly pushed Christy out of the way. One guy was knocked overboard when Alex gave him a sharp karate kick. But the man with the knife was harder to deal with. Alex wanted to believe this guy would be easy to take down, but his gut told him otherwise. And then the tussle began, but out of the corner of his eye he saw the other man, the one he had knocked overboard, was crawling back over the side of the boat, coming up behind Christy.

"Christy! Behind you! Look out!"

The split second that Alex's attention was diverted had been enough for the man with the knife to gain an advantage. It took Alex only a minute to feel the burning pain in his leg where the man's blade had sliced.

Alex knew he had to ignore the pain. Christy was in trouble. With the roar of a fierce lion intent on protecting his mate, he gave the man a hard kick to his midsection, sending him sprawling backward as the knife flew out of his hand.

Alex's head snapped around with the deafening sound of a shot being fired. Christy, her blouse ripped, was holding a smoking revolver in her hand and standing over the body of the man who'd come back on deck.

Alex was about to go to her when he heard Christy's frantic warning and turned in time to see that the man he had knocked down earlier had regained his balance and was wielding his knife again. The man's blade moved in Alex's direction, aiming straight for his heart. Alex ducked and pulled out a gun that was tucked in the waist of his pants and with the anger of a man who had reached his limit, pulled the trigger. The shot sent the man down, and his blade went with him.

Breathing deep, Alex turned and quickly crossed the deck to Christy. Taking off his jacket, he placed it around her as he pulled her into his arms. When he felt her trembling, he pulled her closer. "It's OK, baby. It's over."

He tried not to think of how the man had tried attacking Christy. But in the end she had given him his due. It appeared that both men were dead because of their lust. Alex closed his eyes, not wanting to think what would have been Christy's fate if the men had succeeded in their plans.

He chuckled and when she pulled back and met his gaze questioningly, he reached out and lovingly caressed her cheek with the tip of his finger. "That will teach anyone to mess with the Maxwells."

CHAPTER 25

"Alex, are you sure you're all right?" Christy asked with deep concern in her voice. They had made it to the Kiribati island and were about to get airborne for Honolulu.

She hadn't realized that Alex had gotten injured until they reached the airfield and she noticed the blood that had soaked through his jeans. It had taken a lot to convince him to stand still long enough for her to rip the sleeve off her blouse and use it as a bandage to try to stop the bleeding.

Alex squeezed her hand reassuringly as he strapped himself into the seat. No, he wasn't all right, but he wouldn't tell her that. Right now the pain in his leg was killing him, but he would try to ignore it and get them out of there. He was more than anxious to get back on U.S. soil. Only then would he seek medical attention.

"I'm fine, sweetheart," he lied, and forced a smile over to her. "Once you're all settled, then I'll fly this thing out of here," he said, cranking up the engine.

She smiled over at him as she strapped up. "I'm ready."

For some reason Christy couldn't dismiss the concern she felt as she watched Alex put on a pair of headphones and shift the gears that started the plane moving down the runway. She had tried convincing him to get medical help for his leg before they flew out but he had staunchly refused. As the plane began gathering speed she leaned back in her seat and closed her eyes. She had left the States nearly three days ago very much a single woman but was returning a happily married one.

"I can't believe they left us behind," Syneda Madaris said angrily as she paced the room.

"Yes, the nerve of them," Lorren piped in.

"Too bad none of us can fly their plane," Caitlin added.

"Yeah," Felicia and Corinthians chimed in simultaneously.

A few seconds later all five women turned and gave Tori Warren, wife of Sir Drake and a former CIA agent, a curious stare. Tori was sitting at the table next to Nettie, Ashton's wife, giving her full attention to the little boy she held in her arms. Fifteen-month-old Deke Warren looked so much like his father it was ridiculous.

Tori glanced up when she felt all eyes on her. She raised a curious brow. "What?"

"Can you fly a plane?" Syneda asked. Since getting to know Tori they had discovered the woman could do just about anything.

Tori shrugged. "Sure. Why do you ask?"

Syneda raised her eyes to the ceiling. "Tori, haven't you been listening? Our husbands have deserted us and didn't invite us to go along."

Tori raised a curious brow. "Yes, but aren't they on their way to Honolulu to pick up Christy?"

"Yes," Lorren said, "but trust me there's a lot going on with Christy and when they find out, all hell is going to break loose."

"And we need to be there when it happens," Caitlin added.

Tori nodded. "OK," she said slowly. The former CIA agent in her couldn't help wondering what was going on with Christy that would get her brothers so upset. "And I guess one of you has a plane stashed somewhere that we can use?" she asked jokingly.

Lorren nodded. "Yes, we have a plane. Dex, Clayton, and

Justin own one together. We used it to fly here from Ennis and I see no reason why we can't borrow it."

Tori blinked. She hadn't actually expected them to pop up with a plane and couldn't help but chuckle when she glanced over at Nettie. "So do you think we should fly to Hawaii and keep our men out of trouble?"

Nettie smiled. Like everyone else, she knew how things could get if Ashton, Trev, and Sir Drake got together. Add the Madaris brothers and Trask to that mix and there was no telling what might happen. "Yes, I think that we should."

Tori then glanced around at the group. "OK, as soon as we find babysitters, then we can hit the friendly skies."

"Finding babysitters won't be a problem," Caitlin said. "My girlfriend Beverly won't mind, and then there's Kattie and Traci, who hate flying. I bet they'd love to watch the kids for us."

Syneda nodded in agreement. There was never a problem getting a babysitter in the Madaris family. "And I strongly suggest that we invite Jonathan and Marilyn along. This might be one of those times when they'll need to intervene on Christy's behalf if things get overheated."

Tori raised a curious brow. "What in the world is going on with Christy?"

Syneda chuckled. "We'll give you the scoop on the plane."

They had been in the air for two hours already, and Christy's concern for Alex's injury was increasing every moment. Unease rippled through her as she glanced down at his leg. It had started bleeding again.

She reached out and touched his forehead and found it hot and knew that he had a fever. And the eyes that glanced over at her were glazed. She tried to contain the panic she felt when she said, "You have a fever, Alex."

From the way he was looking at her she knew he was fighting whatever pain he was in. The cut of that knife must have gone deeper than either of them had thought. She quickly glanced out the plane window. They were miles and miles from land, and below all she could was the ocean.

"Can't be sick," Alex mumbled. "I have to get you to safety."

She fought back the tears that misted her eyes. Even now his concern was mainly for her. She wondered how much longer it would be before they could land. Thanks to her uncle Jake and the flying lessons he had given her, she knew a little about flying, but . . .

Driven by concern and fear, she said, "Alex, you're ill, sweetheart. I need to get in touch with the airport to make sure someone will be there to look at you as soon as we land."

She saw that it took a whole lot of effort on his part to nod. "I got to make sure you're safe," he repeated.

Again Christy fought back tears as her fear and concern for him increased. She glanced back down at his leg and noticed blood was soaking through the bandage she had made. She inhaled deeply. Alex didn't need her tears; he needed her to be strong and do whatever had to be done.

Reaching out for the controls, she radioed the air tower: "May Day. May Day. This is *The Golden Seas*. The pilot is hurt and will need medical attention as soon as we land."

It seemed everyone in the tower went silent. Then a deep male voice asked, "What happened to the pilot?"

She sighed deeply. "He's been injured."

"How many of you are onboard?"

"Two."

"And do you have any flying experience?"

Christy sighed again. "A little."

"Do you think the pilot will be able to bring the plane in?"

Christy glanced over at Alex. His efforts were still focused on flying the plane, but she could feel the wing of the plane wavering somewhat. He was fighting to remain lucid. "I'm not sure."

"Then you may have to be his co-pilot." After a few moments the man said, "It doesn't seem that a flight plan was filed. Do you happen to know what model of plane you have?"

Christy gave him the model number located above the console. "OK," the air-traffic controller said. "We're alerting the medical authorities. They will be here when you land. Now I need for you to grab that extra set of headphones and listen up."

Christy prayed that she wasn't putting her and Alex in even more danger, but if she didn't do something there would be the risk of the plane crashing. Already she could feel them losing altitude. She glanced over at Alex and smiled. "We're a team, Maxwell. I'm taking over."

Glazed eyes looked over at her. "You can't fly. I have to keep you safe," he said, studying her with his head cocked to the side, his face completely covered in sweat.

She smiled over at him and didn't think she could love him more than she did at that moment. Taking a deep breath, she said, "And you *have* kept me safe, sweetheart. We wouldn't be in this mess if it wasn't for me. Now please let me handle things. And I *can* fly . . . with some guidance. The air-traffic controller will help me."

"I have to keep you safe," Alex persisted, losing coherency. Then he closed his eyes and she felt the plane take a huge dive. It went plunging downward, seemingly headed straight for the ocean below. Alex was out, probably from the loss of so much blood.

It was there in the back of her throat to scream, but she swallowed it back and forced herself to hold her panic at bay. She went to the panel and pushed a button, prayed for just a little of the control Alex always had, and said, "OK, Mr. Air-Traffic Controller, I need help fast. Pilot is unconscious and plane is going down. I need you to tell me what to do to bring this baby in."

"Are you Jake Madaris?"

Jake, who had just walked into Honolulu's airport terminal after landing, slipped off a pair of sunglasses and glanced at the man wearing an airport security uniform. One dark eyebrow went up. "Yes, I'm Jake Madaris."

"I need you to come with me."

Jake turned and glanced at the seven men who had accompanied him on the flight, saw their suspicious gazes, then turned back to the airport security person and asked, "Why?"

"Not sure, sir," the man said easily. "I received orders from the tower to bring you to them as soon as you landed. It has something to do with a private plane that's on its way here from somewhere in the South Pacific being in distress."

"Alex and Christy!" Jake heard Clayton say behind him.

Jake sighed deeply. "Lead the way," he told the man.

When eight men began walking, the security officer said, "I was only told to bring you, Mr. Madaris."

Jake smiled faintly as he kept walking. "Sorry, but we come as a package deal. Let's go; we can't waste time."

"And there you have it, Mr. Madaris. It appears the pilot is unconscious and your niece is the one who is now piloting the plane. She mentioned she had some flying training from you, and so far she's doing OK with keeping the plane level by following our instructions. The tough part, however, will be in the landing. She mentioned she's never landed a plane before."

Jake rubbed a hand down his face. "She hasn't. I've always taken over before she got to that part." He glanced back over his shoulder at Justin's, Dex's, and Clayton's ashen expressions. They weren't saying anything. He knew their minds were filled with thoughts of Christy piloting a plane with very little experience. The thought of that was enough to make anyone go silent.

"What happened to Alex . . . the pilot?" a very concerned Trask Maxwell asked the man who had identified himself earlier as a senior air-traffic controller.

"I'm not sure. All she would say is that he was badly injured and needed medical assistance as soon as they landed. I have paramedics standing by."

Jake nodded. "What can I do?"

The man sighed deeply, appreciating Jake's calmness in such a serious situation. "I have a layout of the controls of the plane. It's a Cessna Skylane, single-engine, and relatively easy to handle. The air-traffic controller who is walking your niece through everything is doing a pretty good job, but I think when it comes to the landing part, a familiar voice will help under the circumstances. She happened to mention that you were on your way here."

The man took a deep breath and then continued talking. "I can tell by the tone of her voice that she's getting tired, but I have to hand it to her, she's a real trouper and is determined to land that plane. We've taken every precaution and have cleared the runway."

Jake nodded, thinking about the niece who held a special place in his heart, as well as Alex, whom he considered a special friend. "OK, I'm ready to do whatever you need me to do."

"Christy?"

Christy exhaled a relieved breath upon hearing the familiar voice. "Uncle Jake?"

"Yes, Red, it's me," he said, calling her by the special nickname he had given her as a child because of her hair coloring. "How's Alex?"

She glanced over at Alex. His face was drenched in sweat, and as she glanced down at his leg she saw the bleeding had gotten worse. "He's passed out and is in bad shape. It's my fault that he's injured and—"

"We'll discuss that later, sweetheart. The main thing we need to do is help you get that plane down so we can get him medical treatment. Now listen up and follow my instructions, all right?"

"Yes, sir."

Jake smiled. He couldn't help but recall the times when he had given her flying lessons when her brothers had staunchly refused to do so. She had been an eager student and had done pretty well handling his plane, which was a lot larger than the one she was operating now.

He sighed deeply. He would help his niece land that plane or die trying.

CHAPTER 26

Cheers went up in the tower. It was a long way from a smooth landing, but Christy had brought the plane down in one piece.

Inhaling deeply, Jake Madaris leaned back in his chair. He knew his hair was no longer sprinkled with gray but was probably completely gray by now. He didn't want to recall the touch-and-go moment when the plane had dipped and come close to hitting the side of a mountain. He doubted everyone's hearts would be the same after that experience.

"Damn, I'm glad that's over," Trevor Grant was saying, wiping sweat from his brow. Six other men nodded in agreement.

"Mr. Madaris, we have special transportation to take you to the hospital," the airport security officer was saying. "Medical help is being dispatched to the airfield, which will take them to Honolulu General. I'm sure your niece will want to see all of you."

Jake nodded. He then turned to the seven men with him. "Let's go."

"We did it, sweetheart," Christy whispered as she leaned over and cupped Alex's hot cheek and gently kissed him. He was still passed out, but she had to believe he was hearing her words.

Her heart was still pounding from landing the plane, but she had done it. Her determination to take care of Alex had made her do it. It was as if he had unconsciously willed some of his strength and control to her when she needed it most.

She glanced around. The ambulance had arrived with its siren blasting. As soon as the vehicle came to a stop in front of the plane, the EMTs quickly descended, opened the plane's door, and went to work on Alex.

"What about you?" one of the men asked her. "Do you need medical attention as well?"

Christy shook her head as she watched what was happening to Alex. "No, I'm fine; just take care of my husband, please."

The men were taking his vital signs and had started an IV. She fought back tears, calling upon Alex's strength and control once again when they removed him from the plane on a stretcher and she saw how much blood he had lost.

She paused and lifted her gaze up to heaven, closed her eyes, and prayed for God to intervene and make Alex well.

They made it to the hospital in less than thirty minutes, and with Christy following close behind, the medics rolled Alex through a pair of glass double doors. Eight men who were standing in the waiting room rushed out the moment they saw Alex.

"Christy!"

She turned, and from the way everyone was looking at her she knew she must look a sight with her torn blouse and blood-splattered jeans, but at the moment she didn't care.

She was about to say something, tell everyone how glad she was to see them, when a nurse and doctor came rushing forward. A concerned frown covered the doctor's face as he checked Alex's leg. The doctor then glanced over his shoulder and quickly asked, "Who's the next of kin to approve medical treatment?"

"I am."

Both Christy and Trask had spoken the words at the same time. All eyes that turned to stare at Christy were confused.

The doctor also turned around. "OK, which one of you is it?" he asked, his frown deepening.

Trask, who hadn't taken his eyes off Christy, said, "I'm his brother."

The doctor then switched his gaze to Christy. "And you are?"

Knowing everyone was watching and waiting for her response, she said, "His wife."

"Wife!" That shocked exclamation came from seven pairs of lips. Jake didn't say anything. He merely silently looked on.

Christy lifted a very stubborn Madaris chin and met seven very shocked gazes, three in particular. "Yes, his wife." She then gave the doctor her full attention. "Please do whatever you have to do to make him well."

An angry Dex stepped forward. "What the hell do you mean, you're his wife?"

Christy glared up at her brother. "Just what I said, Dex."

Jake thought that now was the time to intervene. He placed a protective arm around his niece. "Dammit, Dex, calm down. Alex had to marry Christy to get her off that island."

Dex's anger quickly vanished. "Oh."

"Then it's just a matter of getting it annulled," Clayton said with a relaxed smile now that he understood things.

"That should be easy enough, since it hasn't been consummated," Justin added.

Christy stepped away from Jake and was in her brothers' faces so fast they didn't have time to blink. But they did have the good sense to back up. "There won't be an annulment," she snapped. "And as far as our marriage not being consummated, you're wrong. It's been consummated several times over and then some, thank you very much."

No one said anything. Startling silence reigned supreme until the doctor cleared his throat and spoke up. "Uhh, we need to get this man to surgery right away. An artery was punctured and he's lost a lot of blood already."

Everyone went into action again as the medics wheeled Alex's stretcher toward double doors. "Hey, Doc," Dex called out.

The doctor glanced back over his shoulder. "Yes?"

Dex's expression looked hard, almost made of stone. "You do just like my sister requested and make him well. Just so I can have the pleasure of killing him all over again."

Trask snapped his head around and glared at Dex. "Like hell you will!"

"Dexter Jordan! Trask Elgin!"

Anyone familiar with the Madaris family recognized that stern and firm voice and all eyes quickly went to the hospital's entrance door. Jonathan and Marilyn Madaris entered the room, surrounded by the wives of all eight men. The men shook their heads upon seeing their wives and knew only one person was responsible for their being there: Syneda. Seven pairs of eyes went to Clayton, who merely shrugged.

The presence of Christy's father unleashed a flood of pent-up emotions. She had tried to be strong and stay in control, but the sound of his voice made her fear of losing Alex that much more real and suddenly she couldn't stop the panic and fear that gripped her.

Christy met her father's gaze and somehow he understood what she needed and automatically he smiled and held open his arms. "Dad." His name came out on a sob and she raced across the room to him and broke down and cried.

"It's OK, sweetheart," Jonathan Madaris was saying softly, tightening his arms around her. "Alex is going to be all right. You got to believe that."

Her father continued to hold her protectively in his arms and she fought to find that strength again. She refused to think that she was losing Alex and that the love they had finally found would be snatched away from them. In the deep recesses of her mind she willed Alex to be OK. She needed him in her life and didn't want to think of a life without him.

• • •

Marilyn Madaris pressed a cold cloth to her daughter's eyes, which were swollen from so much crying. Marilyn had tried to get Christy to drink something and she hadn't. She just sat there, staring at the double doors Alex had been wheeled through a half hour ago, as everyone waited for word on his condition.

Jonathan had his sons somewhere in a private room and probably was reading them the riot act. He was breaking the news to them that Christy was no longer a little girl but a young woman who was old enough to make her own decisions. It was time they realized Christy had a life, and they needed to respect that. Marilyn knew her husband and was sure that by the time the talk ended, Justin, Dex, and Clayton would have a new attitude or would keep the old attitude to themselves. It was a known fact that it took a lot to make her husband angry, but when he reached that point all hell was known to break loose.

She again focused on her daughter. It was evident that she was tired, completely exhausted. And as Marilyn looked at Christy's clothes she didn't want to think of what she'd gone through to bring her to this point. Marilyn had listened to Jake while he had briefed them on how their baby girl had miraculously landed a plane. With mountains looming all around, Christy had somehow brought her and Alex to safety.

Yes, Marilyn thought, there was no doubt in her mind that her pampered daughter had grown up a lot during the past twenty-four hours. And according to what Jake had also shared with them, Christy was now a married woman, a woman who had stood up to her brothers in proclaiming that fact. It seems what may have started off as a marriage of convenience just to get Christy off that island was now anything but that. Christy had gotten the man she had always wanted, and Alex had gotten the woman that he loved.

"Mom?"

Marilyn glanced at her daughter. "Yes, sweetheart?"

"Alex is going to be all right, isn't he?"

Although she'd been told just how serious Alex's condition was, Marilyn had to believe he would be OK. She had to believe it for all their sakes, especially Christy's. "Yes, sweetheart, I believe in my heart that he'll come through this because he knows how much you love him and that you're depending on him to get better."

Christy fought back the tears. "I love him so much, Mom."

Marilyn nodded and smiled. "Yes, and you always have."

Christy smiled, too, through her tears. "Yes, I have." Then a regretful frown touched her features. "I've been so mean to him since that night of the auction."

Marilyn pushed back a lock of hair from her daughter's face. "I'm sure he understood why, sweetheart. He had hurt you and you were protecting your heart from further pain. At some point he realized that, and I think that's why he was so diligent in trying to prove he was worthy of your love. At first he was afraid to love you because in his mind there were too many opposing factors that stood in the way: the differences in your ages; his relationship to our family, especially to your brothers; and your inexperience, just to name a few. Jonathan and I appreciated the fact that he wouldn't take advantage of your love. But now it seems that the two of you have worked through your differences and are a happily married couple just like it was meant to be."

Christy didn't say anything and Marilyn hoped she had given her daughter something to think about. She shook her head, knowing her husband was somewhere giving their sons a lot to think about as well.

Jonathan Madaris stared angrily at his three sons. They had inherited his stubbornness, two of them to the nth degree. But even worse, when it came to Christy, all three were overprotective beyond reason.

"I want to know why you're against Christy and Alex being married?"

It was Dex who spoke up. "Dad, it's nothing against Alex personally of course, but Christy is too young to get married."

"And Alex isn't ready to settle down, either," Clayton added tersely. "Although his business has always been the most important thing in his life, he's still into women. He can hook up with one whenever he wants."

"And I personally don't think Christy is ready for marriage," Justin tacked on. "It's a big responsibility and Christy's priorities are still her hair and nails."

Jonathan turned to Dex and lifted a dark brow. "If I remember correctly, Dex, when you married Caitlin the first time around, she was a lot younger than Christy is now and the two of you had only known each other for two weeks."

Dex frowned. "That's not the point, Dad."

Jonathan leaned against the closed door. "Then maybe it should be."

He then turned to Clayton. "And I don't know of anyone who was more into women than you, so how can you talk? But being all into women didn't stop you from falling in love with Syneda and settling down, thank God."

He then turned his attention to his oldest son. "I remember when Marilyn and I thought that you and Denise weren't ready for marriage, either, but the two of you proved us wrong. Just think how things would have been had we or her parents stood in the way of your marrying her." Jonathan knew he was reminding Justin of how determined he'd been to marry his first wife, Denise. They had shared five years together before she had died of a brain tumor.

"And as far as Christy's appearance being her top priority," Jonathan continued, "I think you'd better take another look at her today. She doesn't give a damn about her hair, nails, or what she's wearing. The only thing she's concerned with right now is the man she loves."

He inhaled deeply before he said, "Your eyes have been

closed to what's been going on with Christy and Alex." Still angry, he was determined to make his sons see reason. "Christy has loved Alex since she was thirteen, when he gave her that ring on her birthday and promised to marry her. To all of us it was a joke, but to Christy it was the most important event to ever take place in her life, and since that day she has been waiting to grow up just so the two of them could marry."

Clayton shook his head. "That's crazy, Dad. Christy was just a kid. Alex didn't think of her that way. He only gave her that ring to stop her from crying. We all knew that."

Jonathan nodded. "Yes, we all knew that and over time we assumed that as Christy got older she knew that as well, but that wasn't the case. Although Alex never encouraged her in any way, your sister went through high school and college actually believing that she and Alex were promised to each other. In fact, she reminded him of his promise three years ago, the night of the private auction at Sisters. Up until then, Alex hadn't had a clue of Christy's feelings."

"What did he do?" Justin asked quietly.

Jonathan sighed deeply. "He made the worst mistake a person could make with a Madaris. In rebuffing her advances, he injured her pride by telling her he had no intention of marrying her and that she needed to grow up, get out of fantasyland, and start dating guys her own age."

Dex shook his head. "No disrespect, Dad, but although I agree with anything Alex told her, I'm sure saying it put him on her shit list," he said. He knew all too well about the Madaris pride since he was full of it. It was only when he had put his fierce pride aside that he had been able to open up his heart to love again and have a new beginning with Caitlin.

"Yes, and Alex would have permanently remained there if he hadn't started realizing something."

"What?" Clayton asked.

"That he was in love with Christy. And when she returned

home from college, if the three of you had been more observant, you would have noticed how taken Alex was with your sister and how hard he was trying to fight it. And knowing Christy, I'm sure it was her intent to play the vixen and put salt in the wound by deliberately making sure Alex knew just what he'd lost."

"Damn, we didn't have a clue," Dex said, shaking his head.

Jonathan shook his head. "Well, it hasn't been easy for him. Any other man would have said the hell with it and walked away. From what I understand, your sister has put him through pure hell, yet he refused to give up on her."

Jonathan sighed deeply. "Alex is a fine young man, and like Trask and Trevor I've always considered him as another son. I can't think of any other man I'd want to have my daughter—a man who would do just about anything to keep her safe, which is proven by the fact he's in there fighting for his life. Not once did he try to take advantage of Christy's feelings and he has always treated her with the utmost respect, and as her brothers you couldn't have asked for more than that."

"But why didn't he let us know how he felt?" Justin Madaris asked.

Jonathan smiled. "Because he knew just how overprotective the three of you were of Christy. And then there was the friendship the four of you shared, which was special to him. Alex knew it wouldn't have been anything personal, but he, like everyone else, had long ago accepted that when it came to a man in Christy's life, as far as you all were concerned, no man, not even him, would have been good enough for her."

Jonathan shook his head sadly. "It wouldn't have bothered the three of you in the least if she grew up an old maid, which I think is kind of pathetic considering the fact that you're all happily married. I think it's pretty damn selfish that you wouldn't want your sister to share that same happiness. It's time the three of you stop treating her like a little girl. If you haven't noticed lately, Christy has blossomed into a woman, and I can't think of a finer man to have as my son-in-law than Alex. I know in my heart he will love her; he's already proven just how far he will go to protect her, and I think you'll all agree he will treat her right. What more can we ask for or expect?"

Jonathan glanced down at his watch. He hoped it wouldn't be too much longer before they got word on Alex's condition. "Over the years I think it has been admirable the way you've always looked out for your baby sister, but the time has come to back off and let her live her own life. I'm going to leave you in here for a moment to think about everything that I've said."

Jonathan then opened the door and walked out of the room.

Trask looked at his wife as they sat in a corner of the waiting room. "How long have you known about Alex and Christy?"

Felicia met her husband's gaze. She sighed deeply, glad everything was out in the open. "For a few years now."

Trask leaned back in his chair and frowned. "And you didn't think I had a right to know?"

"Yes, but it wasn't my place to tell you, Trask. Alex is your brother. It was obvious he had a lot of decisions to make concerning Christy, and the last thing he needed was for you to muddy the waters."

Trask's frown deepened. "I wouldn't have done that."

She leveled her gaze at him. "Yes, you would have, Trask Maxwell. Clayton is your best friend. You knew his attitude regarding any man in Christy's life. You would have tried finding a way to talk what you would have considered as some sense into Alex."

Trask fell silent for a moment. He couldn't disagree with that. "I know it wouldn't have been anything personal against Alex, Felicia, that's the way Justin, Clayton, and Dex are toward Christy. Everyone has known that. That's why I can't really fault Dex for being so angry now."

"Well, it's time for them to change their attitudes. If none of you have noticed lately, Christy isn't a kid anymore. She's a woman. And right now everyone's main concern should be on Alex pulling through. From what I understand, his condition is serious."

Trask nodded and blew out a ragged breath as he stood. "Yes, and I need to call Momma and let her know. I'll be back in a second."

Felicia watched as Trask walked over to the bank of telephones. She hoped and prayed for Christy's and Alex's sake that her cousins came to terms with the decisions Christy had made.

Christy glanced at the clock on the wall. What was taking so long? It had been over an hour already and still there hadn't been any news about Alex.

She had spoken to Trask and he'd told her he had contacted his mother to let her know about Alex. Jake had called his good friend, movie actor Sterling Hamilton, who had agreed to fly Jolene Maxwell Thomas to Honolulu in his private jet.

The double doors opened and the doctor walked through. Christy rushed over to him as fast as she could. "How is he?" she asked. Then panic kicked in at the look on the doctor's face. He sighed deeply and shook his head.

"I can't make you any promises, Ms. Maxwell. There was extensive bleeding and we did all we could to stop it, but your husband has lapsed into a coma. I'm sorry."

Christy sighed deeply, refusing to cry; refusing to believe what the doctor was telling her. She felt strong arms around her shoulders and looked up to see her brothers had come to stand by her side.

The doctor in Justin asked the one question they all needed to know. After introducing himself to the doctor, he asked, "What are his chances, Dr. Shane?"

Christy's heart nearly stopped when the doctor met

Justin's gaze and said, "Not good. Like I said, he lost a lot of blood, and just like I'd thought, an artery was punctured. It's surprising he didn't bleed to death before he got here. One thing: the man has a strong constitution for survival, but still, the human body, as you know, Dr. Madaris, can only take so much."

Christy pulled up all the Madaris stubbornness that she could muster and said, "He *will* pull through. He *will*!" She then inhaled deeply and fought back her tears. "When can I see my husband?"

The doctor had sympathy in his eyes when he said, "In about a half hour. A nurse will come and get you."

The doctor then turned and walked back through the double doors.

Only one person at a time was allowed in ICU to see Alex. Christy knew her family hadn't wanted her to see him alone, but the nurse had regretfully explained that hospital rules were hospital rules.

Christy braced herself as she walked into the small private room and saw him. He was lying in a bed hooked up to all sorts of machines. She fought back the cry that began building deep in her throat, knowing that she had to stay strong for Alex.

She walked slowly over to the bed and took the chair beside it. He looked bruised, barely recognizable, with so many tubes connected everywhere. But she thought the most blessed sound in the room was that of his breathing, and she thanked God for that.

She couldn't stop the tears she felt burning her eyes. It was OK to cry for the man she loved, she inwardly convinced herself. And she knew she had to get through to him and hoped that he heard everything she said.

"Don't give up, Alex. Fight this for us. Do you remember what I told you two days ago? I couldn't take it if anything were to happen to you, and I'm not taking this very well. I need you, Alex. I need you here to love me, be my partner in all things. I refuse to let you leave me. I refuse to go it alone. You are mine and I will fight for you. I will fight for you to live."

Tears she couldn't control any longer ran down her cheeks and the next ten minutes she spent telling him how much she loved him, how much he meant to her, and all about the unfinished business left for them to complete.

Suddenly she felt a hand on her shoulder and turned and looked up. It was Trask. He pulled her up from the chair and placed his arms around her. Moments later she pulled back and wiped her eyes. "How did you manage to break hospital rules without being thrown out of here?"

He shrugged and smiled faintly. "One of the nurses remembered me from my football days and agreed to look the other way if I gave her an autograph for her husband."

He looked down at the brother he loved and inhaled deeply. "We have to remember that the hospital rules are for Alex's benefit. The more rest he gets, the quicker he'll pull out of this and start playing detective again."

Christy nodded and glanced back at the bed. Alex was lying there as if lifeless, but deep in her heart she believed he would pull out of it and play detective again.

She had to believe that.

CHAPTER 27

Christy had remained by Alex's side day and night for the past seventy-eight hours. She used the bathroom connected to his hospital room for those times when she needed to take a shower and change clothes, and she ate her meals in the chair beside his bed. And during those short moments when she was away she made sure someone was there with him.

She had kept up steady conversation with him, refusing to let him slip any further away from her, and she would watch closely for any sign that he was regaining consciousness. He was still hooked up to more monitors, machines, and tubes than she could count, but she knew their use was a necessary part of his recovery.

She stood to stretch her muscles. Alex's mother had arrived a few days ago and had taken one look at her son and broken down. It had taken all of Christy's strength not to break down right along with her.

Christy's brothers had flown back to Texas to handle important business matters regarding the Madaris Building but were to return tomorrow. Trask, Trevor, and Uncle Jake were still there as well as her parents and Alex's mother. The other women had returned to Houston to take care of the children, but Christy talked to them each day when they called to check on Alex's progress.

A couple of days ago Uncle Jake informed her that he'd heard from Rasheed. The FBI sting operation had been successful, and those influential men who'd been members of the Kantar Cartel, including Senator John Harris and Congressman Blair were now in custody. Although Christy had been too busy to read the newspapers, the arrests had made national headlines.

Christy was glad closure would come to those parents whose daughters had gone missing. The teens on the ship that had docked in Vanuatu had been returned safely to the States. Christy intended to write the article for the *Cincinnati Enquirer* and reveal the truth behind Mark Tyler's heroic death. She had shared the news of the arrests with Alex, and although he hadn't given any sign that he'd heard anything she said, she wanted to believe that he had, including news that Bonita's body was being returned to Morganna Patterson for a decent burial.

Christy walked over to the window and looked out. Honolulu was a beautiful island, and she intended for her and Alex to return one day. She thought it would be the perfect place to celebrate their first wedding anniversary.

"Christy."

She froze upon hearing her name and then quickly turned around. Alex was still lying there lifeless with his eyes closed, but she refused to believe she hadn't heard him speak. Her heart began thumping a million beats a minute as she swiftly walked over to the bed. Reaching out, she took his hand in hers and stared at him.

A minute had passed, possibly two, when suddenly she watched as his lids fluttered slightly just moments before he slowly lifted them to reveal dark, glazed eyes. It was as if he had awakened from an overnight slumber instead of three days of unconsciousness.

The only sound she heard in the room besides the clicking of the monitors was the rapid beating of her heart as their eyes held. And then she watched his lips move slowly. "I love you," he said in a deep, grating whisper.

She squeezed the hand she held with as much love as she could exchange in her touch. "And I love you, too, Alexander the Great," she whispered back as tears began flooding her eyes.

Emotions she'd held at bay made her entire body tremble as tears began flowing down her cheeks. "I love you so much. Thanks for coming back to me."

Their eyes held for a long, meaningful moment, and then, as if with a contented sigh, he closed his eyes again. Wiping the tears from her eyes, Christy quickly pushed the button for the nurse. In the time it took Christy to blink, a nurse arrived. With tears still in her eyes Christy turned to the woman, smiled, and said, "Please get the doctor. My husband is back."

For what seemed like an entire day Alex had felt himself wander in and out of the deep throes of sleep. But whenever he opened his eyes, Christy was there smiling at him, talking to him, giving him water when he was thirsty, encouraging him to get better while she lovingly bathed him, and most of all telling him over and over how much she loved him.

He remembered hearing her voice when he had been in the clutches of pain while in some dark place that had tried pulling him into its existence. But in the deep trenches of his unconsciousness he had heard Christy calling his name, pleading with him to come back to her and not stay in that dark place. But most important, he had remembered her words of love. Knowing she loved him had given him a reason to fight to return to the world of the living. Her words had been the catalyst behind his determination to open his eyes. He had wanted to see her again, to be with her, to always love her.

He slowly forced his eyes open again, and just as he had known she would be, Christy was there. She was sitting in the chair next to his bed asleep, but as if she needed the contact, she held his hand in hers. And she was leaning over the bed with her head and shoulders on the mattress as she slept so she would immediately know if he stirred.

Although he felt a sharp pain, he moved his injured leg

just to make sure he still had both legs, and when he did so Christy felt the movement and came awake immediately, lifting her head to stare at him.

Alex knew that with the bad shape he was in the last thing he needed to think about was holding his wife in his arms, kissing her, loving her, touching her all over. But he did. Some things just couldn't be quenched no matter what shape you were in, and his desire for Christy was one of them.

"Come here," he whispered throatily as he felt the slow pounding of his heart as well as the hard throbbing of another part of him.

Evidently clueless to what he was thinking, Christy got out of the chair and moved closer and cupped his face in her hands. "You're awake again."

Mindful of the IV tube, he lifted his hand and let his fingers glide through her hair and said, "You're worth waking up to."

And then with as much strength as he could muster, he pulled her closer and captured her mouth—and not lightly, either. He hadn't eaten since heaven knows when, but at the moment he was perfectly contented to feast on this, the taste of his wife. She didn't resist and was returning the kiss with equal ardor, making him appreciate every second he had fought death to remain alive.

"Hmph."

He heard the sound of someone clearing his throat and was certain Christy heard it as well, but it soon became apparent the both of them had chosen to ignore it, hoping whoever it was would get the picture and go away.

Alex heard someone clear his throat a second time and decided the person wasn't getting the picture after all. That was too unfortunate, since Alex had no intention of releasing his wife's mouth until he got good and ready, and if whoever was in the room wanted to watch, then so be it.

"And I thought you and Syneda were bad," he heard a very deep male voice say.

Recognition of that voice made Alex excruciatingly aware of just who his visitors were—Christy's brothers. Thinking that being flat on his back was not the best time to test Justin's, Dex's, and Clayton's tolerance level, he reluctantly ended the kiss. "We got company," he whispered against Christy's moist lips.

Christy frowned and turned to look at her brothers. "When did the three of you get back?"

Justin Madaris quirked his lips wryly. "A few hours ago. We came straight here from the airfield. We need to talk to Alex."

Christy had an idea what they wanted to say and wasn't having it. "No, I don't like this," she said, taking a few steps away from the bed to confront her brothers. "Alex needs his rest."

Dex Madaris raised his eyes to the ceiling. "What Justin should have said, Christy, is that we are *going* to talk to Alex, whether you like it or not."

Christy raised her brow a little higher. "Alex and I are married and there's nothing you can do about it."

"Christy, it's OK," Alex said from behind her. It was an effort, but he managed to pull himself up straighter in the bed. "It's time your brothers and I talked."

Turning to him, she shook her head furiously. "No, Alex. They don't like the fact that we're married and I won't let them hurt you." Her voice was choked and she forced back her tears of anger.

"They aren't going to hurt me, sweetheart," Alex said to reassure her, although he really wasn't certain what her brothers' intent was. But he couldn't stand the thought of her crying and getting upset on his behalf. "Come here a moment."

He watched as she turned and glared at her brothers once more before walking over to the bed. Her cheeks were wet and it touched him that those tears were for him. "Come closer," he whispered.

When she did, he slipped a hand beneath the thickness of her hair to gently grasp her neck to pull her mouth down to his, deciding that if her brothers had a problem with him kissing his own wife, that was too bad. He figured he was doing them a favor by trying to kiss away her anger . . . and succeeding.

He knew the exact moment she released her fury and claimed his passion, and when she did, it was with such mind-whirling vitality and vigor that he felt a deep stirring emotion. He couldn't wait until he was well again so he could do more than just kiss her.

"It seems Alex isn't in as bad a shape as we thought," Clayton Madaris said in an irritated tone of voice that was loud enough to be heard by everyone in the room.

Reluctantly Alex released Christy's mouth and gently touched her cheek. "Let them have their say," he whispered softly. "Then I'll have mine."

She raised a worried brow. "But . . . but—"

"Christy, I'll be fine. Now leave us alone for a moment."

She looked into his eyes, and after inhaling deeply she pulled herself out of his arms. With one hesitant glance she turned away from him to face her brothers. "Touch him, hurt him, and I'll never speak to the three of you again." And then with her lips compressed and her eyes glaring, she walked out of the hospital room.

As soon as the door closed behind Christy, Alex's attention was drawn to the three men whom he had always considered friends. But from their unreadable expressions he had no idea what they were thinking or feeling; however, he was more than certain they weren't overjoyed with the recent turn of events involving his marriage to their sister.

They would just have to get over it.

He watched as they slowly spread out. Justin moved to stand at the foot of the bed, and Clayton and Dex flanked the sides, cornering him. Alex lifted a dark brow. Did they actually think he would try anything in his condition? Damn, these were men who had shared Trask's role as big brothers to him. Men he loved and respected and men who over the years had always had his back like he'd had theirs. Now it seems they had his back against a solid wall.

"Is there a particular reason why you didn't tell us you were involved with Christy, Alex?" Justin asked with the fine skill of an experienced diplomat.

Alex met Justin's gaze. "Had I told you would I have gotten your blessings?"

Justin shrugged. "Probably not at first, but I'm sure that eventually we would have come around."

Dex snorted. "Speak for yourself, Justin."

Alex wasn't surprised by Dex's comment. He glanced over at Clayton and watched as a wry smile touched his lips. "I'm a nicer guy than Dex. Like Justin, in time I would have accepted it. So why didn't you tell us?"

Alex moved a steady gaze from one man to the other, then said, "My relationship with Christy was already taking a beating. That in itself was bad enough. The last thing I needed was to take a beating from the three of you as well. Christy and I had issues to work out and the last thing we needed was anyone interfering until it was done."

"Yeah, Dad said she didn't make things easy for you," Dex said with a smirk on his face like he actually enjoyed the thought of that.

"No, she didn't. In fact, she went out of her way to make things rather difficult."

"Yet you didn't give up on her," Justin said, shaking his head. He knew how strong-willed and stubborn Christy could be.

Alex momentarily looked away, remembering just how intent he'd been on winning back Christy's love. He met Justin's gaze once again. "No, I wasn't going to give up."

"You love her that much?" Clayton said, raising a brow. He had loved Syneda, too, but he couldn't forget how during the course of pursuing her his pride had taken a beating and how he had made up his mind that you couldn't make someone love you. Unlike Alex, he had gotten tired of trying and had walked away. But thank God he and Syneda had found their way back to each other with his mother's help.

Alex shook his head. "No, I don't love her that much. I discovered that I loved her a hell of a lot more."

For the longest moment no one said anything, and then Dex spoke. "There will be days when you will wonder what you've gotten yourself into."

Alex chuckled, thinking about all the things he'd been through already, and said, "And I'm prepared for those days. But when you love someone you take the good, the bad, and the ugly."

"And you're more than willing to do that?" Clayton asked, meeting his gaze.

Alex nodded. "Yes. I can't imagine my life without her in it."

Justin nodded. "She's grown up a lot over the past few days, the way she's been taking care of you and all, making important decisions and handling business matters. And on top of that, she had to endure an intense inquisition by both the FAA and a representative from the Justice Department on what happened in the waters off Kiribati as well as Senator Harris's and Congressman Blair's involvement in that cartel. We're proud of her."

Alex nodded again. "And you should be. You prepared her well."

An arrogant smile played at the corners of Clayton's lips. "Yeah, we did, didn't we?"

Justin came from around the foot of the bed to stand in front of Alex. Dex and Clayton walked over to join him. "We don't want to tire you out, Alex, but we had to come and talk to you. We had to know, had to be sure, that you really love Christy. She means a lot to us."

Alex nodded. He'd always known that and really couldn't

blame them for wanting to confront him to learn his true feelings. "Well, rest assured that I do love her and I will take good care of her."

"And we believe you." That statement came from Dex, and the others soon concurred. Alex knew whether or not they believed him shouldn't matter, but it did.

"Thanks," he said to the three of them.

Justin offered him his hand. "Welcome to the family. Although we've always considered you part of it anyway, I guess now it's pretty much official."

Alex couldn't help but smile as Dex and Clayton offered their hands as well. "Yes, it is now official."

Christy looked at Alex as he sipped the chicken broth the nurse had given him. "And that's all they wanted to do? Welcome you to the family?"

He lifted his eyes and met her gaze over the rim of the cup he was holding. "Yes. But before that they needed to hear me say that I loved you."

Christy frowned. "Why? Don't they think you can love me?"

Alex smiled. "I guess they know you will be a challenge and wanted to make sure I loved you enough to be up to it."

Christy opened her mouth to say something and decided for once to keep quiet. After all, she *had* been a challenge to him. "I promise not to give you any more problems."

Alex lifted a dark brow, wishing he could believe that, but knew that she would give him more problems eventually. She was a Madaris, a female one at that. But he did believe she would try not to make things too difficult for him most of the time.

"Do you know what I've been remembering a lot over the past couple of days as I've watched you move around the room?" he asked her.

She lifted a brow. "No, what?"

"That night you were on the dance floor dancing in that

club. I know you don't remember a lot about that night, since you were under the influence, but I do. I'd never seen you dance that way before. That song by OutKast, 'The Way You Move,' was playing and it was as if you were dancing just for me, beckoning me to be your mate, claiming me as yours."

Christy smiled. "I probably was but didn't realize I was doing so."

"Well, I can't wait until I get better to take you dancing so I can watch you dance that way again." He smiled. "I definitely love the way you move, Mrs. Maxwell."

Lulled by the deep look of desire in his eyes, Christy moved closer to the bed. "And what else do you love, Alex?"

He caught her wrist in his hand and pulled her even closer. "I definitely love you. In fact, I think Barry White summed it up pretty good with his song 'You're the First, the Last, My Everything.' You're all that to me."

He pulled her closer and their lips met in a long, slow, and deep kiss. Moments later when he pulled back she whispered against his moist lips, "You're all that to me as well."

He held her gaze and by slow, simmering degrees passion mounted. Alex's mouth returned to hers and he knew he would be counting the days, the hours, the minutes, and the seconds until he was physically able to make love to her again.

And he didn't intend for his recovery to take long.

EPILOGUE

Three months later

What some considered the wedding of the year had taken place less than an hour earlier.

It didn't matter that legally the bride and groom were already married. What mattered to everyone was that they were present when Alexander Julian Maxwell and Christina Marie Madaris again exchanged those vows, sealing their lives together.

As much as Alex had wanted to, he could not rush his recovery. After remaining in Honolulu for two weeks he was flown back to Houston. Putting weight back on his leg for the first time had been difficult, and using a cane for a while had been a bitter pill to swallow. But now he was on the dance floor, without any type of aid, while he shared the traditional first dance with his wife.

Christy had practically refused to leave his side during the entire time of his convalescence and would have stuck to him like glue had he not convinced her of the importance of finishing her story. After getting an exclusive from Sheik Valdemon, she had returned to Cincinnati and written the article that brought closure to Morganna Patterson's ordeal as well as giving Detective Mark Tyler the hero's recognition he deserved. Senator Harris and Congressman Blair had resigned from their offices once the nature of their involvement was revealed to all America. A number of other elected officials and world leaders had been arrested in the scandal that had shocked the nation. Indictments had been served and those involved were awaiting trial. Hank Adams had been arrested for Mark Tyler's murder.

Now, Alex thought, as he held his wife in his arms while over five hundred guests looked on, his life could not be more complete. Although he enjoyed their wedding and intended to have a good time at this reception given in their honor, more than anything he was looking forward to tonight—their wedding night.

Because Christy thought that partaking in any extracurricular activities could reinjure his leg, she had insisted that they refrain from making love. And although she hadn't had anything against them engaging in some heavy-duty necking sessions, for him that hadn't been enough. He wanted to make love to his wife. He wanted her bad. And if they continued to hang around much longer, all five hundred of their guests would know just how much.

"When can we leave?"

Christy lifted her head from his shoulder and smiled. She wasn't a fool and knew exactly what was on his mind, since it was probably the same thing on hers. But she wouldn't let him know that . . . until after her surprise.

She was more than aware of how his body was brushing against hers while they danced and knew if they were alone without any guests around he would have stripped her naked by now. The look of heated lust in his dark brown eyes was making her skin tingle from head to toe, since she knew just what that look meant.

Instead of leaving immediately for their honeymoon—three weeks in the Virgin Islands—they would fly to New Orleans to spend a few days there. She knew she could forget about taking in the sights for the first couple of days. The only thing she would be seeing would be the inside of her hotel room, but she didn't have any complaints about that.

"It will probably be another couple of hours before we

can slip out," she finally answered. "But if you're patient just a little longer I promise to make it worth your while."

She watched as the eyes holding hers darkened some more. It hadn't been easy resisting him for the past three months and he had intentionally made things difficult in that regard, but their imposed abstinence would come to an end tonight.

She smiled at him, thinking she had to be the luckiest woman alive. The man who was holding her in his arms, who had vowed to love her forever, till death do they part, for the second time in four months, was everything she could hope for. He was her husband, her protector, her lover, her shield against any storm; the man who would father her babies, and, more important, the man who would always be the love of her life. She had resigned from her job with the *Enquirer* and was back in Houston. Already she had received another job offer, this one from Maxwell Investigative Services. Alex thought they made one hell of a team and figured he would be able to keep her out of trouble if she worked by his side. They hadn't yet decided on all her duties, but she figured once they returned from their honeymoon they could tackle the issue.

She glanced down at the ring he had placed on her finger during the wedding ceremony. It was simply beautiful. But the one he had given her at thirteen had a sentimental value that the ring she was wearing now could never replace. Everything Alex had ever given her was special. As special as he was. Now it was his time to receive some extraordinary treatment.

"I have something special for you," she whispered when he pulled her body closer to his again.

He lifted a brow? "What?"

She smiled. "You'll see soon enough."

"Are you trying to tease me into an early grave?"

She chuckled and shook her head. "No. I would never do that."

When the music stopped, the woman her parents had hired

as their wedding consultant descended upon them to let them know what was next.

A couple of hours later, Alex was chomping at the bit, more than eager to leave. The wait was killing him and he wondered if he would be able to survive the trip to New Orleans. Maybe he and Christy should just stay in town tonight and not leave until the morning.

And it wasn't helping matters as he watched Christy standing across the room talking to the wedding coordinator. As far as Alex was concerned, they should be able to leave now. Christy had done the traditional dance with her father; she had danced with her brothers and with his; they had cut the cake; he had removed her garter and she had tossed her bouquet and they had sat down at the head table and eaten something—although for the life of him he couldn't recall what he'd eaten, since his mind had been so focused on Christy.

"You seem to be in a hurry to leave."

Alex turned and raised a dark brow only to find himself surrounded by the Madaris brothers. "Yeah, you could say that," he said dryly as he took another sip of his champagne.

"Then just go get her and take her out of here," Clayton said, grinning. "You need to establish in the beginning who's the boss."

Dex chuckled. "Yeah, like you've established any such thing with Syneda."

Clayton shrugged. "Hey, there are benefits in being married to a woman wrapped up in this liberation stuff. I knew what I was getting into when I married Syneda, and there's never a dull moment. You never know what she's up to next."

Justin shook his head. "Yes, and that's what worries most of us. Your wife's antics are sometimes outlandish."

Clayton smiled as he glanced across the room at the woman he loved with a passion. "Yes, they are, aren't they?"

As he continued watching her, Syneda turned and caught his gaze and smiled. He winked and knew she understood his signal. Earlier he had cornered her and whispered his plan in her ear. They were to meet in the empty coat closet down the hall in ten minutes.

"May I have everyone's attention?" The loud voice of the wedding consultant poured across the room with the use of a microphone. "Christy and Alex are about to leave . . ."

Thank God, Alex thought.

". . . and Christy has something special she wants to give her husband."

Alex lifted a brow, thinking that an escape to one of the hotel rooms upstairs wasn't such a bad idea, but he preferred taking her away out of the building for privacy. He didn't want her brothers anywhere in the same vicinity when he made her scream.

"Ladies and gentlemen, I present to you Christina Marie Madaris Maxwell as she does a special tribute to her husband."

When the woman walked off, Christy was left standing in the middle of the floor wearing her elegantly beautiful floor-length white wedding gown. The strapless bodice was beaded with sequins, with a matching border around the skirt's hem. Her hair was pinned up on her head and she wore a tiara that gave her the look of a princess. Then there was the elegant-looking diamond necklace that adorned her neck, Alex's wedding gift to her.

She was absolutely stunning, and seeing her standing there took Alex's breath away the same way it had when she had walked down the aisle to him on her father's arm. She had a look of concentration on her face. But more important than that, her eyes were locked on his.

The entire room got quiet as everyone waited and his heart began racing a mile a minute. He recognized that look in her eyes and thanked God for it. She wanted him just as much as he wanted her and tonight they would share something beautiful in each other's arms. They would definitely wrap up any unfinished business between them.

"Do you think she's going to sing?" Dex Madaris asked, chuckling.

"God, I hope not," was Clayton's response as he checked his watch. Seven more minutes before that very important meeting with his wife. "Christy can't sing."

"Do you know what this surprise is about, Alex?" his brother, Trask, came up to ask him.

Alex shook his head, his gaze not leaving Christy's. "I don't have a clue." His body began feeling heated as Christy continued standing there just staring at him. Then he watched, like everyone else, as she unsnapped the waistline of her wedding dress to whip off the bottom portion of her floor-length skirt to reveal a shorter matching bridal skirt.

"What the hell is she doing?" Dex Madaris asked, shocked. "Just look at how short that gown is. That's something like what Syneda would wear."

Clayton laughed. "Yes, it is, isn't it?" He checked his watch. *Five more minutes*.

Alex didn't see anything wrong with his wife's outfit. He would admit it was short, but with her long, shapely, gorgeous legs he thought that she looked pretty damned good.

Then he heard the music; he recognized the tune immediately and ignored Justin's shocked whispered words of, "I don't believe it," and an even more shocked Laverne Madaris asking her youngest son, Jake, "Has my granddaughter lost her mind?"

As the OutKast song "The Way You Move" filled the room, Christy began shimmying her body to the beat of the sound the same way she had done that night in the club. She threw everything she had into it—her breasts, hips, hands, legs. And her buttocks were wiggling just as much, sending Alex's heated lust into overdrive.

Alex didn't care what others thought about his wife's surprise, but personally he felt like he was the luckiest man alive to receive such a special gift. She was letting him know that the only influence she was under this time was him.

"Do something," Trask whispered frantically to him.

Without his gaze leaving his wife's, Alex smiled and said, "I intend to."

Removing his tux jacket, he handed it to Trask. Then Alex removed his bow tie as he slowly began walking toward her, watching her every move; especially how she was working her midriff, and loving every minute of seeing her do so. She was dancing for him and she was right: It was special and only the two of them understood just how special it was.

Desire so thick he could plaster the walls with it was consuming him as he kept walking toward her. When he came to a stop within three feet of her he stood and watched as her body continued to dance just for him, beckoning him as her mate, publicly claiming him as hers.

Then she eased up to him and shimmied her body against him, around him, letting him know that she was truly his. He could only take so much and reached out and pulled her to him and kissed her, ignoring the applause, catcalls, and whistles coming from their audience. She had issued the invitation and now he was answering it.

And when the music finally ended, without missing a beat he swept her into his arms and headed for the nearest exit.

Christy set cross-legged in the bed Alex had just placed her in and glanced around the room. He had carried her out of the ballroom to the nearest elevator, which took them to the tenth floor, and to the room he had reserved for them to use to change into their traveling clothes before leaving for the airport. A private plane, compliments of her brothers, would fly them to New Orleans.

Alex stood across the room, leaning back on the closed door and looking at her. He was missing his jacket and bow tie, but then, she had replaced the floor-length skirt of her wedding gown with a much shorter one. And from the way Alex had stared at her while she was dancing, he hadn't seemed to mind.

Deciding to elicit conversation, she said, "Shemell thought she had died and gone to heaven when Rasheed walked in. But then she actually had near heart failure when Sterling Hamilton arrived." She chuckled. "I think she was upset that I'd never mentioned that he was a close friend of the family."

Christy heard an odd catch in Alex's voice when he asked, "Was she?"

Christy smiled. "Yes, at least she was for a while. Then she set eyes on Blade, Slade, and Lucas. I had to promise her that I would invite her to any Madaris family reunions we have."

She glanced at the clock on the nightstand next to the bed. If they wanted to make it to the airport for their flight they needed to start getting dressed. She slipped off the bed to begin changing her clothes. She glanced over at him. He hadn't moved an inch. "I guess we need to change into our traveling clothes if we want to be at the airport in a few hours."

Still he didn't say anything but continued to watch her. When she discovered she needed help unzipping her gown she said, "Could you come help me please?"

Without saying anything, he moved away from the door toward her. She turned and presented her back to him when he came to stand behind her. She felt her knees weakening when he brushed his lips against her neck before going to work at her zipper.

Alex breathed in deeply as he slowly unzipped Christy's gown. Desire that had been fueled by watching her dance downstairs, as well as by three months of abstinence, began taking over every part of his body. He needed her. He wanted her.

Now.

He turned her into his arms, wanting her to see his eyes, read what was in them. Wordlessly they stood staring at each other; then he knew the exact moment the meaning of what she saw in his gaze became clear.

"We aren't going back downstairs to get showered with rice as we leave for the airport, are we?" she asked softly, holding his gaze.

"No," he said quietly as a fever of deep anticipation flamed through his body. "At least not for a while. When it becomes evident that we won't be coming back down any time soon everyone will get the picture," he said quietly as he pushed the bodice of her gown almost down to her waist, exposing her breasts. "They can continue to celebrate without us for a while."

Christy nodded. Everyone would know what they were up here doing, but she didn't have a problem with that. "Our plane is scheduled to take off in a few hours."

Alex smiled. "I'll call the airport to let them know our flight out will be delayed."

He felt her tremble as he began caressing her bare shoulders and his gaze moved lower to her lush breasts. The sight of her firm and taut breasts did more than stoke his passion. It sent a fire blazing through him, especially when she wiggled out of the rest of her gown, leaving her practically bare to his eyes. The only thing that covered her below the waist was a white silk thong.

He leaned forward and licked a path from her collarbone all the way down to her breasts. Then tenderly cupping her breast in his hand, he lowered his head for his mouth to cover the hardened brown tip. He heard her murmur his name, and the sound made the deep compelling need within him increase.

Deciding her torture was his own, he released her and took a step back to remove his shirt. When his hand went to the buckle of his belt, she walked over to him and said, "Let me."

He inhaled deeply as she undid his belt with smooth, gentle hands. And when she began easing down his zipper he felt his strength dissolve and knew he had to take over or he would definitely lose it. He gathered her up in his arms and placed her back on the bed. After removing his pants and briefs he joined her in bed, whispered her name as he pulled her to him to remove her thong.

Christy's heart was pounding wildly in her chest and an intoxicating weakness was melting her bones. He moved his body over hers and leaned in to kiss her. It was a kiss that further stoked their passion, escalated their desire, and made their bodies a mass of quivering flesh. Her tongue mated with his voraciously, stroke for stroke, and Christy traced the heavy muscles of his body with her fingertips, needing to touch him any way she could.

He pulled back and met her gaze. "I love you."

She struggled to catch her breath and whispered, "And I love you, too."

When he moved his body to rest between her thighs their gazes held as he slowly entered her. "Three months was a long time without you," he moaned, gritting his teeth against the overwhelming emotion he felt, being back inside of her again after so long. And when she tightened her inner muscles to hold him within her, he threw back his head and let out a deep masculine growl of pleasure.

Then he began moving, his strokes long and hard, making love to the woman he loved, his wife, his life. He leaned down and began kissing her mouth over and over again, taking her bottom lip into his to suck on it while his body continued to move back and forth, in and out of hers. He continued the process, prolonged the torture, taking them to the brink of pleasure time and time again, stoking the passion between them that kept building and building.

And then when they couldn't take any more, he felt it—the heat, the fire, the flames. She screamed his name as a shudder ran through her, and he quickly followed, groaning out as an explosion of gigantic proportions went off inside of him. His arms tightened around her hips and held her to him as he spilled inside of her.

But he didn't stop there.

Over and over again, he stoked her fire and then fed her the pleasure they both needed. It was if they were making up for lost time. He loved the sound of the moans being wrenched from her lips as they satisfied their unending needs.

A very long time later, he pulled her into his arms while lying beside her, sighing contentedly.

"Alex?"

He didn't think he had the strength to lift his head, so he merely answered her, "Yes?"

"I definitely like the way you move."

A smile touched Alex's lips. "Thank you, sweetheart."

Then moments later she asked, "Is there still unfinished business between us?"

He pulled her closer into his arms. "Our business is finished, but a new phase in our life is just beginning."

She leaned up and kissed the pulse at the base of his throat, then lifted her head to stare down at him. "And what phase is that?"

"The phase that's called now until forever," he said, gently combing his hands through her tousled hair.

A smile touched her lips as she gazed down at him. "Now until forever. I like that."

And then she eagerly proceeded to show him just how much.

Dear Readers:

When I introduced Christy Madaris in my very first book, *Tonight and Forever,* I knew her story would be a very special book. She was the sixteen-year-old baby sister of three very wonderful but intense men who were not ready for her to grow up.

Over the years you have seen her mature and you know that one thing has remained constant—her love for Alex Maxwell. Falling in love at a young age is a beautiful thing. I know because I fell in love with my husband when I was fourteen. However, Christy soon discovered that having Alex reciprocate that love was not going to be easy because there were too many obstacles that stood in her way; more specifically, her brothers and Mr. Maxwell himself.

I hope you enjoyed Christy's and Alex's story in **UNFINISHED BUSINESS,** and getting the chance to revisit with some of the characters from my earlier books in the Madaris Family and Friends Series.

There are more Madarises out there—Blade, Slade and Lucas—just to name a few, and I look forward to sharing their stories with you.

I love writing connecting books. Individually, every book I write will be a totally satisfying love story. And together, the entire collection of my books in this series will create a compelling saga of one family's love and deep devotion, which will extend to their friends as well. I hope they will be stories you will enjoy and cherish forever.

If this is your first Brenda Jackson book, then welcome, and please visit my Web site for a list of the others. With all my books I intend to give you an enjoyable read and leave a smile on your face.

You can write to me at the following:

Brenda Jackson
P O Box 28267
Jacksonville, FL 32226

I would love hearing from you, and promise to write back as time permits if you include a business-size, self-addressed, stamped envelope. Also, please check out my Web Site at *www.brendajackson.net*. If you would like to receive my monthly on-line newsletter, please send me your e-mail address at *WriterBJackson@aol.com*.

Take Care,

Brenda Jackson